On the Road from Burns

Stories from Central Oregon

Ted Haynes

"On the Mountain" won second place in the Fourth Annual Bartleby Snopes Dialogue Story Contest, and was published in the January 2013 issue of Bartleby Snopes semiannual magazine. "Boondoggle" was awarded honorable mention in the New Millenium 2012 short story contest. "Living Well" was named a finalist in the Glimmertrain Fall 2011 Short Story Contest for New Writers. "Do No Harm" won honorable mention in the 35th annual Moonlight Mesa Cowboy Up Short Story Contest. "Kubali and the Vampire Cowboys" was a finalist in the 2011 Fencon Short Story Contest.

ISBN 0-9646506-3-0

Book design by Jim Bisakowski of BookDesign.ca
Cover photo by Christian Heeb. U.S. Highway 20 approaching Bend and the Cascade Mountains from Burns.

The Robleda Company, Publishers
1259 El Camino Real Ste. 2720
Menlo Park, CA 94025

www.robledabooks.com

For

*the people of Central Oregon,
real and imagined*

CONTENTS

Bridges

Caleb Johnson decided, at age thirteen, that haying was a necessary evil. His family needed hay to feed their cattle through the winter. But late July was always hot. Bits of hay, swirling in the air, stuck in Caleb's clothes and made him itch. The dust and the chaff clogged his eyes, nose, and windpipe. He squinted, sneezed, and coughed all day long.

Caleb and his father wore handkerchiefs over their mouths and noses. From time to time they dipped the handkerchiefs in water. But dust still coated their throats and got in their eyes. The boy imagined he would invent goggles for the sake of everyone who ever hayed. Maybe instead of goggles he would invent a special cloth that he could see through. Goggles or cloth, it would have to let air in and out. That would be the difficult part. But Caleb would find a way. Thinking of his inventions made the pain of haying easier to bear.

The start of haying season was pleasant, even satisfying. The work horses, Margie and Daisy, pulled the mower while Caleb's father sat on it and drove. What chaff there was fell behind the mower. The mower was a perfect invention. The two Johnsons could harvest ten times as much as they could have with scythes.

Caleb's goggles would make loading hay tolerable. The invention would help again when the ranchers wrapped slings around bundles of hay in the wagon and hoisted them into the loft above the barn, the chaff falling straight down on them as the hay rose. In the winter, when they threw the hay down to the cattle, they wouldn't need the goggles. The job didn't take long and the chaff would be falling away from them.

Caleb believed cold weather was better than hot. He judged it as impartially as he could, carefully remembering when the temperature reached forty below. Caleb and his father chopped up the river ice so the cattle could drink. His exposed skin hurt but working hard made him warm. It was, overall, much better than haying. Cold weather rewarded hard work. Hot weather punished it.

In the winter, Caleb arrived early in the schoolhouse to light the iron stove. He got the schoolroom warm before the other students and Mr. Handley arrived. "Prometheus," Mr. Handley called him, "the Bringer of Fire."

This fall he would start ninth grade at Bend High School fifteen miles away. He was impatient to start his science courses. Mr. Handley had taught him beginning algebra and started him on physics. They had replicated some of Galileo's experiments with falling bodies and spheres rolling down ramps. But the one-room schoolhouse had no chemistry equipment and no slide rules.

Mr. Handley, as much as Caleb liked him, could not teach all of the things Caleb wanted to know. He could not explain the difference between force, energy, and power well enough for Caleb to understand it. Mr. Handley knew of Einstein but could not explain his theories in even the most general way. The school library in Bend had sent a book on trigonometry to Mr. Handley at Caleb's request. But Mr. Handley did not know trigonometry and Caleb could not get very far in it on his own.

Caleb feared he might not be smart enough to be an engineer, scientist, or inventor. He had not been challenged in the right way to know. Ninth-grade science would be the critical test.

When Caleb and his father hoisted the day's last load into the barn the air was still hot and both of them were tired. They took towels down to the little river that ran through the ranch. Out of sight of the house, they shed their clothes and stepped into the cold water. They sank up to their necks and relaxed before they started to wash. The ice house hunkered on the bank above them. There was enough ice left even now to make ice cream two or three more times.

"You know, Caleb," said his father, his head resting on top of the river as though there were no body below it. "They've started building the Crooked River Bridge to be ready when the railroad gets that far. I thought after we've got the hay in we might go see it."

Caleb would have fallen over if he hadn't been neck-deep in water. "That would be great, Dad." The bridge was a feat of modern engineering set down in the wilderness. It would carry the long-awaited railroad to Bend. Up until now everything that shipped between Bend and the outside world had to go eighty miles by wagon. The railroad would finally put Bend on the map. The bridge was the critical link. It would be the second highest railroad bridge in the country when it was done.

"Of course," his father said, "we don't have to go. The railroad won't reach Bend until after you start school. You can see them bring the tracks right into town."

That wasn't what Caleb wanted. Watching men lay track over the last flat mile into Bend with everybody in town looking on would not compare. Besides, that was still at least two months away.

"They will only build the bridge once," said Caleb. "Now is the only time we will see it this way." He thought of all he might learn about forces, structures, and working with steel. How great it would be to bring that knowledge with him to science class.

"Two more days to finish haying. Then the weekend. We'll leave on Monday."

Any amount of haying was worth it. Caleb's fantasies swelled as he coughed, sneezed, and sweated through two more baking hot days. He would become a railroad engineer, deciding where the road would go, which hills would be climbed and which tunneled through, how much earth to use building a causeway and where the fill would come from, how many men and machines he'd need and how they would be organized. Better yet, he would be an inventor, busy in a laboratory, like Thomas Edison. The laboratory would be in Bend and he would make Bend famous. He would visit the Masonic Lodge from time to time to tell his father's friends what he was working on.

Caleb and his father left Monday after breakfast. Caleb's uncle would come by the house on Wednesday to see if Caleb's mother or the cattle needed anything. Caleb and his father took blanket rolls and some food for the road. Caleb brought a dozen fresh eggs carefully wrapped in straw to give to Mr. and Mrs. Stuart, the people they would stay with that night in Bend. The Stuarts had a house on the Deschutes where the river had been dammed and formed a big long pond. Mr. Stuart owned a shipping company with six wagons. Caleb was going to live with the Stuarts during the school year. "When I was your age," his father said as they rode north, "the project that got my attention was the Brooklyn Bridge. It took thirteen years to build. The man in charge was injured and his wife supervised the construction. She had studied engineering and she knew what she was doing. Maybe someday you'll see it."

"Do you think some day they will bridge the Amazon?" asked Caleb.

"I suppose someday they will," said his father.

"I'd like to be the man to do it."

Near Bend they crossed the fast-flowing Central Oregon Irrigation Canal. The canal, raised above the level of the surrounding land, ran faster than the river by the Johnsons' house. The water came close to the tops of its artificial banks. Caleb imagined standing on a raft, floating through the countryside at a rapid rate, watching the scenery go by, and catching the astonished eyes of onlookers.

When they dismounted in front of the Stuarts' house Caleb lifted the eggs from his saddlebag. He stood holding them in one hand and the reins for the two horses in the other. The Stuarts came down off their porch, shook hands with his father, and began a conversation about everything, it seemed, except Caleb and the eggs.

"Caleb, why don't you take the horses back around to the stable?" said his father. His father took the eggs from Caleb and handed them to Mrs. Stuart.

"Marjorie's hens always lay the best eggs." Mrs. Stuart seemed to be as nice as Caleb remembered her. But she wasn't paying as much attention to him as before. The last time he had visited Mrs. Stuart gave him sugar cookies and told him he was already becoming a man.

"Take the hay you need for your horses," said Mr. Stuart.

Caleb walked the horses around to the back. He put the horses in a small empty corral, separate from the Stuarts' horses. He took the saddles off and carried hay out of the barn. He pumped the water trough full with the hand pump.

Caleb and his father slept in the room that Caleb would have in September. His father slept in the bed and Caleb in his blankets on the floor. In the middle of the night Caleb woke up thinking of Mr. Stuart. Mr. Stuart had never gone beyond sixth grade. He could read, write, and do arithmetic and that was it, he said himself. But he was a successful man with a dozen men working for him. Running the freight company was not a simple thing. Loads were unpredictable. Wagons and horses broke down. Competitors cut prices. Soon no one would need wagons to bring goods from the railhead to Bend. Mr. Stuart thought that with more freight coming to town there would be more wagons than ever between Bend and towns the railroad still wouldn't reach. He was willing to bet on it. Caleb realized there were things worth knowing that he would never learn in school. How had Mr. Stuart learned them? Was Caleb capable of figuring them out? He didn't know and wondered how he ever would know.

Mrs. Stuart scrambled Caleb's mother's eggs for breakfast. She offered coffee to both the Johnsons. His father said Caleb did not drink coffee but he himself would have some. Caleb had not, in fact, begun to drink coffee, but he thought he should try it. He was disappointed at the lost opportunity.

"Do you think I could start drinking coffee?" he asked his father as they rode out of town.

"Not while we're traveling," said his father. "It can make you sick if you're not used to it. Someday when we get home."

Fair enough, thought Caleb. But he had another concern.

"I don't think Mrs. Stuart likes me as much as she used to."

"She likes you fine," said his father. "But she's going to see you every day like a member of her family. You're not going to be a guest. And you're older now. You'll get less affection and more respect. And that's what you should want. If you can earn it and keep it."

The country north of Bend was a thousand feet lower in altitude than his parents' ranch. Instead of tall pines there were ragged junipers. Dry grass and sagebrush filled the space between them. But here and there were flat, lush fields unlike any Caleb had seen before.

"Potatoes," his father said. The crops were irrigated with water that came from the river upstream. A canal ran beside the road. "The Morgans grow potatoes."

Mr. Morgan came upriver to hunt deer and elk every fall and he stayed with the Johnsons. Mr. Johnson and Mr. Morgan both belonged to the Masonic Lodge. Caleb and his father were going to spend a night with the Morgans in Redmond and then camp out by the railroad bridge the next night. His father said the Morgans had a daughter named Marilee who was Caleb's age.

Caleb did not think he would have much to say to Marilee, or she to him. He had two younger sisters and a girl cousin who was three years older. But there were no children his age at Mr. Handley's school. Perhaps Marilee would be impressed that he was going to see the bridge being built. But maybe she had already seen it herself.

The Morgans were building a new house. They had bought their land before irrigation arrived and the land's value had gone up. They sold their potatoes for good money. The Johnsons arrived in the late afternoon to the sound of hammers. The two-story frame was up and two men were working on it. The new house covered four times the area of the older and much simpler house right next to it. One of the men working on the new house was Mr. Morgan.

Behind the old house the barn and the corral fences were brand new. Caleb washed his face in a bucket by a pump and drank handfuls of water to quench his thirst. Then he watched Mr. Morgan and the other man work on the framing. He had never seen a house being framed before. The vertical two-by-fours ran two stories high to the tops of the walls. The men were up on ladders nailing boards between the two-by-fours to hang the floor of the second story on the frame.

The men stopped working and the second man left. Mr. Morgan came and sat with his guests, looking at the new house from the porch of the old one. Mrs. Morgan brought them fresh-squeezed tomato juice. She had cooled the pitcher in a basin of water. There were too many frosts to grow tomatoes at the Johnson ranch, even at the height of summer. He had never had tomato juice before. It tasted strong and he wasn't sure he liked it.

The adults talked about how much the area would grow when the railroad arrived. Their cattle and potatoes would profitably compete in Portland and even further away.

But the owner of the railroad, Jim Hill, wasn't building it to ship cattle and potatoes. He wanted to carry lumber. The area around Bend, particularly south of the city, was a virgin forest. The railroad would be shipping lumber for decades.

"You ought to buy up the forest around your ranch," said Mr. Morgan.

"It's gone," said Mr. Johnson. "Bought by lumber companies from Minnesota who saw what was coming. I didn't have any cash. I got the ranch in the first place by homesteading it."

The girl had not come out to join them.

"She helped me make dinner but now she's reading a book," said Mrs. Morgan.

"She can be shy," said Mr. Morgan.

"She isn't shy," said Mrs. Morgan. "She would simply rather be in dreamland than out here in the real world." Mrs. Morgan got up and went inside the house. She came back with a tall, freckled girl in a simple but new-looking dress. The girl held her head high as she regarded Caleb and his father. She made a short curtsy when she shook Mr. Johnson's hand and said "How do you do?" in an even tone. She said the same to Caleb and shook his hand with a stronger grip than he had expected. Then she turned away.

"Why don't you and Caleb go pick the corn for dinner?" said her mother. Marilee nodded and marched off the porch without looking back.

"Go," said his father, and Caleb started after her. She walked down a slight hill to a vegetable garden enclosed with chicken wire. She opened a loosely hung gate and waited for Caleb to pass through. She shut it quickly behind him.

"These are peas and those are tomatoes. These vines will have pumpkins. This is lettuce. And here is the corn." She stopped and waited as though she expected Caleb to do the picking. Caleb had seen pictures of corn cobs and nothing he saw looked like one. He approached the corn stalks warily, as though hunting a skittish animal.

"Here," she said, pulling a fat pod of green downwards, wrenching it off the stalk, and handing it to Caleb. "Hold on to this." She picked three more and gave them to him without saying anything.

"Now you pick one," she said. The ears of corn were the same color as the stalks and leaves. After careful searching Caleb found one and put his hand on it.

"Not that one," she said. "It isn't ready yet." Marilee put her hand around an ear on another plant. "Pick this one."

"How do you know when it's ready?" he asked.

"The silk at the end gets darker and it starts to dry out."

Caleb searched the corn plot for five more ears that looked right. Marilee kept a close eye on him and then acted bored.

"That's enough," she said. Caleb picked up the ears he had stacked on the ground and they started back to the house.

"Have you read The Idylls of the King?" asked Marilee. Mr. Handley had assigned The Death of Arthur to Caleb, but it was the only one of the Idylls he had read. That is what he told Marilee.

"You need to read The Holy Grail," said Marilee. "That one is the best."

Caleb had never thought his reading assignments would ever be relevant outside the classroom.

"Did you read The Wizard of Oz?" asked Caleb. He had read the book three times. He liked the Tin Man, the machines that the Wizard rigged up to impress people, and he liked the Wizard's departure in the balloon. If Caleb had been in Dorothy's place, however, he would have handled some things differently and would have figured out the shoes much earlier. Dorothy certainly did have courage, though, and he had to admire that.

"That's for children," said Marilee. "like Old Mother West Wind. But it's good. I've read all the Oz books." Caleb did not know there was more than one.

Caleb and Marilee shucked the corn outside the kitchen door. Stripping the leaves off was easy but removing the silk was frustrating. Caleb would think he was done with an ear and then find there was still more silk sticking to the cob. Marilee carried the corn in to her mother. Caleb took the leaves and silk over to the garbage pit.

The adults sat around one end of the small table while Marilee sat opposite Caleb at the other end. There was a platter of baked chicken and a bowl of peas on the table. The corn cobs were steaming in a white china tureen and there were tongs to pick them up with. Caleb watched his father put the corn on his plate and spread butter on it. Then he sprinkled it with salt and pepper. When his father picked the cob up with his hands Caleb stole a look at Mrs. Morgan. She was picking her cob up too. The adults gnawed on their cobs, starting at one end and working along the side of it. Caleb did what they did. It was delicious. He judged it was the best thing he had ever tasted after ice cream. Marilee was eating it the same way and she seemed to enjoy it. Dessert was strawberry shortcake. Mrs. Morgan and Marilee had picked the strawberries the day before.

Caleb and his father slept on their blankets on the floor in the living room. It was a hot night and all the doors and windows were open with screens to keep out the insects. Neither of the Johnsons slept well until it got cool in the early morning. The ride from Bend to Redmond had been long and hot. They were tired. They were still asleep when Mrs. Morgan and Marilee started making breakfast, keeping their voices down and sliding the heavy lids on the wood stove quietly.

Caleb wanted to get going, to see the bridge, but his father was in no hurry. He wanted to enjoy his breakfast and talk with the Morgans, as though it were a Sunday morning. Caleb did not ask for coffee. Maybe he would on the way back.

Mr. Morgan was first to leave the table. The man he had hired to help him with the new house had arrived. Marilee stepped away from helping her mother in the kitchen and told Caleb she had something to show him outside. On the shady side of the house, away from the kitchen and from where the men were working on the new house, she pointed to a patch of blue flowers growing in the neglected soil. Caleb struggled to understand what was so special about the flowers. Then Marilee turned to him and looked him in the eye. She slid an arm over his shoulder and pressed her hand on his back. She kissed him full on the lips. Caleb stood as still as a tree. Marilee pulled herself away and ran around the corner of the house.

The kiss had felt new and strange. But it was the arm grazing the side of his neck that flung Caleb into confusion. The touch had galvanized his entire being. He felt there was something he should do, immediately and at any cost. He was not sure what it was. Here was one more thing he did not understand. He did not think he was going to learn about it in school. He went around the side of the house after Marilee. She was gone and his father was cinching the saddle on his horse.

"Time to get going, Caleb," his father said. The boy saddled his horse and mounted. Marilee did not come out of the house again. He looked back one time as they rode away.

The bridge was only seven miles away but they would have to strike off across the sagebrush to get there. The wagon road went down into the canyon on a steep slope miles away from the bridge. The railroad bridge would be where the canyon was narrow and the walls were vertical.

Mr. Morgan told them to turn off where a big juniper tree bent down to the ground but was still growing. Then head northwest.

They had not brought their chaps along so they skirted around the taller bushes.

After a mile they could see what looked like the frames of two very unusual houses facing each other in the distance. The houses each had a single second story wall that was wider at the top than at the bottom. The side walls on the first floor were braced with giant X's. There were ropes and pulleys running through the frames like the rigging on a ship. Caleb saw a heavy girder being hoisted up inside one of the structures and then lowered again. He could hear the huffing of a steam engine and the clang of hammers striking iron.

"Watch where you're going," said his father, "or you'll ride right into the canyon." The land looked seamless until they rode up to the canyon's edge. The ground dropped away and the river was far below them.

The workmen were building from both canyon walls to where the bridge would meet in the middle. Each half was anchored in the cliff face. There was one long plank between the two structures but nothing more. Some engineer somewhere had figured out where the forces would go when the bridge was built, where the girders must connect to support the bridge and the trains that went over it. That person, whoever he was, had also determined how the two stubs of the bridge would support themselves before they could lean on each other in the middle. There were equations the engineer used to do this. Caleb told himself he could learn those equations. He would work hard. And it would be worth it.

Three men clung to the steel where a girder had been lowered down to them. A man on top of the bridge used tongs to pull a red hot rivet out of a fireplace and toss it down to the men. One of them caught it in a big funnel. The catcher used tongs to put the rivet in a hole that went through two girders. Then another man pushed on one end of the rivet while the third man hammered on the other end. After putting five rivets in one end of the girder they moved to the other end and put in six more. The men moved quickly with no ropes to catch them if they fell.

Caleb could not take his eyes away. His father told him to get down off his horse and stay away from the edge. His father left him there and led the horses away to graze on the sparse wild grass. After watching the men work for an hour, and tracing the line of every girder with his eyes, Caleb walked along the edge of the canyon to the near end of the bridge. He wanted to get as close as possible, to walk out on the stub of the bridge if he could. There was a barb wire fence and a sign that said "No Trespassing". Caleb stood outside the fence, directly in line with the bridge. The men were quitting for the day. They had stopped feeding wood to the steam engine and charcoal to the furnace where the rivets were heated. They laid their tools down on the wooden floor around the furnace and the men on Caleb's side of the bridge walked over the plank to the other side. There was a rope ladder hanging from the far section of the bridge and men were already climbing down it. Caleb could see tents at the bottom near the river. The largest tent had a pipe coming out of the top of it and smoke coming out of the pipe.

"Why do they camp all the way down at the bottom of the canyon?" Caleb asked his father when he found him sitting by the horses.

"Probably because it's cooler down there and they have all the water they need."

On the flat land above the canyon it was still hot and the sun had hours to go before it set. They unrolled their blankets and sat on them. They built a small fire to fend off mosquitoes. The matches were in a glass jar to keep them safe and dry. Caleb and his father had a cold dinner of bread, hard cheese, and sliced meat the Morgans had given them. Mrs. Morgan had included a Mason jar filled with fresh strawberries, a little squishy but still good. Caleb's father brought out two books and handed one to Caleb.

"It's by Rudyard Kipling," he said. "The first story is called The Bridge Builders." Caleb thanked his father with a look of surprise on his face. Both his parents were pleased to see him reading but his father had rarely picked out a book for him. This one was from the library in Bend. When and how had his father gotten it? They had not stopped at the library when they went through town. His father must have thought of it way in advance.

"What are you reading, Dad?" he asked.

"It's a novel about railroads and politics. It's called Mr. Crewe's Career."

Maybe his father was not taking this trip solely for Caleb's sake. Maybe his father had been looking forward to this trip as well.

They lay on their blankets with their heads on their saddles and read as the sun set. The hero of The Bridge Builders was an engineer. He was in charge of building a bridge with multiple stone piers over the Ganges. Terms whose meanings he could only guess at – borrow-pit, crib, spile-pier, truss – beguiled him. The story wasted a lot of time, Caleb thought, on the debate among the Hindu gods over whether to help Mother Ganges destroy the bridge. Ultimately the bridge withstood the river's flood and that had to be a good thing.

When it was too dark to read they put the last few twigs on the fire, shed their boots and trousers, and pulled their blankets up.

Caleb resolved to wake up when it was still dark and he succeeded. He dressed quietly and picked up the little bottle that had the matches in it. The desert night was cold and he snugged his bandana around his neck.

Mr. Handley had told Caleb that the bridge was so high and the air was so dry that if you dropped a match off the bridge the match would light before it hit the bottom. Caleb wanted to tell Mr. Handley that he had proven it by experiment, that he had seen it for himself. He climbed through the barbwire fence and walked toward the bridge. Caleb could barely see where he was going by starlight. This wasn't dangerous if he went carefully he told himself. He got out to the floor where the steam engine and the furnace were. It was too dark to examine them.

He walked over to the edge of the platform and steadied himself with a hand on a crossbeam. He realized that if he simply threw a match over the edge he would not be able to lean over far enough to see it ignite. He lay down so most of his body was on the platform but his shoulders and head extended over the edge. He took a match out of the bottle, held it out as far as he could, and dropped it. He watched intensely for a flare of light but nothing happened. He had calculated that, in a vacuum, it would take 4.47 seconds for the match to hit the river. He waited what he thought was three times as long. The next match he threw down as hard as he could while lying on his stomach. There was no flame.

Perhaps the match needed to be attached to something heavy so it would fall faster. A rivet would be ideal. If he used a rivet he would have to pay for it and he did not know what a rivet cost. He went back to the land and found a small rock and a little bunch of grass. On the platform he tied the match to the rock as tightly as he could. There was no point tying a loose knot after he had come so far.

He stretched out over the edge, threw the rock down, and started to count. When he got to four a flame winked up at him from the darkness below.

Boondoggle

Sheila had three assets. She was ambitious. She was pretty. And she could work long hours without getting tired. She had used her strengths to earn a degree in accounting at Golden Gate University and then a CPA. It had taken hard work and a curtailment of her social life.

McAllister, Balcolm and Marano had hired her as assistant to the law firm's business manager. His name was Tim Runyon and he kindly invested extra time to ensure Sheila would be successful. She received a good six-month review and a raise. She was pleasant to everyone and joked with the attorneys.

One limitation, which Sheila accepted, was that she was not as smart or as quick as the attorneys. She always did the best she could. The other limitation, which she felt more acutely, was that she lacked sophistication. The attorneys, immaculately dressed and always confident, spoke of Broadway shows, skiing in Aspen, family trips to Italy, Porsches and Audis, and playing golf at private clubs. When she heard of something new she would look it up. But she knew she was merely scratching the surface. The attorneys, both men and women, had ways of speaking and acting that went beyond politeness. They had class. It was not easy to come by.

A professor had told her, and Sheila believed it, that it was important to her career that the senior partners know who she was. Balcom and Marano still came to work every day. They now recognized her and said hello in the hallways. They even had friendly conversations with her while maintaining a businesslike distance and a certain dignity suitable to their age and positions. Their familiarity, she felt, was an important accomplishment.

Burton McAllister was retired and only came to San Francisco for meetings of the partners. Some meetings he attended by phone or missed altogether. He lived somewhere in rural Oregon and was frequently off fishing or traveling the world with his wife. Yet it was Burton who had founded the firm and made it grow. He was highly respected in the company and in the San Francisco business community. In his prime he knew everyone important in the city. He and his wife had led a busy social life and raised money for multiple charities.

Sheila had never met Burton McAllister and she decided she needed to find a way to do so. It would give her more credibility within the firm and outside it. For years to come she could drop his name into conversations. No one else her age would be able to claim they knew him.

Sheila spent long hours, on her own time, examining old accounting records from the years when the firm was growing rapidly and Burton himself was acting as the business manager. He oversaw the finances, hired attorneys, brought in business, and held the hands of the most important clients. Sheila searched the records for issues that would not have a readily apparent answer. Then she would ask if she could pose the questions to Burton himself. Fly up to his home in Oregon if possible.

The records were, in fact, surprisingly sloppy. It took an inordinate amount of work to follow transactions between the ledgers, the income statements, the cash flows, the balance sheets, and the bank statements. Cash seemed to flow back and forth between accounts for no reason at all. After two months Sheila compiled a long list of issues. She thought if she told Tim there was five million dollars missing he would think she had not looked hard enough. She told him one million and gave him a detailed report.

Tim agreed that the person to talk to was Burton. "We're not going to pay a team of accountants to unsnarl this," said Tim.

"Burton should be able to cut through most of it in a few hours. You should go see him. I'll call to tell him you're coming."

Sheila took an early-morning commuter plane. No luggage, just a briefcase. She rented a compact car and followed the directions she had printed from the Internet. The landscape near the airport was drier than Northern California. The brown grass was sparse. The pine trees were short and scraggly. In the distance there were pyramidal snow-capped mountains.

McAllister's place was thirty-five minutes west of the airport and at a higher elevation. The pine trees were taller and straighter and there were more of them. The land didn't look quite so dry.

The driveway was a long one, a strip of black asphalt between the trees. The house was log and timber with a complicated roof and massive stone pillars flanking the front door. There was a spot of green lawn between the driveway and the house. Sheila parked her car next to an old green pickup. In the pickup's back window there was a gun resting in a gun rack with the trigger facing up. There was no sign there was anyone around. She stepped up the walkway, into the covered entryway, and rang the doorbell.

It was half a minute before Sheila heard footsteps and another ten seconds before the steps reached the front door. The door was opened by a tall silver-haired man. He wore a freshly ironed plaid shirt, blue jeans, and loafers without socks. He seemed to make a quick appraisal of her. She felt for a moment that she was on a fool's errand and he knew it. Then the man smiled at her. He was going to be nice about it. McAllister had won over so many people in his career.

"Welcome," he said. "I'm glad you made it all right. I hope you don't mind the jeans. We're pretty informal up here."

"Not at all," said Sheila. "It's good to get out in the country. And I love all the rockwork in your house."

"Would you like some fresh coffee before we start?"

Sheila had drunk enough coffee on the plane but she did want to see more of the house. She thought it unlikely she would ever see it again. Most of the junior partners had never been there. They called it "Burton's Retreat."

Through the living room window Sheila glimpsed a pond and a meadow dotted with pine trees. There were mountains in the distance.

"I thought I left adequate records of everything the firm did," said McAllister, "but of course I'm glad to explain whatever you think needs explaining. My memory isn't perfect, but I think it's pretty good."

The kitchen had a large central island with a wooden top. There was a heavy black stove with six burners and a griddle. Sheila did not see a refrigerator until she looked closely at a large wooden cabinet with a long vertical handle on it. The pot in the coffee-maker was full and there were two mugs beside it. Cream and sugar were in simple matching china. McAllister poured the coffee for both of them and asked Sheila to help herself to what she wanted.

"Why don't we sit at the breakfast table where we can catch some sunlight?"

"Thank you for taking the time to do this," said Sheila. At the circular table they sat across from each other, sideways to the window. Sunlight reflected brightly off the table between them. Sheila pulled a thin folder from her briefcase.

"First let me ask you about some companies the firm wrote checks to. I cannot find invoices or notes on what these checks were for." Sheila placed a single sheet of paper on the table in front of McAllister. There were twenty companies on the list with dollar amounts next to them ranging from ten thousand to five hundred thousand. Sheila had ten more pages listing the individual checks written to each company but she kept those details in the folder. "Can you shed any light on these?"

McAllister brought a pair of horn-rimmed glasses out of his shirt pocket and put them on. Now he looked more like an attorney. He pulled the paper toward him and tipped up the top edge. An intense look entered his eyes. He looked, thought Sheila, the way he must have looked at the height of his career, the managing partner of one of the top law firms in San Francisco. He studied the paper carefully for about half a minute.

"There should be records for all of this – what cases these companies worked on for us and what work they performed. Do you mean to tell me you cannot find them?"

"I'm sorry. I can't find them and Tim can't find them." McAllister's face tensed and he looked darkly at the paper.

"Did you look at what we billed clients in the same timeframes? These companies and the amounts we paid them appeared on the billings. I realize it's a lot of work to match them up. But did you give it a try?"

"We looked thoroughly. This list started with over a hundred names on it and we eliminated most of them by finding them on the invoices we sent to clients. But we are left with these." McAllister picked up the paper again.

"Most of these firms were consultants or other law firms we hired," he said. "The law firms had special expertise or they handled our work in other cities. I would not have thought, though, that our business with Thomson, Seagram and Locke added up to four hundred thousand. Are you confident that the checks you have total that much?"

"Yes, absolutely."

"Well, I'm sure you're right. Thomson was a law firm in Winnipeg that worked with us for F & S Foods. F & S bought grain from Canadian companies on long-term contracts. We drew up contracts that had to conform to both U.S. and Canadian law. We dealt mostly with Bill Locke. He came to San Francisco several times and I expect you can find some expense reports that show lunches and dinners with him. Would you like me to go through all these companies and tell you about them?

"If you would, please. It would help us a lot."

"Very well," said McAllister. Sheila imagined he was well practiced in suppressing his feelings. He must have hidden his annoyance in countless client meetings. Of course, when he had been a practicing attorney, plodding through details like this was billable.

It took an hour for McAllister to work his way down the list. His memory appeared to be excellent and his statements were clear. He seemed to speak at exactly the maximum speed that Sheila could write. Her hand hurt by the time they were done. For each company McAllister gave the city it was in, what clients their work was billed to and, for about half the companies listed, who the principal contact was. The one company he could not recall had been paid thirteen thousand dollars.

"All of this business happened more than fifteen years ago," said McAllister. "The IRS can't go back more than six years, even if they find a substantial error." He took a sip of coffee. "I have to wonder at Tim's persistence in pursuing these questions."

The man was a gentleman, thought Sheila. He could have asked whether there wasn't more useful work she could be doing. He could have asked whether her trip was really to give her a day away from the office and let her meet the grand old man of the company. He could have been insulted at the implication that something had not been done correctly on his watch. What could she do if he chose not to answer any more questions? He could show her the door anytime.

"Some of those companies are out of business now," he said. "I'm sure some of the people we dealt with are retired." McAllister gazed out the window without seeming to look at anything in particular. Then he gave her a wry smile and almost winked.

"These days, you realize, I think mostly about golf and fishing. I spend time with our friends and, when we can get them here, our children and grandchildren. When I think about past years I think more about hunting than I think about the firm."

"Do you keep up with the charities you supported while you were in San Francisco? I think you were on the board of the symphony and the Modern Art Museum."

"Sometimes the people I met through charities brought us business or helped us one way or another. But when Maureen and I moved to Oregon it got harder to stay involved and, as we cut back on our giving, the charities politely encouraged me to leave the boards."

Sheila still had not seen the hunting trophies and she asked if she and Burton could take a break to see them.

McAllister brightened at the suggestion. "They're in my office. Come along." They went back past the front door and down a long hallway. The office was large and looked out into a forest of pine trees. McAllister flicked on the lights. It was very much a man's room. Wooden wainscoting ran around the room about four feet high. The wall above was green and held paintings of outdoor scenes. One portrayed a vast dry plain with low hills in the background and hundreds of grazing animals. Camouflaged in the grass in the foreground, and almost the same color, was a lion, crouched for the hunt. Another painting showed a rocky mountainside with water cascading down it in complex waterfalls. But most of the wall was covered with animal heads. There was a lion, a mountain goat, something that looked like an ox, and a number of deer or antelope.

"Tell me about the fish," said Sheila. It wasn't the biggest trophy but it had pride of place over a stone fireplace.

"It's a steelhead, a kind of trout that lives in the ocean but spawns in fresh water. I caught that one in the Deschutes River, about two hours north of here. It weighed twenty-four pounds. That's not a record but it's still a big steelhead."

"Did you shoot any of these animals on your own land?"

"Oh, no. No hunting here. We see elk here all the time but we have to go a hundred miles to hunt them."

"Do you still hunt?"

"I do more fishing now. But Maureen and I go bird shooting in England every year. All very English. You have to wear tweeds and a tie. I've made some lifelong friends hunting and fishing. I know them better than people I saw every day at work."

Sheila had never left the United States. She had never been hunting or fishing or to the symphony. She didn't have friends she expected to have for the rest of her life. She envied McAllister his life, his house, and his place in society. The money was secondary, she thought, a means to an end.

"Thank you for showing me all this," she said. "I've never seen a room like it. Do you mind if we go over a few more questions?"

"Not at all," said McAllister. "That's why you're here." They walked back to the breakfast table. He offered more coffee and Sheila declined. He took the mugs to the kitchen and put them by the sink. He took the same chair as before.

"What's next?" he said.

"There are several cases where it doesn't look like the firm collected all it was due when we won in court or we negotiated a settlement. The client agreements and court records say one thing but the bank statements have a different amount."

"Fees like that are often paid over time, not all at once," said McAllister. "Have you looked at later years?"

"Yes, I did, but I still could not find the missing amounts."

"Well, they must be there," said McAllister in a reassuring tone, as though he was not concerned about them and Sheila should not be either. She would find them eventually if she kept looking.

"In the Galvan case," said Sheila, "where our client was injured in a small plane accident, I don't see where we received any fee at all – not from the airplane manufacturer, not from our client, and not from the court."

"Have you asked Paul Galvan?"

"He died a year after the settlement," said Sheila. "His son says his father was paid the settlement but he doesn't know anything about the fee. He was fifteen at the time."

McAllister steepled his hands beneath his chin and gazed down at the table. "You said there were several?"

"For Lucatero Manufacturing the firm won a fifty million-dollar judgment when their insurance company refused to pay claims for environmental damage. The firm persuaded the court that it was equivalent to property damage and that the insurance policy covered it. The firm should have received four million dollars but I can only find three."

Sheila went on. "Then Pittman Tools went bankrupt right after our firm won a judgment in their favor. It isn't clear whether we should have been paid prior to the bankruptcy or we lost our chance along with the other creditors. There are four or five more."

"Are there four more or five more?" McAllister asked. He spoke calmly but a harder edge had entered his voice.

"Five," said Sheila. She called out the client's names but did not go into details.

"What does Tim think about all this?"

"He told me to ask you about it."

"And the partners?"

"Tim says we owe it to them to make a report after I get back. He says he doesn't know whether the partners will want to pursue these questions further or to forget all about them. I told Tim about one million dollars. Actually, there is five million I can't find. I may have overlooked something but I'll have to include everything I know in the report."

"Well, Sheila, the partners were satisfied at the time with the reports they received. And very satisfied with their payout when we won Lucatero." He continued looking at Sheila with a thoughtful and slightly pained expression on his face. Then he straightened up in his chair.

"I suppose," he said, "the only way to clear this up is for me to come down to San Francisco and go through the books myself." Burton sighed. "I thought I was well past having to do that sort of thing."

"I know it would be a pain but it would be great if you would."

"I think I can get down there in the next few weeks." He smiled a tight-lipped smile. "I'm sure the firm can wait that long. They've waited a long time already."

"I'll tell Tim."

McAllister gave her a reassuring smile. "Are there other questions you'd like to ask? Anything else you need my help on?"

"Yes, there is one other mystery, though it isn't a big dollar amount. The year we won the Galvan settlement, the Christmas Party cost almost three times as much as in other years. I don't know why that would be."

"That's easy," said McAllister, broadly grinning. "That was the year we invited our clients. Bigger room, fancier dinner, and, of course, more liquor. It was an experiment that we never repeated. The party was too stiff and formal, not fun the way it had been in the past. And the wilder behavior of some employees, which we would have tolerated or handled quietly in an employee party, was embarrassing in front of our clients. One poor young man we had to keep in a back room for a year until we had some new clients we could assign him to. Any other questions?"

"No. That's it."

"Well, I hope you will stay for lunch. Maureen made us a salad and some sandwiches before she went into Bend. I took them out of the refrigerator when I took the mugs to the kitchen. I'll have some wine with you, if you like. But there are all kinds of sodas and fruit juices in stock for the grandchildren. We could sit out on the deck overlooking the water."

"Thank you," said Sheila. "I'd like that." She knew, and she suspected that McAllister knew, that the next direct flight to San Francisco did not leave until evening. Having lunch at this beautiful house, overlooking the water and the meadow, would be a taste of the good life. Maybe she could get McAllister to talk about the places he had been and the people he knew.

"I'd like to hear what you think of the firm as it is now, coming in as a new person," said McAllister. "Of course, digging through all these old records can't be much fun."

"Well, it's given me a sense of the history of the company. And what the attorneys I see every day have worked on in the past."

"That's good," said McAllister. "Still, I'm sorry for the messiness you still have to deal with."

"Not at all," said Sheila.

"The powder room is by the front door if you want to wash up." McAllister started down the hall toward his office.

In the spotless half-bath there were fresh flowers by the sink and two landscape paintings on the walls. Both the hand towels, cloth and paper, had flowers on them. Sheila chose the paper and dropped it in the little lacquer wastebasket. She thought of giving Tim a quick call but it could wait. She was still Burton's guest.

There was a salad bowl covered with plastic wrap in the kitchen and a jar of homemade salad dressing next to it. There was a plate of sandwiches under another plastic wrap, two glasses, two plates, cloth napkins, and two pairs of silver salad forks and small knives. The plates looked to be hand-painted with images of flowers. Sheila lifted the plastic wrap, served some salad on a plate, and chose half a sandwich. It looked elegant.

She decided not to take the food to the table without McAllister and she waited in the living room, her hands clasped behind her, casting her eyes over the art. There was a half-abstract painting of a group of Indians in garish colors over the fireplace. Over the wet bar was a painting of a skull that looked like a Georgia O'Keefe and, on closer inspection, had her signature on it. By the front door was a wooden sculpture of an owl painted in multiple colors like a totem pole. The light had moved since she first arrived and she admired the fabrics on the couch and chairs. She wanted to try sitting on the big soft couch but did not. After five minutes of wandering around the living room and dining room Sheila walked slowly toward the office. The light had changed there too and something else as well. There was a spray of tiny red dots on the wall behind the desk chair.

"Burton?" she said. There was no reply. She walked up to the desk. The specks on the wall were wet and glistening. The chair was pushed back from the desk. Between the desk and the chair McAllister was lying on the floor with a pool of red beside him. The back of McAllister's head had burst open. Sheila leaned over the desk. There was a revolver on the floor beside the body.

She backed up slowly from the desk and left the office. She picked up a wall phone in the kitchen and dialed 911. She told them that Burton McAllister had shot himself. She was very sure he was dead. She hadn't touched anything in the room when she found him but she had been in the room earlier. She identified herself and her employer. She said Mrs. McAllister would be coming home some-time that afternoon but she did not know when. The 911 operator asked Sheila to wait outside the front door. A deputy sheriff was on his way.

Sheila found a pitcher of iced tea in the refrigerator and poured herself a glass. She took the glass and a napkin to the bench in the outdoor entryway and went back for her plate and a fork. Though her hands shook slightly nothing spilled off the plate. She sat on the end of the bench in the sun. The bench was comfortable, the sky was blue, and the lawn was freshly cut. The only sounds were the scrabbling of a squirrel on a tree and the occasional call of a jay. The salad was very good. Someday, Sheila said to herself, she would live like this.

Do No Harm

My great uncle Walter grew up on a cattle ranch near Rosland on the Little Deschutes River. When he became a doctor he returned to Rosland and set up a medical practice. The next doctor was thirty miles away. Seeing patients paid well but the population was too small and too healthy to take up all of Uncle Walter's time. That made births doubly welcome and deaths doubly sad. Thanks to his efforts though, and the fact that he was readily available to those who could pay and those few who could not, there are people alive today who would not be here if Walter had not saved the life of their father or grandmother or someone else from whom they descended.

Walter drove a Model T Ford when cars were still new in the area. The dirt roads, some of them little more than wagon tracks, threw the car around. But Walter was a good driver and he rarely went fast. He was a good mechanic too and he needed to be. Cars were so rare in that part of the country that sometimes families were as excited to see the car as to see the doctor. The car had carriage lamps and a loud horn that sounded when Walter squeezed the rubber bulb. The horn was mostly to entertain his patients' children.

After being up most of the night and finally delivering a rancher's baby girl on a clear blue August afternoon, Walter was driving back to town when he was waved down by an eighteen-year-old boy on a foot-sore horse. The boy was wearing ragged clothes and a dirty broad-brimmed hat. Walter had never seen him before.

"My friend fell off his horse and is busted up bad," said the boy. "His arm is broken and the bone is sticking out. He needs you right away, as fast as you can come."

"When did this happen?" asked Walter. The question seemed to flummox the boy.

"Yesterday. He was just ridin' along and his horse spooked and threw him."

"Where is he now?"

"About six miles east of here in an old house we found." Walter knew which house it was. A family named Fancher had attempted to homestead the place but the poor soil would not even grow rye.

"Where were you headed when your friend had the accident?"

"We were riding from Reno to Bend to find work," said the boy. "There are supposed to be sawmills starting up in Bend and looking for workers. We've all had it with punching cattle."

"How many are you?"

"Six of us all riding together. Henry's the boss."

"What spooked the horse?"

"Rattlesnake," said the boy.

Walter did not say anything. There were no rattlesnakes near Rosland. The winters were too long and too cold. Walter knew the boy was probably lying about more than rattlesnakes. But there was someone out there who needed a doctor. He was sure of that. He thought of going home first for an early dinner. On the other hand he could save at least an hour if he went to the patient directly.

"I'll drive on ahead," said Walter. "I'll meet you out there."

Walter considered buckling on the revolver that was under his seat but left it where it was. If there were five men at the house the gun would be useless. Wearing it would show he was afraid of them. As long as they needed a doctor he would be all right.

Except for the recent hoof prints in the front yard the log house looked abandoned. There wasn't even smoke coming out of the chimney. The double doors to the barn behind the house were shut. A man came out the front door with tall boots and a leather vest on. No gun. The man looked down the road past the car to see if there was anyone else coming.

Walter shut the engine, stepped out of the car, and retrieved his black medical bag from the back seat. "Are you Henry?" he asked.

"Henry Cahill at your service. We are glad to see you, Doctor. Your patient is right inside. His name is Homer."

"How was he injured?" asked Walter.

"He was shot in the arm," said Henry. "It was an accident."

They went into the front room that took up half the little one-story house. The room was dark and full of dust. There was a cast-iron stove but no furniture. Three men were sitting on the floor, their backs against the log wall, and one man was lying on a pile of blankets.

Walter unwrapped a bloody cloth that tightly circled the arm. There was a big hole in the man's arm but no exit wound. The bone did not appear to be broken. The man had lost some blood but was still conscious.

"Homer, are you hurt anywhere else?" asked the doctor.

"Just the arm," said the man in a bitter voice.

"We need to get you into the sunlight so I can see what I'm doing."

"You fellows lift those two blankets he's on. Don't let them slip," said Henry. They settled him in the front yard. Walter gave Homer a shot of morphine and began to clean the wound.

"How did this happen?" asked Walter.

"Damn fool shot me," said Homer.

"One of his buddies, fooling around with his gun," said Henry. Walter did not ask which one.

"Can you feel this?" asked Walter as he pinched the arm above the wound.

"Nope. It's stopped hurting." Homer look relieved, as though the whole problem were solved.

"Good. Now lie down while I get that bullet out of there. You men hold on to Homer so he doesn't move while I'm working. Mr. Cahill, please hold on to his arm, firm but not too tight."

Walter tried not to cut anymore flesh than necessary but the bullet was lodged against the bone. He pulled it out and held it up to the light. Forty-five caliber bullets were uncommon in 1913 and Walter tried not to show his alarm in seeing this one. The only 45 that he knew of in the area was a pistol that belonged to his brother, my grandfather. As far as Walter could see, none of the guns the cowboys had were 45s.

The shot had been fired at long range. A short-range shot would have broken the bone or gone all the way through the arm. Whoever fired the shot could not have been certain of hitting the arm. The shooter had to be willing to kill this man if not specifically intending to do so. What threat had this bunch posed to Walter's brother or his family that a family member had shot to kill? Had the family come to harm?

Walter dropped the bullet in his medical bag and turned back to clean and bandage the wound. "What happened to the man who fired the shot?" he asked.

"Nothin'," said Henry. "It wasn't a quarrel. It was an accident. Is Homer going to be all right?"

"If it doesn't get infected he should be fine. He's lost some blood and the wound needs to start healing. I'll change the dressing this evening and then again in the morning. Then I'll drive him to my place where I can look after him for a while."

"Why not drive him there tonight?" asked Henry.

"The wound has got to seal itself or he'll lose more blood. I'm going to have to drive very carefully in the daytime to keep the wound from opening up again. We'll never make it in the dark."

"Well, doc, I guess you will be our guest for the night," said Henry. "I'm afraid all we have are beans and dried beef for dinner; bread and coffee for breakfast."

"I think I'll drive myself home tonight and come back in the morning," said Walter. Henry gave the sky a sour look.

"Suppose you don't come back," said Henry. "Suppose you get hurt driving or you decide some other patient is more important? Then we'd be left here with a man we can't take care of. I'm afraid we can't take that chance, Doc. You fix up Homer again in the morning and then be on your way. It will save you having to come back out here."

"Keeping me away from my office and my own bed is not going to make you popular around here," said Walter.

"We're not too popular already," said one of the other men. Henry told him to shush.

"Let's get a few things straight, then," said Walter. "First of all my fee is fifteen dollars. I would as soon you pay me now."

"Fair enough," said Henry. He reached into his jacket pocket and pulled out a large brown wallet. There were a lot more bills in it than anyone would expect a bunch of cowboys looking for work to have. He gave Walter fifteen dollars and put the wallet away.

"Thank you, Henry," said Walter. "Any of the other men have complaints that need looking after?"

"Clem's got a bad blister," said Henry. "Any of the rest of you need the doc?" No one answered. Walter swabbed the blister and put a dressing on it. He told Clem to keep it clean and dry. There was another man who had some aches and pains to complain about. It was nothing serious and there was nothing for Walter to do but listen. He told the man he would give him something later to help him sleep.

"I have some smoked pork sausages in my car," Walter told the men. "My last patient gave them to me. There are enough to feed all of us for dinner with a few left over for breakfast."

"That is welcome news," said Henry, "and we're much obliged to you." The sound and smell of sausages frying on the wood stove lifted everyone's spirits. They ate dinner outside off tin plates. Some of the men had forks and some used their knives to eat with. Henry found a fork for Walter that the doctor washed and doused with alcohol. He unfolded his pocketknife to cut his sausage.

After dinner the men watched the sun set over the mountains to the west. The sun lit up one small cloud in the sky, first gold then red. Walter told the men how much he and his wife enjoyed watching the sunsets from the porch of their house. The couple had early dinners before putting their one-year-old son to bed. Now that the days were getting shorter they were thinking he might like to watch the sunsets too. Walter told them about meeting his wife when he was a student in Eugene and how they were married while he was in medical school in Portland. His wife could sing and she was a good piano player.

"You know, Doc," one of the men said, "you're not a bad man." Walter mentally completed the statement for him. "It's a shame we have to shoot you in the morning."

Henry told Walter he could sleep by the stove, which was still giving off heat. Walter thanked him. Henry slept by the door. About two o'clock Walter got up to visit the outhouse. He stepped over Henry and the man did not stir. Clem was knocked out by the sleeping draught and Homer was in dreamland from the morphine. The others seemed to be asleep. Walter did not go near his car. They had probably taken the crank away and even if they had left it, the noise of starting the Model T would wake the men up before he got it in gear. Besides, there was no moon and he would not see the road well enough to drive.

He walked to the barn and slowly opened the door. A horse whinnied quietly. Walter shut the door behind him and lit a short fat candle he had taken from his medical bag. He put it on a crossbeam at the far end of the barn and examined the horses. They all looked skinny and tired except for one. It was a young paint that Walter recognized. Its name was Jackson and it belonged to his nephew Vincent. Walter picked out a blanket and saddle and put them on the horse. He had just put on a bridle when he heard footsteps. He stepped quickly and quietly to the wall beside the door. The door opened and Henry stepped in. He was holding a pistol at his shoulder, pointed at an angle toward the roof. He peered toward the back of the barn where the candle was glowing and the horse was saddled.

"Going somewhere, Doc?" said Henry in a false friendly voice. Walter slammed him in the nose with his fist, blocked Henry's arm as it swung weakly toward him, and followed with a knee to his stomach.

"Oof," said Henry. He tried to shout but his voice had no volume. "Bob, Johnnie, the doc is trying…" Walter gouged him in the eye with his knuckle. Henry cried out in pain. Walter pulled the gun from his hand but, having no holster for it, threw it into a dark corner. He scooped up all the bridles for the other horses and mounted Jackson. He kicked hard and the horse shot out of the barn. There were two men rounding the corner of the house.

"Henry's been kicked," he shouted. "I'm going for help." The men were half-asleep and had not brought their guns. They had not even put their boots on. Walter rode past the house and headed for the road. The boy was coming out of the front door with a pistol in his hand. Walter angled behind the car to get it between him and the front door and then charged away. He heard a bullet whistle past him and heard the report of the revolver. He galloped blindly in the direction of the road, counting on the horse to see better than he could in the dark and trusting it not to stumble. He leaned down along the horse's neck to reduce his silhouette against the stars.

"The boy's got one more shot that might possibly hit me," he thought. He heard another bang but the bullet was wide. Fifty feet further he slowed the horse to a trot. He thought he was safe but the boy had run after him and took another shot. Missed again. Walter galloped another hundred yards and led the horse to the right. Then he turned to the west again and put Jackson into a brisk walk. He could hear urgent, angry voices behind him. Another shot rang out but it was just for show. They would never catch him. The other horses would be useless without the bridles. When he got to Paulina Prairie he pointed Jackson toward his brother's ranch. The horse caught on quickly and Walter let him pick his own route.

It was cold, as even August nights can be in the high desert. Walter had left his coat behind and he hugged himself to keep warm. By daybreak he was at his brother's ranch. His nephew was up early to get milk for breakfast from the cow.

"Where did you find my horse?" Vince shouted.

"Is everybody here all right?" answered Walter.

"We're fine, except that some rustlers stole my horse."

Walter was cold and tired. He climbed off Jackson and gave the bridle to Vince. "They're at the Fancher place. I need to call the sheriff and I need to get warm." He walked into the house and went to the phone. He turned the crank but no one answered.

"Millie doesn't get in 'til six," said Eleanor, his brother's wife. She had a sweater on over her nightgown. "Sit by the stove while I fix you some breakfast."

"Hot coffee to start, if you don't mind Eleanor," said Walter. He sat down and closed his eyes. She did not ask him how he came to be there so early in the morning.

Walter tried the operator ten minutes later and Millie was in early. She woke the sheriff up at his house in Prineville thirty miles away. Walter described the men and their location. He told the sheriff where he had dropped the bridles.

"I'm sure they're the men who held up the bank in Antelope the day before yesterday," said the Sheriff. "They shot the bank manager and Doc Thompson is looking after him."

Walter slept upstairs for two hours and borrowed a horse to get home. The sheriff found all the men still at the abandoned homestead. Bob now had a broken arm from trying to start the doctor's car. The men gave up without a fight. Henry had an enormous black eye. The sheriff brought the men into Rosland where Walter changed the dressings on Homer and Clem and set Bob's arm. He gave Henry an icepack.

The boy went to prison in Salem. The bank manager did not survive and the rest of the gang was hung for murder. Walter testified at the trial in Prineville.

Walter's wife told him Rosland was no place to bring up children and she wanted to leave. Walter said nothing like this would ever happen again and there was no healthier climate for children. They stayed. The story of the gang's escapades appeared in all the papers from Seattle to Santa Fe. It put Rosland on the map. The population grew, first with more cattle ranching and then with timber once the railroad arrived. The sheriff got money to station a deputy in the town. It was not a good place for the lawless. Walter's practice filled up and he made good money on the land he owned. He and his wife lived in the same house another forty years.

Kubali and the Vampire Cowboys

W hen Oregon was not yet a state, citizens of another planet oc-
cupied a lush meadow by an attractive little river right in the
middle of the territory. The aliens were young men and women –
none of them over nine hundred years old – out to see the galaxy
before turning to careers and families.

Their parents had told them not to do anything risky and no
hanky-panky. But they were as high-spirited as anyone nine hundred years old could be, looking to push the limits while they had
the chance and to have some new and different experiences.

Their BBZ-13 Deluxe Interplanetary RV circled Earth while the
group looked out the windows. Humans were the most advanced
animals on the planet but still had a long way to go. They had rudi-
mentary steam engines but cable TV had not even crossed their
minds. Nonetheless, as the aliens' attention wandered from the nov-
elty of large marine fauna, the varieties of human experience began
to intrigue them.

"We should go down there and try living like they do for a while,"
said Kubali, an independently minded young woman who was getting a little cranky sharing the RV with her friends. She had taken
a degree in biological engineering. Most of the others had studied
sociology. Recognizing that stepping on the surface of the Earth
was something their parents would definitely not want them to do,

Kubali's friends voiced immediate enthusiasm. They searched with rising excitement for a human way of life they might emulate.

The hunter-gatherers in Africa and Australia looked interesting. The young men wanted to stalk wild animals and kill them with spears and arrows. But the women said the humans in those places wore few clothes, the gathering part of hunting and gathering looked boring, and, besides, there were a lot of bugs.

Some of the Trombolinians were attracted to the incipient culture of France and Italy. But careful consideration led the group to realize that, after all, they did not really want to associate with humans. Mankind was still backward and the humans might not respond well to short blue-green creatures who were much smarter than the humans were.

Two of the males, whose names are too long to spell out here, watched men herding cattle in Texas and called their friends over to the window. The humans were riding big animals and bossing other big animals around. The men wore wide-brimmed hats and waved ropes around in the air. It looked like fun. The Trombolinians, using more powerful lenses now, began evaluating which cowboys seemed better at directing the cattle and which looked most impressive sitting in the saddle.

Kubali was the first to suggest the Trombolinians take up the cowboy life. They would be outdoors in the Earth's weather most of the time and associate with the big animals that were, she said, only slightly less intelligent than the humans. At night they could have fires outdoors and still tuck themselves into bed in the spaceship. They could range far and wide on their horses. This ranging among the rocks and rills, fields and streams, it occurred to some of the group, would allow private encounters between boys and girls that could lead to special experiences.

Kubali's friends thought she had a great idea. Some of them wrote a manual on horse riding and cattle herding based upon their observations. Others went out to find the ideal site.

There was still a faction that wanted to be hunter-gatherers in Africa. Humans, they said, had lived as hunter-gatherers for thousands of years. The domestication of animals was recent, even trendy, and it might fall into the dustbin of galactic history before the Trombolinians even got home again. The boys, and they were mostly boys, talked of facing lions with nothing but a spear and a shield. It was, they felt, the one chance any of them would have to experience such a fundamental, simple, and physically challenging way of life. Their friends listened attentively but were not persuaded.

It was Fitbor, a young man of no particular talent, who surprised his friends by proposing a compromise. He noted that the Masaii tribe in Eastern Africa were cattle herders. The Trombolinians could combine the practices of the Masaii and the Texas cowboys to have a richer experience. They would use horses and lassos to herd their cattle. But like the Masaii they would bring all the cattle into a big corral made of piled brushwood every night. The Texas faction said this was a silly gesture since there were no lions around to attack the cattle. The Africa faction countered that branding cattle, which excited the Texas faction no end, was absurd when they would inevitably choose a place with no humans and, therefore, no other cattle. Finally branding was agreed to and the brushwood corral was dropped on the condition that the Trombolinians, like the Masaii, would bleed the cattle periodically and mix the blood with milk. They would drink the mixture in gourds teleported in from the Serengeti.

The Trombolinians had been bioengineered to run on an implanted nuclear energy pack. But a love of mojitos and potato chips, or substances very similar, had sustained an ability to ingest food. The Masaii concoction had no kick to it but most were game to try it. It seemed, as one young woman said, "pricelessly authentic."

The group picked a site in Texas that had water, good grass, and not too many people. But their survey team said that humans traipsed through regularly and the heat was "meaner than a neutron star." Kubali, on her own, spotted a sliver of land east of the Cascade Mountains that had grass, a river, a better climate, and no people. There was a large meadow there surrounded by a deep forest. There were mountains to the west, miles of desert to the east, and deep river gorges to the north and south. It looked like humans would leave the place alone for many years to come.

They called the place "Mahali Furaha" which means, more or less, "Happy Acres" in Trombolinian. They cleared a landing zone in the nearby trees to hide the spaceship.

As always in the American West, fences generated much debate. Remnants of the Africa faction, led by a young man named Uuujinda, argued that fences were unnatural and that the cattle, as they came to love the Trombolinians, would stay close to home. Others doubted they could win such affection from the beasts. There was a wooden fence faction, with sub-factions arguing the relative merits of post-and-rail, buck-and-rail, and zig-zag fencing. The Trombolinians could have built walls out of almost anything – stone, steel, nano-tubes, or dry spaghetti. But true cowboys never used these things. Barbed wire did not occur to the group and humans had not yet invented it. A fact unknown to most historians today is that barb-wire was the first human invention that had not been developed by the Trombolinians thousands of years earlier.

"Let's just use a force field and say 'the hell with it,'" said Kubali. Her friends were so tired of debating fences they accepted her proposal on the spot. Uuujinda insisted they take the force field down during the day so they could rely on the herding skills they were about to learn. Taking the force field down would also allow the wild animals to come and go.

The group needed cattle, horses, saddles, bridles, ropes, blankets, horse medicine, and other things they learned about as they went along. They needed hats, chaps, and shirts with pockets. They made lists. They decided they would take a little bit from different owners all around the world. They would leave gold nuggets behind in payment. Sometimes the wrong person would find the nugget but the Trombolinians decided they could not solve that problem. They had taken from humans and given to humans. The two races were even overall.

They preferred small horses because they wanted to control the animals with their arms and legs, like human cowboys. Using brain waves would have been easier but it wasn't the experience they were aiming for. They still made compromises. They did not mind using brain power to float the saddles on and off. When a horse lost a shoe they swapped the horse out for a new one.

The cattle herd was a motley one. They had Durhams, Holsteins, Herefords, and Brahmans. The Masaii cattle were narrow and scraggly. The Charolais were enormous and intimidating. All the cows got along but the bulls, regardless of breed, fought all the time and chased the cows into the river. The Trombolinians sent all but one of the bulls away. A Masaii tribesman, surprised by the sudden appearance of a Texas Longhorn in his herd, decided the wisest course was to eat it immediately.

The group had a wonderful time charging around on horses, in and out of the willows and lodgepoles, chasing down errant cattle. Smashing across the river, with noisy splashes of water and the risk of falling off the horse, was a particular treat. When their days ended, they sat on their horses on a rise above the meadow, watching the sunset. The cattle grazed contentedly at that hour, some lying down and chewing their cud. The cowboys and cowgirls rolled cigarettes and smoked them. They called each other "pardner" while they "palavered" about doggies, critters, pulling leather, and which horses had "bottom." They referred to their spaceship as the bunkhouse. When branding time came, some said, it was the highlight of the entire experience. They hypnotized the cattle so the animals would not feel the hot iron.

One morning they saw a tall cloud of dust rising in the north. Kubali, Uuujinda, and another man, Elemika, volunteered to ride out and see what was causing it. They found a thousand humans coming right toward them in a long wagon train. If the people settled in this place, the idyllic summer of the Trombolinians would be over. Elemika addressed the humans in the front wagon as politely as he knew how. He explained how glad he was to see them, that his people wished them well on their journey, that his people would even help them on their way. But they should understand that this land was unsuitable for them. That the Trombolinians could barely scratch out a living here.

The humans stared blankly at Elemika. His auto-translator was still set to Spanish from a trip to Spain. He had brought back a bull from a bullfight and the bull had given no end of trouble. Elemika was not the sharpest tool in the Trombolinean toolbox. But one of the humans had been captured in the Mexican-American War and began to reply in halting, half-remembered Spanish. By this time Elemika's auto-translator had picked up English mutterings and it delivered his speech for him again, this time with a Scotch accent and quotations from Robert Burns.

The emigrants were in sorry shape. Some were sick and all were tired and hungry. Their cows and oxen and horses were dying. They were trying to find a place called Willamette. They believed there was a pass over the mountains about thirty miles to the south.

Kubali used a planet scanner to find a suitable volume of food that was instantly available. She took all the food about to be served at an enormous banquet in New York. She spread it up and down the length of the wagon train. The food saved lives and the dinner wine lifted spirits. The Trombolinians let the settlers' animals graze in their meadow and drink from the river. They swapped their healthy cows and horses for wagon train animals that were weak. During the night, a few switches and turns of a dial in the spaceship silently transported the entire wagon train south and erased the emigrants' memory of the Trombolinians. The wagon train struggled toward the mountains and was eventually rescued by settlers from the other side. Without the Trombolinians, however, the settlers would have ground to a halt about where Gordy's Truck Stop stands today.

Elemika sent the used plates and the silverware back to New York but he missed some. Even today pieces emerge when the ground thaws in the spring.

The cowboy life, the discovery of so many new life forms, and the encounter with the humans rejuvenated Kubali. She explored and catalogued all the natural life around her, like a Trombolinian Audubon. The names she gave the plants and animals, and the pictures she drew of them, are enshrined today in the Trombolinian Central Library. The snow-clad mountains, the rippling waters, the majestic trees, and the waving grasses worked their magic on her. She also did not fail to notice how gracefully one of her male friends rode a horse.

The first sign of a pregnancy among the Trombolinians is a red mark on the back of the neck of the mother-to-be. It is considered impolite for anyone but her own mother to mention the mark to the woman. As a result, many of her friends often know a woman is pregnant before she does. The implications of this phenomenon ripple all the way through Trombolinian culture, from seating arrangements on public transport to the fundamentals of constitutional law. Elemika assumed someone else had told Kubali and he mentioned it to her in casual conversation. Friends now admitted to her they were torn between admiration for her daring, envy for the experiences she'd had, and dread of her parents' reaction when they all got home.

The group did not have the authority to marry the couple but they went through the motions hoping it would ease re-entry to the wider community. Unfortunately, the pseudo-marriage created a new problem.

"If we are married we can cohabitate," said ersatz husband. He began building a crude log cabin.

Everyone could see he was motivated. The half-built cabin – evidence of his passion – can still be found today, falling apart in the woods. Wiser heads agreed, however, that reports of a couple playing house would cause even more trouble at home. They gave the marriage a special status that did not permit private quarters.

As the nights grew longer and colder Uuujinda had a dream. He saw more English-speaking humans coming from the east, out of the desert. They smoked pipes and looked for places to settle. They traded with the Indians until there were enough settlers to drive the Indians away. Sometimes the Indians fought back and killed settlers. In the dream the Trombolians were repeatedly asked to take sides, to get involved.

"We have to leave," he said.

"But we like being cowboys," said Fitbor, "and we like this place. We love the horses, the land, even the flowers."

"I would miss the cows," said Elemika.

"We've had our fun," said Uuujinda. "We were lucky we got to this planet when we did. In a hundred years they will have nukes and post-modernism."

"I'm staying," said Kubali. "I'm going to raise my son here." By that time she knew it was going to be a boy. Her friends were incredulous. Some eyes grew so big their owners had headaches for a week.

"Your boy won't have a power pack. How will he live?"

"Won't you miss us?"

"Nobody will come back all this way to pick you up."

"Is the boy's father staying with you?"

"No," said Kubali, "I'm staying by myself. I like it here. I'll have my son for company."

"It's still very primitive here," warned Uuujinda.

"At least I won't have to spend light-years in that RV with a chemical toilet."

"We'll all worry about you and wonder what you are doing," said Elemika.

"I'll send you Twinkles," said Kubali. A Twinkle is an interstellar Tweet that can include small food items. Kubali's friends had acquired a taste for filet mignon and the prospect of tasty Twinkles allayed their concerns somewhat. The BBZ-13 rose to the height of a ponderosa and shot away into the cosmos. A blue-green cowgirl waved to it cheerfully from the back of her horse.

Kubali's gaze fell from the sky to the meadow below her. She now possessed a log cabin built by amateurs, some odds and ends left by her friends, twenty horses, a still for making grain alcohol, and about a hundred head of cattle. Plenty of water, a great view of the mountains. She was ecstatically content.

Though Trombolinian gestation is longer than an elephant's, birth is relatively simple, analogous to punching a microwave to open it when the food is cooked. Kubali named her son Pierce because the humans whom she had rescued said their president was named Franklin Pierce.

Pierce's mother foresaw that he was going to have to deal with humans when he grew up. She set her translator to English and kept it there. As she heard it translating for her she learned the language herself. When Pierce was five, she turned off the translator and they both spoke English from then on. To make Pierce look more human Kubali took up cosmetic surgery. She used razor-sharp kitchen knives and she consulted a vast medical book Uuujinda had left her. She practiced on the cattle, recreating faces of pioneers she remembered from the wagon train. When the cows chewed their cuds they appeared to be chewing tobacco, getting ready to spit.

Pierce's face was modeled on a portrait of George Washington that the settlers had left behind. He thrived on milk, blood, and grass-fed beef. He was five-foot five when he was ten years old, very tall for a Trombolinian. He walked with an erect posture and powerful muscles. He was a masterful rider and his horse would do anything for him. His skin retained a greenish tinge but he could pass for a human. An unusual human, but a human.

Pierce liked to talk. He and Kubali would sit by the fire in the log cabin and talk the evenings away. The boy would relate the events of the day – whether the cows were well and peaceful, how the horses were behaving, what wild animals he had seen, and whether there were fish in the river. Kubali would fill his head with stories of life on Trombolinia. Every year, at the winter solstice, their home star sat right above the outhouse and she would point it out. In the summer they watched a big yellow moon rise over the ridge. It lit up the landscape in a way that the two little moons of Trombolinia never could have.

The two sat out the American Civil War without knowing it was going on. The Transcontinental Railroad came nowhere near them. A famous Shoshone raider, Chief Paulina, attempted to pay them a visit but Kubali quickly snapped on the force field and he went away.

A family that settled fifteen miles downstream of the Trombolinian cattle ranch had a red-haired seventeen-year-old daughter named

Alice. With so few young people around the possibility of a match with Pierce was obvious to all. But it was not love at first sight. Alice, a tall girl, referred to Pierce, when discussing him with her parents, as "the green troll." While Alice was quite attractive by human standards, Pierce was not human. His hormones did not rise above idle when he saw her. This deficiency endeared him to her even less.

What brought the two together was music. Alice's family had brought a piano across the country and her parents taught her to play. Pierce had never heard anything so heavenly. He asked Alice to teach him and he took to it immediately. He visited her house often from that time forward.

Kubali's cosmetic surgery extended to equipping her son to consummate a marriage. She wondered later whether she had made a slip along the way since her son seemed to be very taken with his novel appendage, weighing its capabilities when he should have been minding the cattle. After Pierce met Alice, the hours sitting together on the piano bench somehow led him to suspect that greater intimacy with Alice might allow him to put his addition to its highest and best use.

The couple was married at Alice's home by a passing preacher. Though Alice had come to love Pierce, and relations between Trombolinians and humans had made a giant step forward, Kubali knew that the only DNA on Earth that was remotely compatible with that of Trombolinians was that of shiitake mushrooms. Like a witch with caldrons and beakers, Kubali toiled for months to create human DNA that would carry along Pierce's most desirable features. The couple's first child, a small but very cute girl with green eyes, was named Bonny. Bonny lived a long and happy life.

Kubali and Pierce are still on Earth today and, barring accident, will outlive all of us by many centuries. They live like humans now, voting and paying taxes. From time to time they create new birth certificates and change location, leaving their neighbors to wonder why they never aged. They have already outlived Bonny's children and her grandchildren. Pierce has taken six more wives in succession and has over a thousand descendants. Many of them have green eyes and an ear for music. Not one is a vegetarian. Pierce and his current wife are now living on the land the Trombolinians first settled. This wife, Kimberly, is one of the few who knows his true origins. Their children can speak a few words of Trombolinian and can find the star their grandmother came from.

Kubali lives on the slopes of Mount Kenya. Her neighbors think she looks rather odd but her mixing of milk and blood for breakfast seems quite reasonable. She keeps in touch with her friends back on Trombolinia. Uuujinda is now a highly respected university professor. Elemika works on an offshore drilling platform. He has pictures of cows and the Cascade Mountains over his bunk. Kubali says she would love to see her friends. But if they sent a spaceship she would not get on it. She likes it where she is.

On the Mountain

He's not moving.

We have to rappel down to him and see.

He's dead. That's a hundred-foot straight fall onto a flat rock ledge.

We can't be sure he's dead. If it were you or me we'd want some-body to come down and check.

What if we can't climb back up? The rock is a sheer face.

I'll go down. You can belay me while I climb back up.

I can't haul you up if you don't find places to put your hands and feet on the rock. And my trying to get off this mountain and go for help by myself is risky. We might never get help and all three of us could die up here.

So what should we do?

Finish the climb.

Are you kidding? Shouldn't we get back down to a phone and tell someone?

All Search and Rescue can do is get his body. They're going to need a day to plan for it. Whether we go down now or finish the climb and tell them later won't make any difference.

You want people to know Chris died and we just went on with the climb?

Climbing is a dangerous sport. Everyone knows that. Things go wrong. You go on.

But climbers don't die every day. This is going to be in the news.

Chris would want us to go on. It's what he would have done if one of us were down there.

If I were down there I'd want you to come down and check on me. You wouldn't really want anything. You'd be dead. Listen. The whole point of climbing is to test your nerve. When you're hanging out over thin air and you're holding on with your boot tips and fingernails, are you going to carefully and rationally think through what your next move is? Or are you going to panic? That's the essence of the sport. If you wimp out, you die. Or you get injured. Or you have to quit without making the top. I agree something bad has happened. But that's just the point. Can you suck it up and still make the climb?

If a storm comes in or someone gets injured you're supposed to get off the mountain and try it another day.

It's a clear day. You and I are fine. We're both roped in and you are standing on a rock as big as a parking place.

We had a team of three. Two of you were experienced climbers. Now we're left with only two of us and I'm not as experienced as you.

Don't knock yourself because you're upset. You're a good climber. You and I have climbed pitches that were much tougher than anything we're going to see on this hill. Come on. Let's bag this peak and go home.

I thought Chris was your friend. Aren't you upset about this too?

We were climbing buddies, that's all. He knew the risks he was taking.

What the hell happened anyway? How did an experienced climber like Chris suddenly fall off the mountain like that? One minute he had you on belay. You were climbing up the pitch he'd climbed ahead of you. Then you slipped five feet and the next thing I knew he was sailing through the air.

He tied a bad anchor. He tied his anchor rope around a rock or to an old piton somebody drove into the ledge and left there. When I slipped all my weight went on the belay rope and it jerked him forward. That wouldn't have been a problem if he had been securely anchored. Either his anchor rope slipped off a rock or a piton pulled out. We'll see when we get up there.

Maybe the anchor rope broke.

No. I checked it carefully before we started. It was a good rope.

I saw you slip but it happened so fast I didn't understand what was going on. I'm surprised he didn't yell or something.

He's a climber. He didn't panic. He was trying to think of a way to save himself. He did the only thing he could.

What was that?

He hung on to the belay rope. It was the single thing he had. But I was attached to the rope. He almost took me with him. Then you would have been up here by yourself with no rope at all.

I'm glad you're here. But how come he didn't pull you right off the rock?

I was lucky. When I slid I grabbed onto a piton. As soon as Chris started to fall I wrapped the rope around the piton. When the rope straightened out the piton took the strain instead of me. But Chris couldn't hang onto the rope. He was already going too fast.

I couldn't be sure what I saw.

Chris knew he would probably take me with him. But he hung on anyway. He made a mistake with the anchor rope and he almost killed me as a result. I don't think I owe him.

In a way I suppose you don't. I didn't realize what happened.

So are we climbing?

You are tough. I don't think I'm anywhere near as tough as that.

Now's the time to find out. I'll belay you from the top of the pitch. I'm already halfway up.

How are you going to anchor yourself when you get up there?

I'll use the sling I'm carrying my pitons on.

Is that strong enough?

Stronger than rope.

Wait a minute. Before you start up, I've got to think about this.

Take a minute. But not too long. Daylight won't wait.

I'm done. I am sorry but I am just flat not willing to climb any further. As rationally and as calmly as I can think it through, I see the risk as being too great. On top of that I'm still shaken by Chris's fall. I don't have the confidence I started out with. If Chris can make a mistake like that so can either of us. I want to climb but I have a lot of other things I want to do. I'm not willing to risk them.

Fair enough. I understand. I'll come down to where you're standing and we'll leave the mountain for another day. But we've learned something. If this is the way you react you're not cut out to be a serious climber. You don't want it enough. You don't want to test yourself to that point. Most people don't. It's okay.

Sorry.

No problem. I've just got to do a better job picking the people I climb with. I've got one guy who makes a fundamental mistake, kills himself, and nearly kills me. Then I've got another guy who I thought had the nerve for climbing but turns out not to.

Sorry.

Now do you still want to check on Chris? You can belay me and I'll go down.

We're still not sure either one of us can get back up once he's down there. That's not the way we came up.

If I can't get back up then I'll just have to wait until you get Search and Rescue.

You think I can get down off this mountain by myself?

If you want to badly enough you will.

You sure know how to make a guy nervous.

So the hell with Chris?

Well, I don't want to say that.

It's your choice. I've even offered to go down there myself. Are we going to check on Chris or are we going to get off this mountain?

We're going to get off this mountain.

So the hell with Chris.

The hell with Chris.

Bloodlines

My father started with the lumber company as a knob-knocker. He chopped the branches off the logs so they could fit close together on the company's rail cars. Later he became a tree faller which was a higher paying job. My father teamed with another man on a two-man saw. I was a four-year-old girl then and was very proud of my father. I assumed all the gigantic logs that went past our camp had been cut by my father.

The company built temporary railroads into the forest to harvest the timber. When the company had cut all the trees in one area they took up the tracks and moved them somewhere else. Every few years they moved the camp we lived in as well. All the buildings in the camp were designed to fit on the rail cars. The cranes that lifted logs were used to put the buildings on the rail cars in the morning and take them off in the afternoon. Two houses could fit on one rail-car but the schoolhouse took up one car by itself. The entire camp was moved in one day. The crane operators were so good that if you left a glass of water on the table in the morning the glass would still be there with the water in it when you went into your house again that evening.

My best friend in the camp, and the only other child in my grade, was a girl named Elyse Jensen. Elyse's family came from Minnesota and, before that, from Norway. Mr. and Mrs. Jensen spoke Norwegian at home. In the camp where we were in fourth grade there was a clothesline on pulleys that ran between the Jensens' house and ours. When our mothers didn't have wash hanging on it Elyse and I sent messages back and forth in a bucket. We could see each other as we did this and we could have shouted to each other if we wanted to. But the messages were secret. Our secrets didn't amount to much but we liked the idea that no one else knew what was in the bucket. And wouldn't they like to know!

We played baseball with the other children, boys and girls. First base was the corner of the schoolhouse. Second and third base were pine trees that had been left standing in the camp for shade. I couldn't hit as far as the older boys but I wanted very much to win. I tried to hit the ball to the worst player on the other team. When Elyse was on the other team she was usually the worst player. Her attention wandered. I don't think she ever figured out that I hit the ball to her on purpose.

Elyse was blond with blue eyes. We were both good students but Elyse was better than me in math. She seemed to have a part to her brain that I didn't have, or part of her brain worked much better than mine. I talked more than Elyse and the teacher sometimes reprimanded me for talking too much.

Families like mine and Elyse's tended to stay with the company year after year, even when work was slow or the temperature got down to twenty below in the winter. The families lived in the narrow little houses that fit on the rail cars. The wives kept house and cooked the meals on wood stoves. There was no running water in the houses and no electricity.

Bachelors lived in bunk houses that could also fit on the rail cars. Bachelors came and went all the time. They argued with their boss or they heard of higher wages elsewhere or they simply got restless. Bachelors ate in the company dining room. The company gave them good food in big quantities so the men would be satisfied and want to stay.

There wasn't supposed to be alcohol anywhere because of Prohibition. But there was local moonshine and whiskey smuggled in from Canada. The company would destroy any still it found in the forest because it was worried about forest fires. They would let a man go if he drank on the job. The company motto was "Safety First."

There was a lot of drinking on the weekends though. We accepted that people were going to drive drunk, just as they had driven horse-drawn wagons drunk. The cars didn't go more than twenty miles an hour and the men were tough. Some men wrecked a car every year and traded in what was left for a new one.

The summer Elyse and I were fifteen the camp cook died driving home from East Lake on a Saturday night. The men said the cook was not as tough as the rest of them and not as skilled with machinery.

The company asked my mother if she would cook for the bachelors until they found a new cook. She did a better job than the cook had ever done and she didn't drink. After three days the company hired her. She liked the job and suddenly we had more money, newer clothes, and better food. Mom fired the two waitresses and hired me and Elyse. We served breakfast in the morning before we took the bus to high school and dinner in the evening after we got back. The elementary school had been in the camp but the high school was in La Pine.

My mother said having us around made the dining room more civilized. She said the men made more of an effort to shave in the morning and clean up before dinner. And we didn't get into trouble with the men like the earlier waitresses. The men worked with our fathers every day and my dad often ate in the dining room. My mother was right there in the kitchen to know if anyone misbehaved, including Elyse and me.

I learned to flirt. Not outrageously but subtly. I'd catch a man looking at me and give him a little smile. Then I would ignore him. The next day I would suddenly show up beside him with a special helping of dessert. It was very safe and very limited. If a man overestimated how special he was I would go pay attention to another man, usually older, who had a better sense of what was going on. When my mother could see what I was doing she told me to cut it out.

Elyse was pleasant and polite but she didn't really flirt. If a man asked her a question about herself or made a comment she didn't quite understand she was off like a shot. But if he adopted a serious tone and asked Elyse a seemingly rational question, like what the eggs were fried in or if she knew the derivation of the word "isosceles," Elyse would give him the best answer she could and, if we weren't too busy, would keep answering questions until my mother or I interrupted.

What Elyse lacked, my mother told me, was feminine intuition. She was oblivious to so much that was going on around her. Her bright blond hair and curvy figure were very attractive to men. One boy at high school walked right into a wall and I had to explain to her why it happened. I don't think she fully believed me. Another girl said nasty things about her and Elyse told me she could not understand why anybody would say something that was so bad when it wasn't true.

In tenth grade we had world history with Mr. Finch. We learned about kings, queens, emperors, and the dates of famous battles. But Mr. Finch's recurring theme, which he warmed to as we came down the centuries, was the inevitable rise and dominance of the white race and particularly of northern Europeans. The sweep of Americans across North America was an excellent illustration of this overarching concept. Among his heroes were Otto von Bismarck for unifying Germany, Thomas Jefferson for the Louisiana Purchase, and James Polk for annexing Oregon. The worst villain I remember him talking about was an Indian named Chief Paulina who broke treaties he'd made with the United States and raided ranches all through Central Oregon in the 1860s.

According to Mr. Finch, people of northern European descent were best-suited to ensure the progress of the world. Ideally they should produce more children than other races. I was willing to repeat these ideas in the essays I wrote. But I knew that adults sometimes got ideas that they liked and they attached more importance to them than other people did. One thing that sank Mr. Finch in my estimation was his dismissal of Sacajawea. Lewis and Clark never would have succeeded without her because she could speak to Indian tribes they met. She tromped all that way carrying a baby, and she was only a year older than me. I thought Mr. Finch under-estimated her importance because she was an Indian.

Another thing that caused me to lose respect for Mr. Finch was a quote from Cecil Rhodes that he printed on heavy paper and hung above the blackboard. It said, "I contend that we are the first race in the world, and that the more of the world we inhabit the better it is for the human race." Cecil Rhodes sounded like one of the bachelors who kept telling people about all the great things he had done in some other camp.

Mr. Finch did, however, find a disciple in Elyse. She never asked so many questions, or offered as many comments, in any other class. Mr. Finch loaned her a book called Applied Eugenics. Eugenics was the idea that the human race, or maybe just the population of the United States, could be improved over time by preventing "defective and delinquent" people from immigrating – and preventing the ones who were already here from having children. I read part of the book and Elyse read all of it. It was over four hundred pages long. The book was easy to read and it said very interesting things about how men and women selected their mates and how they might do a better job for themselves and for the human race as a whole. It had tables and graphs that Elyse fell in love with. It was logical and mathematical. It sounded rational to me and I was caught up in the idea despite my misgivings about Mr. Finch.

Armed with our new insights we compared the men in camp on their eugenic merits. We evaluated apparent intelligence, character (being honest, reliable, and not drinking too much), height, strength, and physical appearance. Our analysis led us to a mechanic named Kurt Willemoes. He could fix anything and he never drank. All the other men respected him. He had thick shoulders and a square face. But he hardly talked and he always looked grumpy. I was repulsed by the idea of kissing him and could not imagine spending time with him. Elyse said that didn't matter if he had truly good genes.

Elyse's own bloodline was Nordic and that was the best type. My family was of English descent except for one grandmother who was French Canadian. My bloodline included Nordic roots, but it did not seem to be as pure as that of the Jensens. My mother told me that her French Canadian mother was part Algonquin or Ojibwe or some other Indian tribe. I didn't tell Elyse.

We often went to a place we called "the beach" in the summertime. It was about a mile away from camp on the Little Deschutes River. The river was slow and shallow and there was a grassy meadow next to it. Where the river was deeper on the other side there was a diving board. People would cool off in the river and have picnics on the grass.

The summer we graduated from high school the cattle rancher who owned the land built a dance floor in the meadow and hired a four-piece band to play on three or four Saturday nights. We could use the beach for free but it cost a quarter to get our hand stamped to use the dance floor. People came from our camp, other company camps in the area, and from the local ranches. After the sun went down the rancher lit bonfires to keep everybody warm.

Elyse and I were very popular with the bachelors, though we also danced with the married men. Our parents told us the rules, not as dictates but more in the sense of passing along tradition. The rules applied to everyone. You couldn't dance with the same partner more than two dances in a row and you couldn't dance with anyone more than four songs in any given night. Of course, if you were married you could dance with your husband or wife as much as you wanted. The other rule was that if a man who was drunk asked you to dance you were supposed to say no for everybody's sake. The men who could dance the best were our favorites. Some men did not know how to dance at all but we would dance at least one dance with any man who asked us as long as he was sober. Elyse liked dancing because she didn't have to talk.

The rancher's son, Clay Martin, was a gangly boy with dark brown hair. He was a year older than we were. Clay's job at these dances was to man the refreshment stand and stamp the hands of people who paid to dance. While people were dancing he tended the bonfires. I liked the look of him. I told a man who asked me to dance that I needed a rest and I went over to talk to Clay.

I learned he was going to start his second year at the University of Oregon in the fall. He was studying to be an engineer. He loved the ranch and enjoyed helping his father in the summer. But he didn't want to spend his life that way. "Too much muscle and not enough brains," he said.

"Are you sure you've got enough brains to be an engineer?" I asked him. He liked that.

"My back-up plan is to marry a rich woman."

"You muscles will help you there," I said, "but you'll need a better haircut."

Elyse came over to join us and I introduced her to Clay. I told him that she was going to start at U of O in the fall and that she was really good in math. Clay was delighted. He told her how much he enjoyed the university and how much she was going to love it. He told her about the math courses he had taken and about professors she should try to get. I think he was more excited about college than he was about Elyse but still I was jealous. I told him I was starting college in the fall too. Elyse and I were going to be the first in our families to go. But I was going to Oregon State and Clay couldn't tell me anything about it.

"Do you suppose Elyse could watch the refreshment stand so you could dance a little?" I asked.

"Sure," said Clay. "We only sell five things and the prices are on the sign."

"I've never done this before. I don't think I'd get it right," said Elyse. I knew it wasn't making change that would bother her. It was dealing with so many strangers. I wished for once she would show more courage. She was not sly or selfish enough to have calculated her response. But the inevitable result was that I manned the refreshment stand while Clay danced with Elyse. When their two dances were over, though, he thanked me and shook my hand.

When I got to college I wrote to both Elyse and Clay. Elyse wrote back within days and Clay wrote back within the week. Elyse had seen the campus as part of freshman orientation and Clay had given her a special tour of the math and engineering departments. As time went on they wrote less about each other. I didn't know whether that meant they didn't see each other that often or their friendship had continued to develop and they didn't want me to know. Elyse wrote about her classes, her daily schedule, how long it took to walk from class to class, and the weather. Clay wrote about his science labs and intramural sports. He played halfback for his dorm's football team. I wrote about the new friends I was making.

We all got a little slower about answering each other's letters but Elyse asked me to come visit her when Oregon State played football against U of O in November. I lost a little weight before I went and I paid more than I could afford for a new dress. I wanted Elyse to be proud of her friend.

My visit was the happiest thing that had happened to Elyse in a while. She had not made any friends. All the other girls were more outgoing than she was. There was too much to read in her English and history classes and she wasn't very interested in them to begin with. The courses she liked were calculus and physics. Clay was still the one person on campus she felt she could talk to.

"Is he your boyfriend?" I asked.

"Oh, no," she said. "He's just a friend."

I talked with Elyse's dorm mates late into the night, comparing our two schools. I saw the whole campus. I enjoyed the football game even though my team lost. I had a great time. Elyse enjoyed it too, though sometimes it seemed like I was the host and she was the guest. I even imagined that I was showing her how to enjoy college. Maybe I did a bit. After that her letters said her friends always asked about me. At least she had some friends. She took an anthropology course in the spring that she said she liked, especially what scientists had discovered about the difference between races.

The summer after our freshman year we came home to work in the camp dining room and save money for college. We got breakfast and dinner for free. I read a lot. I liked being with my parents. I spent time with Elyse. I had to admit, however, that she did not contribute much to the friendship. I asked her so much about her anthropology course I felt I had taken the course myself. We still went to the beach but we didn't see much of Clay. His father didn't put up the dance floor because some of the drinking the previous summer had led to fights and one man had even brought out a knife.

I saw our lumber camp in a new light that summer. I saw how hard the work was on the men. I was tired of seeing injured men trying to recover in camp. Some might never find work again. I was tired of worrying whether my father would become one of them. Even if he weren't injured my father would someday be too old to work in the forest.

One bright spot that summer was the picnic the company put on for all its workers on Labor Day. It was held at Dillon Falls on the Deschutes River. The trains that took the logs to the mill went right past the falls. The company put benches on the flatcars and we all rode down there together. Trains came from the company's other camps and a big train brought all the mill workers and their families upriver from Bend. There were games and races and lots of food. There was no beer because of Prohibition but many of the men brought liquor. The company built a big dance floor and hired a twelve-piece orchestra.

There was a very handsome man there who worked in the mill. He had blond hair and blue eyes like Elyse and a strong face. His name was Kjell Rasmussen. He was in his late twenties but he wasn't married. His father was Swedish and his mother was German. His job at the mill was to sort boards for quality. He was certified by the Western Pine Association to grade lumber and had the best-paid job in the mill, aside from the managers.

Kjell was pitching horseshoes when we saw him. We went to the opposite pit where we could watch Kjell and he could see us. He threw his horseshoe the same way every time, with a gentle step forward and an easy swing of his arm. His horseshoe made a lazy spin in the air and ringed the stake more often than anyone else's. His friends slapped him on the back and they walked off to get some food. Kjell was a head taller than the rest of them. I remarked to Elyse that if anyone were looking for a perfect Nordic type, Kjell was it.

We were waiting for the band to start up when Kjell appeared beside us and asked Elyse to dance. She blushed but kept her poise. "There's no music," she said. Kjell looked right in her eyes with a big smile on his face. He was so calm and confident, just happy to be there looking at Elyse. Then he cocked his head toward the band and the music started. It was as if he commanded it. I went weak in the knees and I'm sure Elyse did too. The two tall blonds with athletic figures made a striking couple on the dance floor. Kjell, I'm sure, knew it. They danced three dances, more than they were supposed to, and he brought her back to the side of the dance floor. I could see them from where I was dancing, completely ignoring my partner. Kjell bent down to kiss her and she stood on her tiptoes to kiss him back. Then he disappeared into the crowd and we didn't see him again.

When Kjell drove into our camp the next Saturday Elyse smiled a contented smile. He invited her for a ride and she got straight into the car. She told me to tell her parents. They were surprised she hadn't told them herself. I was too.

They were back in time for dinner but Kjell did not stay. Elyse said they had driven to the top of Paulina Peak. They could see all the land where the company had cut trees, where the old rail lines for logging had been, and where some of the new ones were. They could see the Great Northern rail line that had just been built south to Chemult. They talked about how much the company was accomplishing and how prosperous Bend was.

"I'm going to have a baby with him," Elyse told me.

I sat right down on a stump to keep from falling over.

"You mean he asked you to marry him," I said, "after seeing you twice?"

"No," said Elyse. "Maybe we will get married but that's not important."

"Did he force himself on you?" I said.

"No," she said. "At the picnic I told him I wanted to go all the way with him and, if he came back next Saturday, I would. I told him I knew all about contraception."

Elyse had skipped a few grades. I had kissed a boy once. She did know all about contraception because we had written away to The American Birth Control League in Brooklyn, New York. We wanted to see what they had to say about eugenics. They were proposing forced sterilization of the insane and retarded. They wanted people with genetic diseases to volunteer for sterilization. And they wanted to discourage poor women from having children. Among all the pamphlets they sent us were two about contraception.

Kjell and Elyse went for rides the next two Saturdays. Then Elyse and I left for our sophomore years. I asked if she were pregnant and she said she didn't know. She was going to work hard at college until she knew. If she weren't pregnant she would look for another boy who had a superior bloodline. She seemed so full of purpose and confidence, more than I had ever seen in her before. I was in awe of her and frightened for her at the same time.

That November I rode the train down to Eugene to visit Elyse again. She looked puffed up and she said her back hurt. She seemed to have lost energy and she didn't cheer for Oregon the way I cheered for Oregon State.

"I'm very glad you came," she told me before I left on Sunday. "This will be my last college weekend. I'm going home to have my baby."

"Is Kjell going to marry you?" I asked.

"He doesn't answer my letters," she said. "I think that means he won't. But it doesn't matter. I'm going to be doing what's best."

"I'm sure it will be a beautiful baby," was all I could think to say.

As soon as Elyse got home my mother wrote to tell me that Elyse had ruined her life and that my parents would be very disappointed if I followed in her footsteps. But Elyse held her head high. She told my mother that she had made a deliberate decision, that she had not been misled.

Elyse named her son Frederick after Friedrich Nietzsche. He was, in fact, a beautiful baby. Blond with blue eyes, like Elyse. Kjell saw him for the first time at the company picnic the next year. He never came to the camp to visit, though he continued to work in the mill in Bend.

That summer I tried to get a job in Corvallis or Portland. But that was 1930, the start of the Depression, and there were no jobs to be had. So I was back at the lumber camp carrying food. In August my mother told me the company could not pay both Elyse and myself. They were cutting less lumber and there were not as many men to feed. So I stopped waitressing, got a student loan, and scrimped my way through the rest of college.

I wanted to become a teacher and it was looking like a better idea all the time. Depression or not, there were still as many children to be educated every year. I trained in Corvallis and then got a job teaching second grade in La Pine. That year, 1932, the lumber company my father worked for consolidated all its camps into one big camp six miles from my school. For the first time my parents had electricity and running water. All the children from the camp came into La Pine to go to school. I taught the children of many people I knew. I didn't make a lot of money but it was steady and I helped my parents out with things they would not have otherwise had.

In my third year of teaching, one of my students was Frederick. When we had parent-teacher conferences in the fall, Elyse took the last appointment of the day. I always looked for positive things to say about each child. Frederick was the most handsome boy in the class, though that is not a judgment teachers are supposed to make. I made an exception because Elyse was my friend and I knew it would be important to her. He was a good student – always kept up with the class. But I couldn't say he was the smartest. I said he had a promising future.

Frederick followed the rules and he was cheerful about it. Any teacher would have been glad to have him. I did not think Elyse entirely welcomed this observation. Superior people were expected to be willful, not so agreeable and perhaps not so quick to laugh.

Clay Martin, the rancher's son, went to work for the telephone company in Portland. I wrote to him and he wrote back. I couldn't ask him much about his job so I asked him about his co-workers and his friends. And about his father and the ranch. His father was not a good letter-writer so most of the news Clay got about people and events around home was from me. I told him all I could about Frederick, Elyse, and Kjell. I made sure not to sound too gossipy or in any way critical. I told him what a beautiful, happy, and healthy baby Frederick was. Kjell had gone to work for a lumber company in Montana and married a woman from Missoula.

When Clay visited his father's ranch one time he invited me to come for dinner and spend the night. His father was there so it was all right. His mother had died before I ever met Clay.

Mr. Martin said the ranch was getting by. The price of cattle was down and he could barely pay his bills. But I could see the house was much bigger than my family's, he had acres of land around it, and he had good food to eat from the cattle, sheep, and chickens. He bartered some of the meat for vegetables and fruit. Mr. Martin didn't have electricity but he had all the firewood he needed for heat and cooking. He owned the ranch free and clear.

Mr. Martin and Clay made dinner for me. Clay's father knew how to cut and cook a good steak. He asked about my parents, whom he knew slightly, and we talked about the dances he and Clay used to have by the river.

"It sure is nice to have a woman in the house," he said, and he thanked me for coming. Of course I thanked him for having me. He wouldn't let me wash the dishes so Clay and I sat in the kitchen while he did them. At least I dried them. I asked where the dishes went and put them away.

In the middle of the night I got up and went to Clay's room.

"Can we just talk?" I said. I sat on his bed. I told him how much I appreciated his friendship. I told him how much I liked and admired him. And how touched I was to be invited to his house and how much I liked his father. I did not tell Clay I wanted to spend the rest of my life with him but that, of course, was why I was in his room.

"Can I lie down beside you for a minute?" I asked. "It would mean a lot to me to be able to remember this moment."

"You mean under the covers?"

"Yes."

I got in his bed and lay next to him. It was a single bed and he was as far away as he could get. But we were touching, lying there quietly for a few minutes looking up at the ceiling.

"Thank you," I said. Then I rolled toward him, pressed my breasts lightly against his chest, kissed him, and left.

Clay said he had always liked me and, after that night, he knew I liked him. We were married in June. We drove to Vancouver, British Columbia on our honeymoon. Neither of us had ever been out of the United States before. And we'd never seen anything as beautiful as the wildflowers on Mount Rainier either. Clay got the telephone company to move him to Bend. We had a house there and I transferred my job to the elementary school on Idaho Street.

Elyse moved to Weaverville, California with her parents and Frederick. She went to work as an operator for a little local telephone company. It wasn't part of AT&T. We wrote to each other a few times a year and then Elyse stopped writing. My letters were not returned so I knew she was still getting them.

I think Elyse stopped writing because of the Nazis. Eugenics sounded horrible when it came back to us as "racial hygiene," the "Master Race," and "Final Solution." It was racism and prejudice dressed up as science. I could pretend my ideas had been a passing fashion, like a crush on a movie star. But Elyse had taken the course of her life from Mr. Finch's opinions. The result of her eugenic convictions met her every morning at breakfast. Perhaps Elyse managed to think of Frederick only as the son she loved and not as her attempt to breed the übermensch.

I remember Frederick as a sweet boy. I hope Elyse is happy with that. He will make some girl a good husband someday. The world would be a better place if there were more people like him.

Local Rules

The gate guard looked like a golfer himself – lean, athletic, and neatly dressed. In his sixties, retired from some other job. The club's name appeared on his golf shirt and on his hat. I told him that I was a guest of Charles Spurr and our tee time was 9:06.

"I have you on the tee sheet," said the man, "but your clothes aren't right. Are you planning to change in the locker room?" I was not a little put out at this remark. I was wearing a new, and not inexpensive, Izod golf shirt with a collar. Clean Arnold Palmer khaki Bermuda shorts. I'd played Pebble Beach in the same outfit. How fussy could a club in the middle of Oregon be? I was driving a Mercedes for Pete's sake.

But I don't enjoy arguing. My objective was to get through the gate and I knew how to do that.

"Yes," I said, "I'm going to meet Mr. Spurr and change in the locker room."

"Mr. Spurr hasn't come through yet," said the man. But then, with a smile, "You can wait for him in the pro shop. Follow the road to the parking lot. There's a bag drop right there. Drive straight I always say." He smiled a professional smile. I was the guest of a member after all.

"Thanks," I said. I smiled too. Yes, my smile said, we were now the best of friends.

The view driving into the club restored my good humor and my eagerness to play a course I had heard so much about. The road went over a little river with geese in it. Unblemished grass undulated down a long fairway to my right. A swath of taller grass ran between the fairway and the river. There was a rustic bridge beyond the green and, towering above it all in the distance, was a snow-capped pyramidal mountain. The landscape seemed like a photograph, perfect and unmoving. The aspens by the road stood still as footmen.

I found the parking lot and spotted a green wooden rack beside the asphalt. I opened the trunk of my car and looked around for an attendant. When I saw no one I lifted out my clubs and put them on the rack.

The lot was nearly empty. I had my choice of parking place. I put my golf shoes on in the car so I would not have to find the locker room and guess at the protocol for guests using it or finding another place to leave their shoes. I didn't see the clubhouse but behind the bag drop there was a building like an old ranger's cabin. I locked the car and walked over to it. There were simple flower beds in front with daisies, blue flax, and a few big orange flowers with rays like sunbursts. I had to duck my head to get in under the porch. I opened a screen door and went inside. A woman with her back to me was examining a blackboard. She had chalk in her right hand and an eraser in her left. There were four columns on the blackboard. The entries in each column consisted of numbers followed by scribbles that I could not read. From time to time she would erase a scribble and write in something else. Or, for all I could tell, she rewrote exactly what had been there before.

"Good morning," I said. "I'm playing with Mr. Spurr at 9:06. Is this where I check in?"

"Mr. Spurr will be a little late," the woman said. "He said you should go ahead." Her tone was pleasant enough but she did not turn around.

"I'd like to pay my greens fees if I may," I said.

"Well, of course, sir," said the woman, now turning and throwing the chalk and eraser under the counter that ran between us. To my surprise I recognized the woman. Her name was Deirdre Tunnelwood and she was a film actress from my youth. I had been smitten with her. She had wide eyes and a full lower lip like Ingrid

Bergman but she had red hair. As I considered how she ought to have aged by now she seemed to age before my eyes, her hair thinning and losing color, her body shrinking to where her chin barely cleared the top of the counter. Her smile seemed to slacken.

"Cash or check?" she said, pleasantly enough. Even her voice was familiar.

"American Express, if you please."

"Good," she said. "Do you need any balls, clubs, or shoes? A bag perhaps?"

"Just a bucket of balls to hit on the range," I said.

"Range balls are free today," she said, "because of the tournament." She handed me the credit card slip and I signed it without looking.

"Even if I am not playing in the tournament?"

"Oh, but you are," she said. "Mr. Spurr was one of the first to sign up. He's been to the range every day this week. He's told me several times how much he is looking forward to the tournament and playing in it with you."

"Tough but fair," is what Charlie had said of his course. "We'll have a good time," he said. I did not remember anything about a tournament. Why would he want a weaker golfer for his partner, a man who had never seen the course before?

"What is the format for the tournament?" I asked.

"Oh, I couldn't say," said Deirdre. "The starter has a sheet with the teams and the rules. He'll explain everything to you before you tee off."

Deirdre's name tag simply read "Dee" and I considered whether to tell her I recognized her and remembered her films fondly. She might prefer to be a private person now, tucked away in rural Oregon living a different life.

"I'm glad you enjoyed my pictures," she said with a smile that I remembered. Of course, I thought, I was not the first person around my age to come into the shop. She had gotten good at telling who recognized her.

"I did enjoy them very much," I said. "When I was a teenager I was in love with you."

"So much spilt milk," she said as if calmly resigned to it. "Well, if you go down those stairs and outside you will find a cart with your name on it and Mr. Spurr's. Your clubs should be on the cart by now. I'll tell Mr. Spurr you are on the range."

"Thank you, Deirdre," I said, "or do you prefer 'Dee' these days?"

"Dee will be fine," she said. "Have a good round." She turned to her blackboard and I saw she had the chalk and the eraser back in her hands.

The stairs were thickly carpeted. The balustrades were polished logs. When I made the turn at the landing, however, the steps changed to stone and led down through walls of dark rock. The tunnel leveled out into what I took to be an old lava tube. The walls were smooth and the ceiling rose and fell as I walked along below it. Low-wattage ceiling lights, widely spaced apart, gave just enough light to keep me from walking into a wall. I walked for a full minute until a pile of rough, dark rocks blocked the tube. To my left I saw a steel door with no window in it. I pushed the bar that ran across it and stepped out on a round grassy lawn with a single golf cart on it. On its windshield was a card that had our start time, 9:06, and our two names, Charlie's and mine. My golf bag was on the cart, on the passenger side.

I don't go around checking my clubs every time they have been out of sight for a minute. Something must have caught my eye. My putter, with its black head cover that read "Scotty Campbell" on it, was missing. In its place was a beat-up old putter with a wooden shaft and a narrow head. The grip was smooth leather and perfectly round. Any experienced golfer finds a putter he likes and develops a feel for it. The "touch" is critical to success. I was disheartened and angry, as though an old friend had moved away leaving no explanation or forwarding address. Or had been kidnapped. I decided to ask Dee for help tracking down my putter. I turned to retrace my steps only to find a wall of solid rock without a hint of a door in it. I saw no handle or knob. I found cracks that had formed when the lava cooled but no combination of cracks looked in any way like the outline of a door.

There was a path leading into the woods opposite the wall and, having no alternative, I got into the golf cart and followed it. My watch said the time was now 8:40.

The path popped out on to a large open space where I saw the range. Every tee was taken with men swinging away. More men were on the practice green. More yet were standing behind the practice tees waiting to hit. I took a place among them and cast my eyes over every man looking for Charlie. Charlie was nowhere to be seen. I noticed in my survey, however, that four colors reappeared over and over in the outfits the men were wearing. No red. No blue. Khaki, but very little white. The colors were yellow, orange, green, and black. Sometimes the green and yellow were paired together and sometimes the orange with the black. My powder-blue shirt and tan cap did not fit the pattern. This must have been why the gate guard did not approve of my outfit.

I no sooner thought of the gate guard when I felt a presence at my elbow and found him standing beside me, holding a Japanese black lacquer box out to me. Was I to take it or merely examine it, perhaps admire it?

"The balls are included in the tournament fee," he said. His tone suggested that he thought this was a very silly idea, not worthy of serious golfers. It seemed that he, an employee, was providing them against his better judgment. Maybe to compensate for forcing this foolishness on both of us he did not mention that I was still wearing a shirt the color of a UN helmet.

"Why thank you," I said. I accepted the box and lifted the lid. The surfaces of the five balls in the box were covered with interlocking designs of green, white, black, and orange patterns. The closer I looked the more intricate the designs appeared to be, like mosaics on a mosque.

"Titleist?" I asked.

"No, no, no," said the man. "These are cloisonné. They are a memento. You wouldn't want to use them on the course."

"Well thank you," I said, "and my thanks to the club." I looked him in the eye to hold his attention. "But let me ask you," I continued.

"Someone has swapped out my putter for this one. Who can I see about getting my own putter back?"

"Oh, your putter is safe in my guard shack. I'll put it in your car when you leave."

"But I would like to play with it," I said. "I've been using it for years."

"Yes, of course," the man said. "But as you must have seen in the invitation the committee decided the gross scores will be used to determine the tournament winners. Everyone will compete on how many shots they actually hit, without regard to handicap. The committee thought this would be very interesting."

"Interesting for some," I said, a little testily. "Most of the competitors will know before they start that they can't possibly win on gross score. What does the committee think handicaps are for?"

"That is what some members said," replied the man, "but the committee allowed for that. Every player is given a set of clubs precisely commensurate with his ability. Or, I should say, conversely commensurate with his ability."

"Perversely commensurate," I thought but said nothing. I was trying to calm down but it was becoming more difficult. I looked at the clubs on the practice tees, and up and down the row of carts. Dotted among them I could see old clubs with wooden shafts. Some of the heads on the drivers were much smaller than modern drivers and some of the woods had heads that were actually made of wood. I spotted some antique putters more or less like mine.

"The committee calculated everything to ensure an even field. Some players do not even have a full set of clubs. Can you imagine being in a sand trap without a wedge? You'll see that it all works out."

"I'm sure it will," I said, though I rather doubted it. I resolved I would pay no attention to the ridiculous tournament. I would enjoy the course and play a friendly game with Charlie.

I gave up waiting for a spot on the range and went to the practice green to get a feel for the antique club I had been assigned. I had a putter like this when I was boy. It was old even then. How long had I lived and how hard had I worked to afford a really good set of clubs? Now the most important club in my bag was back to the beginning.

The green was busy but I found a vacant hole and hit three short putts toward it. They all went in. Not surprising at that distance but still moderately encouraging. I retrieved the balls and dropped them a little further away this time. I was settling into my stance when I heard my name and Charlie's called to come to the first tee. I whacked the ball and watched it over my shoulder as I started toward my cart. The ball missed the hole I had been aiming for but crept up on one further away, hung on the lip, and slowly tipped into the cup.

Still no Charlie. His clubs were not on the cart. I hoped he might still arrive in time for us to tee off together.

There were two bands, not one, and they were sitting on bleachers on either side of the first tee. The green and yellow band had its back to the sun. The black and orange band members had the full sun on their faces and it made their uniforms look snappier than the other band.

A man in a light tan uniform and a brimmed hat like a Forest Service ranger stood beside the tee. His name tag read "Wally" and he was the starter.

"Welcome," said Wally. "Mr. Spurr called to say he will start when he gets here and play through the other foursomes until he meets up with you. He said not to worry."

Wally introduced me to the two men I was to play with. I forgot their last names immediately. Their first names, or nicknames, were Bert and Slammer. We shook hands. They seemed friendly enough. Bert was a thin wiry man with black slacks and an orange golf shirt that fit him perfectly. He had short black hair and an evenly tanned face. He looked like a golfer. Slammer, I learned later, had played defensive tackle for Oregon State. He was over six feet tall and heavily built. He had longish light brown hair and an overgrown moustache. His golf clothes were tight in some places and loose in others, a generic extra-large black golf shirt.

"U of O tees off first," said Wally. I did not go to the University of Oregon but Charlie did. I was on this team. I grabbed my driver and started to focus. The hole was pretty straight and the fairway was wide.

"Be calm," I said. But the second I stepped on the tee a great fanfare burst forth from the green and yellow band. I stopped and stared at them until it was over. Then, working harder than ever to be calm, I teed up my ball and took a practice swing. I glanced at the band. Their instruments were down and another salvo looked unlikely. My drive went a good distance down the left side of the fairway. Not my best, but not in trouble either.

Bert took the tee with a blast from the black and orange band. He lined up his shot while the trumpets were blaring and struck the ball precisely as the fanfare reached its climax. His drive landed exactly in the middle of the fairway, three yards beyond mine. I sensed he wasn't going to miss a shot all day.

Slammer got no fanfare. I suppose it was one per team, not one per person. He stepped up to his ball and waggled a big square-headed club in front of him. He swung his driver back to about the level of his knee, and turned ferociously forward. The ball flew off the tee, climbed to altitude, and banked to the right like a jet fighter. The ball got smaller and smaller and harder to see. It went way past Bert's ball and mine but was in the deep rough if not in the woods. We were going to be looking for Slammer's shots on every hole.

"That's good," said Bert. "Just a chip and a putt from there."

Before we drove off there was a question I wanted to ask Wally. "Dee said you could tell me the rules of the match. Do you have a sheet or something that explains them?"

"It's a team and partner Shackleton Cha-Cha with an Over-Under," said Wally. "Banjo Bingo Boing."

"I haven't heard of that before," I said. "Can you give me the gist of how it works?"

"I'm afraid that is all the committee told me," said Wally, embarrassed. He reminded me of a student who puts up a brave front for the teacher but is forced to reveal, when finally asked a direct question, that he does not know the answer. "They said all the players would know what to do."

"Haven't a clue," I said. All I could do, I decided, was mark down my score on each hole and hope that someone would figure out what it meant at the end of the match. I didn't want to let Charlie down but I was coming to hate this tournament.

"Good luck," said Wally, and I was off. I had a hundred and twenty yards to go on my second shot and the ball stopped inches short of the green. Bert put his ball in the middle of the green and we all went to look for Slammer's. It was under some bitterbrush and I didn't think Slammer had a shot. But he backed into the bush and hit the ball off the dirt with a deep divot. I would have needed a pickaxe to make a divot like that. The ball and a shower of dirt exploded out of the woods. The shot landed in a sand trap right next to the green. Slammer got out of the trap in one shot and was on the green in three.

"Just get near the hole," I said to myself as I lined up with the old putter. "See if you can sink it on the next shot." Ready to blame the putter for whatever happened, I hit the putt as well as I could. It went straight for twenty yards, made a little turn to the right, and went in the hole. I'd gotten a birdie on the first hole. Bert and Slammer congratulated me. Bert made par and Slammer got a bogie. I was enjoying the game very much, if not the confounded tournament.

The course was beautifully laid out. I always had a shot, challenging as it might be. The weather was sunny but not hot. My companions were congenial. I did not mind that I did not know how the match was scored. I parred or birdied every hole on the front nine except for one. There was tall grass in a deep hidden swale and I hit my ball right into it. Slammer found the ball but I had to take a stroke to get a playable lie. Bogey.

Bert made a choice on that hole that was surprising and revealing. With his great accuracy he could have easily hit over that same swale and landed on the green. But he chose to hit to the right and come into the green from the side. He used two strokes where he could have used one. He was unwilling to take the slightest risk if he could avoid it. I could see him steeling himself on other holes when we had to hit over the river. A player as consistent as Bert, I imagined, should never give the water a second thought.

Somehow my old putter turned out not to be a handicap but an asset. Ten, twenty, or thirty feet away from the hole I hardly ever missed. I'd never putted so well.

"Sandbagger," said Bert in a jocular way. It was sporting of him and Slammer, I thought, to be enjoying my success. I admired Bert's accuracy and Slammer's reckless power. We were having a good time and I wished Charlie were there as well.

My luck continued well into the back nine. And then it stopped. After another birdie putt on a short par 4, my companions went into their bags and pulled out rain gear. There wasn't a cloud in the sky. I stood there gaping at them, looking for all the world, I suppose, as though I had never seen a man put on a pair of pants before.

"The ocean hole," said Slammer.

"You must be joking," I said, trying to sound puzzled, in a thrilled sort of way, instead of argumentative. "The ocean is a hundred miles away."

"Special for the tournament," said Slammer.

"It's simulated," said Bert.

There was a great noise coming from around the corner but it didn't sound like an ocean. It sounded like a locomotive powering a hundred leaf-blowers.

"It's supposed to be like Bandon Dunes," said Slammer. I knew the Bandon Dunes course. I'd played it. It was a terrific course on the Oregon coast. But its consistently horrible weather was its least attractive feature. I thought we were in the high desert to avoid weather like that.

We had just put the windshields up on our carts when a man stepped out from behind a pine tree and stood on the cart path in front of us. He had long gray hair with a full beard like an Old Testament prophet. He had on a white robe with a belt of dull green rope. Two animal horns stuck out from a bowl-shaped hat on his head.

"You are doomed!" he said. He raised his arms and shook a long stick he held in his hand. "Go back! Go back!" He looked over his shoulder at the hole ahead. He turned to us with lunacy in his eye. "The ducks shall go to Sodom. The beavers shall go to Gomorrah."

"I'm a golden bear," I said.

"Pillar of salt," he said.

We drove around him while he ranted at us. Slammer yelled an explanation to me.

"Portland State."

The noise picked up. There were huge fans set alongside the entire hole, from the tee to the green. Nozzles sprayed water in front of the fans and the droplets were blown across the hole. Rainbows danced in the mist. This must have cost a lot of money, I thought. I pulled Dee's receipt from my back pocket and looked at it for the first time. It was a shocker. I could have flown first-class to London and back for less money. Dee had written another dollar figure on the receipt and labeled it "Tax Deductible". That was some consolation but I had no idea what I had donated the money to.

"I don't have any spare gear," shouted Bert through the artificial storm. Slammer nodded as if to say the same. They would have given me a windbreaker or something if they had it. But they took a certain guilty pleasure in my lack of preparation. I was soaked before I teed up my ball.

"That's okay," I said. "But help me watch the shot. I don't want to lose it in the fog." I managed to par the hole but I left it dripping wet and freezing. While Bert and Slammer removed their rain gear I took off my shirt and socks, wrung them out, and put them back on.

I was still chilled and wet. Bandon weather beats you down. My putter kept coming through but my drives weren't getting the distance they should. I settled for par on the last three holes. The three of us shook hands and signed each other's scorecards. We didn't know who had won and made a joke of congratulating each other. None of us understood the rules of the tournament. We said how much we had enjoyed playing together. It was certainly true for me.

Bert and Slammer went on to the clubhouse and I sat on a hill behind the green to wait for Charlie. When the drink cart came I bought myself a cup of hot tea and a beer. I drank the tea to warm up and started on the beer. I laid the old putter on the grass beside me. I was determined to take that putter with me when I left.

It was an ideal Central Oregon day – clear and dry as gin. The river sparkled beside the green and the Cascades shone in the distance. My excitement in playing well ebbed into a deep contentment. I found it harder and harder not to lie back on the grass and shut my eyes. The next thing I knew it was late afternoon and Charlie was bending over me shaking me awake. The sun lit up his thick hair from behind like a halo.

"Let's go," he said, "we're going to miss the awards." We drove my cart to the parking lot and put our clubs in our cars.

"Do we need to drive to the clubhouse?" I asked. The only building I'd seen was the homely little golf shop.

"Oh no," said Charlie. "We're here." He laughed at my unsettled look. "The parking lot is on the roof." He pushed a button on a post and I heard a rumbling sound beneath us. Two steel plates that I would have assumed were covering a utility vault opened before us and a platform with a tall hoop over the top rose up out of the hole. We stepped on to the platform and Charlie pushed another button to lower us.

"Take off your hat," said Charlie. "We're going to chapel." We entered a large room with pews facing a raised platform. There was a table on the platform that was covered in a green cloth and had cut-glass trophies on it. We sat in the fifth row from the front. There was no altar or pulpit on the platform and no cross anywhere to be seen. But a stained-glass window in front of us appeared to be a biblical scene. A man raised his arm as if to strike a heavy blow – Jesus casting the moneylenders out of the temple, perhaps, or Sampson slaying a thousand Philistines. After staring at it for a while the image resolved into that of a golfer about to start his swing. His club was outside the frame of the window but between his feet was a little white ball on a tee. The man was wearing a tunic that bore no resemblance to the shirt, pants, sweater, or jacket a golfer might wear. Charlie must have seen me studying the image and commented on it.

"Quite fine, isn't it? But where are his pockets? There must be a caddy who isn't in the picture."

On the back of every pew there were fold-down tables, like those on airplanes. On the tables were bowls of bar snacks and glasses of beer. The beer ranged from dark to light and varied in color. The men talked to their pew mates and laughter burst forth from spots around the room. A shapely young woman with long red hair stepped onto the platform and faced the crowd. I saw that it was Deirdre as I remembered her from the movies. Or it was her daughter, a remarkable resemblance. She stood patiently watching the crowd.

"There will be no more beer and no dinner until they quiet down," Charlie told me.

The woman began to speak and I recognized her voice. It had to be Deirdre herself, though how she managed to look so young I could not imagine. She acknowledged the honor bestowed on her by the committee in asking her to announce the awards. She noted the long and noble history of the tournament and the even longer rivalry between the two schools. She stood with one hand resting on the table behind her, as if on the tiller of a boat. It reminded me of a scene in one of her movies. It was called Damnation at Sea. Deirdre's ship sank and she was left in a lifeboat with two men and a dozen children. The men quarreled and killed each other. Deirdre took over the helm and piloted the lifeboat to safety through a terrible storm.

Deirdre began to recount the history of past tournaments, where they had been played, the unique rules under which they had been played, which team had won and who the individual winners had been. She started in 1925 and went on, year by year. My head felt heavy. Charlie and the others, I could see, were wide awake, taking in every twist and turn. I tried to adopt an enthusiastic expression and feign a special interest in the year I was born. But realizing that sleep would surely overtake me I slumped in my pew, shifted left to hide behind the head of the man in front of me, balanced my body carefully, and contentedly dozed off.

I woke to thunderous applause. I raised my hands to join in. But Charlie and the others seemed to be directing their applause toward me and I halted with my hands in the air.

"Congratulations," Charlie shouted. He seemed quite sincere. He gestured for me to stand up and walk to the platform. Deirdre was holding up a glass chalice and smiling at me. I stepped out of the pew, looking around for confirmation that I was doing what was expected. Bert and Slammer, whom I spotted in the room for the first time, seemed particularly eager for me to go forward.

I stepped up, took the chalice, turned toward the room and raised the trophy high. The applause continued with cries of "Speech! Speech!" I gestured to Charlie. He waved his hand to the crowd. I made a fancy bow to Deirdre as the applause continued. I waved like a candidate for office to the multitude and stepped off the dais. The applause continued. I raised the chalice once again and looked over my shoulders to the left and the right. Finally the clapping abated and we turned to hear about other awards. There was longest putt, closest to the hole, and lowest individual score. Every award occasioned loud and sustained applause. I glanced down at the chalice but there were no words on it. I had no idea what the award was for.

Deirdre gave away the last award and thanked everyone for coming and said she hoped we all enjoyed the tournament. Charlie told me that after dinner we were going to see one of Deirdre's old movies, Heartache on the Klamath. I didn't remember that one. Charlie said Deirdre played an Indian princess who betrays her chief for the love of a white man.

The green tablecloth was replaced with a white one. Doors in the sides of the room swung open and waiters in black tie and tails appeared carrying platters. In less than a minute the table was covered with a smorgasbord of meat, fish, turkeys, salads, vegetables, and dozens of other dishes.

"No duck," said Charlie to me behind his hand.

Each pew stood in turn, shuffled to the center aisle, and queued facing the table. The waiters served food on to dinner plates and handed a plate to each contestant as he filed past. We circled back to our original pews so that we sat where we started. On our fold-down tables there was silverware, a napkin, and a glass of beer waiting for each of us.

I did not know which team had won. All the men were happy whether in green and yellow, orange and black, or, in my case, powder blue. The beer kept coming. My plate was piled so high it still looked full when I had eaten all I could. Waiters brought coffee and cigars. I don't smoke cigars but I took one and gestured with it, placing it in my mouth and pulling it out with great exhalations of smoke-free breath. Slammer chewed his cigar as much as smoked it and spat into an empty beer glass. The cigar smoke grew thicker and obscured the far reaches of the room, though I could still hear laughter from every direction. The smoke became so dense I could hardly see Charlie next to me. Through the din I heard a fire alarm going off in the hallway. The cigar smoke must have tripped it. There was no real fire, I reasoned, and the club staff would find a way to shut off the alarm. We were all having such a good time.

I could not hear what Charlie was saying. The alarm would not stop and I became annoyed. I wanted to call out for someone to turn the stupid thing off. I was unable, however, to rise and speak. No longer sitting, I found myself lying face down on something soft. I'd drunk too much beer I decided. The alarm continued, an intermittent buzzing. I lifted my head and realized, dark as it was, that I was in my own bedroom and the alarm was my alarm clock. I had drunk so much, I thought, that poor Charlie had brought me all the way home. What a burden I must have been.

"Can't you turn that alarm off?" my wife mumbled. I turned it off.
"Sorry," I said.
"Have a good game," she said drowsily, and went back to sleep.

It was still dark outside. Why had I set the alarm for so early? I must have a golf game. Yes. Yes, I did. It was two hours away and my tee time was 9:06. With Charlie Spurr. I got out of bed and checked the weather in Central Oregon. It would be a sunny day. I packed my rain gear anyhow. And I resolved to be on the lookout for an old hickory-shafted putter.

A Trick of the Light

When the company I worked for built a railroad bridge over the Crooked River, I woke up early every morning to heat rivets before the other men started work. We were camped at the bottom of the canyon and climbed a 320-foot rope ladder to get to the bridge.

Before dawn one morning in August I looked out over the river, eyes half-open, and saw a tiny flame streak down below the bridge. Right behind the light came a shadow. I could make out a splash when the shadow hit the river. I ran downstream, clambering over rocks in the dark, to see what it was. It either sank or floated away before I could spot it.

Mike, the boss, stuck his head out of his tent when I walked back to camp. "What are you doing?" he asked me.

"I saw something fall off the bridge. Might have been a person. But I can't see anything down here."

"Who went up on the bridge at this hour?" he asked.

"Don't know. I just woke up."

"Well, I'm not waking up the men for a head count," said Mike, as though that were exactly what I had suggested. "Go back to bed."

I went over to the cook tent and got an early breakfast.

When the other men came for food we were all accounted for. Nobody missing.

Mike banged a spoon on his metal cup. "Tom says he saw someone or something fall off the bridge early this morning. Any of you know anything about that?"

Steve Cotter, a riveter and my closest friend on the job, asked me what it looked like.

I said there was flame falling ahead of it and it looked like a black blob with arms and legs.

"Maybe it was a piece of canvas," said Steve.

I looked at him and shrugged my shoulders. "It looked like a person," I said.

Nobody accused me of imagining it or losing my eyesight, even as a joke. Working on the bridge was dangerous and we had to trust each other. If I said I saw something, then I did.

I climbed up the ladder while they were eating. When I got to the top there was a man standing near the south end of the bridge. I had seen him with a boy the day before. They had watched us work. He waited while I started the fire and I went to talk to him once it was going.

"Hi," I said. "If you're looking for railroad work you'll want to go north to Opal City."

"I'm not looking for work," the man said. "I'm looking for my boy. He got up in the night and he didn't come back. I figured you might have seen him. He was mighty excited about this bridge."

If you have bad news you might as well tell it.

"I saw something fall off the bridge into the river a little bit before dawn this morning. I only saw a dark shape but I'm pretty sure it was a person."

The man went weak but he did not stumble. He lifted his head and looked me in the eye.

"My son was thirteen years old, about five foot seven, big shoulders."

"I couldn't see how big it was or much of anything," I said. "There was a flame that fell right before."

"Stupid, stupid," said the man. He looked toward the mountains and his face tensed up.

"I don't mean my boy," he said. "I mean I should have thought he might try that. I could have told him not to."

"You think he went to drop a match?" I asked. It had been in the newspapers. The bridge was so high and the air was so dry that if you dropped a match from the bridge it would light before it hit the river.

"Yeah. His teacher told him about it."

"Well sir, we can look for him after work but he may have washed way downriver."

"You figure he's dead?" he asked. It was a desperate question but I understood he had to ask.

"From that height he'd have to be. All the men know that."

"Stupid."

"You can stick around if you want," I said, "but there's miles of river to search and some parts you can't get to. He may have sunk. You should get word to the sheriff and I'll tell the railroad. Tell me how to reach you if we find him."

He said his name was Johnson and he gave me the name of a man in Redmond who could relay a message. I told him my name and how to get a letter to me. He thanked me and looked past me toward the bridge.

"He had to have some guts," I said, "to get out on a half-built bridge in the dark." The man nodded and we said goodbye.

The men all watched me walk back to the furnace. When I got to where I could use a normal voice I said, "It was his son." I had not told the man that I had a thirteen-year-old son too. I thought he might resent it. My son was in Portland with his mother. Last I heard he was alive and well.

My concentration wasn't perfect that day. I lost five rivets to the river. It was good I wasn't climbing from girder to girder with a steel hammer in my hand. When we quit Mike asked for volunteers to look for the boy. Half the men raised their hands and Mike picked Steve and John. John was a rivet-catcher. One rivet that went in the river that day was a rivet I had thrown way beyond his reach. I raised my hand but Mike didn't pick me. He told Steve and John to look carefully, not only for a person but for anything that might have fallen in the river. And he told them to look out for rock slides. He didn't want either of them injured. They were gone about an hour. They got to a place where the river came right up against the canyon wall and they couldn't go further. They said they looked carefully both going and coming back. They found nothing. The cook served them a late dinner and I sat with them. Mike came over too.

"I wanted to finish this job with nobody hurt," said Mike, "and now this kid comes along."

"There's nothing we could have done," I told him. "The boy got on the bridge in the middle of the night."

"The bosses still won't like it," said Mike, "especially when it gets in the newspapers. They won't care that we put up signs and a fence."

"At least it wasn't one of us," said Steve.

"It better never be one of you," Mike reprimanded. Steve and John left the table. Mike and I sat watching what we could see of the sunset between the canyon walls.

"Do you think we should do something for the boy's family?" I said. "Send them a letter or take up a collection?"

Mike put his hand to his jaw and then slid it away. "I don't see how a letter or money would make the boy's death any easier. They might not even like hearing from us."

"It might make the men feel better to do something. Settle them down."

Mike set his hands on his hips. "You're probably right. But money makes it look like we're guilty of something. We'll tell the men about the letter tonight and you write it tomorrow."

"When we talk to the men we could have a short prayer for the boy," I said. "I think some of the men would appreciate it."

Mike didn't like this idea. "The men think about steel and they think about getting paid. Sometimes they think about their families. They pretty much stay away from religion."

"They've just been reminded they could fall to their deaths any day. I think it would help to show we care about that. Even if it's a stranger. That we'd regret losing each other even more. That we want each other to be careful."

"Okay. You lead it. Make it short."

"Okay." I thought about what I would say. Sympathy for the boy. Comfort for his family. Gratitude for our lives and for our work. Hope that we would be safe.

I was thinking of words when the rope ladder jiggled. We looked up and saw a figure making its way down. The person was moving slowly and not as confidently as one of us would.

"Jesus Christ Almighty," said Mike. It was the boy we had seen the day before. His clothes were dirty and had little rips in them. "Hey kid, what do you think you're doing?"

The boy looked over his shoulder from thirty feet off the ground. "Climbing down your ladder, sir," he said. We could see he was tired. Mike and I went over to the ladder to make sure he didn't stumble when he got to the bottom.

"Do you know your father thinks you're dead?" said Mike. "We've been worried about you all day, sent out men to look for you."

"Sorry," said the boy.

"Where have you been?"

"Opal City. I went to see the railroad. I was coming back when I smelled the food cooking in your camp. I'm awful hungry and thought you might spare me some dinner."

"You walked to Opal City?"

"Yes, sir."

"Come over and sit down," said Mike. He asked me to see what the cook could still give us.

Mike and I watched the boy eat. He stopped after three mouthfuls. "Much obliged to you," he said.

"I've a mind to give you a good hiding and save your father the trouble," said Mike.

"I understand, sir."

"Well, you'll have to spend the night here," said Mike. "You can walk out to the road in the morning and we'll give you some money to get to Bend. You better catch up to your father as quick as you can."

"Yes, sir. Thank you."

Mike got up and started to move away. "And if you as much as touch that ladder tonight I will personally come after you and throw you off the bridge myself." The boy kept eating and I sat with him alone. He looked like he couldn't decide whether to eat another mouthful or put his head down on the table and go to sleep.

"I was up early this morning," I told him. "I saw a flame come down to the river from under the bridge." He stopped eating and looked at me.

"You saw it?" he asked.

"Yes, I saw it," I said. "Just me and the fish in the river. And apparently you." He looked at me without speaking and without eating.

"And there was a dark shape that came down right after the light. What was that?" I said.

The boy closed his eyes and opened them again. "I didn't see that," he said.

"I thought it was you," I said. "That's what I told your father. I told him that his son was dead, that anyone falling from that height would certainly be dead. He knew about the match."

Tears came to the boy's eyes and he smudged them away with the palms of his hands.

"Did you lose your coat or throw something down after the match?"

"No," he said.

"Well," I said, "you think about it. I'd like an explanation in the morning." He was done eating and I showed him where he could sleep. I took his plate back to the cook tent.

I never got an explanation. He left right after breakfast. He spoke to no one and no one spoke to him. We were mad at him for making us worry about him. I, at least, resented the pain he caused his father.

Mike asked me what I had seen falling if it wasn't the boy. I said I didn't know. It was too big to be a bat and wasn't shaped like an owl. I couldn't imagine a coyote or a deer choosing that exact moment to leap off the cliff. All I know is I saw it and it sure looked like a person to me. If it was a person then nobody ever missed him. He was gone and forgotten.

Fatal Errors

I wanted to buy a lot but Jocelyn wouldn't commit. She thought there might be someplace better. I said we'd looked all over and a place on the ranch would be perfect for us. The ranch had a forest, meadows, a horse barn, and a small river that ran right through the middle of it. It had good views of the mountains.

The developer, Roland Timmons, organized a picnic on the Fourth of July for his best prospects and for the people who had already bought. We came to see what our new neighbors might be like. Roland, a short, anxious man, had fashioned a rustic celebration for the city dwellers. Heavy log picnic tables were covered with blue-check tablecloths. The napkins were red. Mason jars sat on the tables with wildflowers in them. There was a fiddle, a guitar, and a harmonica playing Hank Williams music. The trio sat on wooden chairs on the porch of the old log house. We were down by the river in a grassy meadow. There were two fat white clouds in the sky and a clear view of the mountains. Timmons could not have asked for a better day. As contrived as the setting was, I loved it. Jocelyn said the ranch was lovely but that we should be wary of whatever Timmons told us.

The guests eyed each other, wondering what attracted the other people to the ranch, what kind of community the place would turn out to be. Jocelyn picked out a couple that was about our age, younger than the others, and asked them to sit with us. Their names were George and Marie Nelson. George turned out to have an English accent. Jocelyn asked them where they lived.

"We live on planes," said Marie. She was American. "We travel all the time for business. George flew in from Istanbul and I was in Singapore. We met in the Portland airport."

"But where do you live when you are not traveling?" asked Jocelyn.

"My head office is in London and I share a flat there," said Marie. "George's work takes him through Los Angeles a lot. So he has an apartment there. We meet each other all over the globe."

"Better than taking out the garbage at home," I said.

"We both have jobs we love," said George. "We talk every day or two and, when we do see each other, it's usually at a luxurious resort. We have some great weekends, even long weekends."

"Not just a quickie at the Hilton O'Hare," I said. I heard an embarrassed "Oh" from Jocelyn but the Nelsons were amused.

"It's too hard to schedule," said George.

"So you're really looking for a first home, not a second home," said Jocelyn.

"That's why we're here," said Marie. "We want a place we can put down some roots. George is in love with the American West."

"There's so much space here," said George. "It still seems like the frontier. You can make of it what you want."

"I'm sure Roland would like to get you on tape," said Jocelyn.

"We'll never tell," said George. "I dream of saying to him, 'You know, Roland, there's this lovely place in Australia we're thinking about.'" George looked off at the sky with a pleased expression on his face. We all thought that was very funny. None of us wanted Roland to think we were too eager.

"We've already had an adventure on the ranch," said Marie. "I almost died."

"Was it a snake?" said Jocelyn. "Or a mountain lion?"

"Oh no," said Marie. "We borrowed Roland's canoe. He drove us upstream to where we could put the canoe in the water and told us to stop when we got back here. He said we couldn't get lost." Marie's yellow ponytail swept from side to side as she told the story.

"I'm not a good swimmer but it wasn't a very big river. I figured George could always save me. Once I was sitting in the canoe it was easy. I learned to paddle right away and to do the draw stroke when we needed to make a turn. The willows hang over the river and they were full of birds going about their business, not paying us the slightest attention. It felt like a wilderness. Every once in a while we could see the mountains.

"Then we made a sharp turn and the boat started tipping. It kept tipping and I kept thinking it would stop. Next thing I knew I was in the water. The water was cold and the current pulled me away from the boat. All I had ever done before was paddle around in the shallow end of a pool. I was trying to keep my head above water. Then my foot got caught on a root or something and the current pulled me under. I thrashed around like mad trying to get loose. I told myself to be calm. Can you imagine trying to reason out how to swim while you are already under water?"

"That's awful," said Jocelyn. "You must have been terrified."

"I thought of animals that would chew off their foot to get out of a trap and I decided I would gladly do that if I could. Do you know the phrase "pay any price, bear any burden"? It came to me and I decided the situation was important enough for it to apply. I thought if I were serious enough I could solve the problem. But it didn't do any good. I pulled at my foot until I couldn't pull anymore. I was too exhausted to move. I just lay there trying to put off breathing in water as long as I could.

"Then whatever it was let go of my foot. I was tumbling along in the current again and I couldn't figure out which way was up. I wanted to breathe so badly. Then I felt the bottom beneath me. When I pushed up the water was a few inches deep. I was on a mud bank. I barely had the energy to lift my head and shoulders out of the water. I started coughing but I was sucking in all the air I could between the coughs. The current tried to pull me away and I fought to get my knees under me. I was kneeling there coughing when George came and helped me stand up. He saved me. It felt like the hand of God had reached down and picked me up."

I had to admire Marie. Death almost claims her and a few hours later she is bright and cheerful and enjoying telling her story. I could imagine her telling it for weeks to her business friends around the globe. Someday she would tell it to her grandchildren.

"My God," said Jocelyn, "how did you get back here?"

"We walked," said Marie. "We certainly weren't going to get in that canoe again. And we only had one paddle. We lost the other one. We walked home."

"It was a long walk," said George. "The river meanders so much. There was no trail and there were deep holes hidden in the grass. We kept thinking we'd see the house but it took forever to reach it."

"I'm surprised you didn't leave Roland behind and never look back," I said.

"We decided it made us glad to be alive," said Marie. "And we're going to be more careful in the future."

"Did you think you were drowning too?" Jocelyn asked George. We were the one table that was having a real conversation. People looked at us quizzically.

"George hit his head when the boat went over," said Marie. "I insisted we go to the hospital because he might have a concussion. The doctor said he probably didn't but I should keep an eye on him." There was a small bandage on George's left temple.

"It must have been the canoe," said George. "I was dazed for a bit. Then I came to and saw Marie kneeling on the sandbar. We were lucky."

I wanted to know how Roland retrieved the canoe in time for the picnic. It was there on the dock by the river, clean as if straight from L.L. Bean, with two paddles propped against a seat. It was a wooden canoe with green sides and woven cane seats. Very old-fashioned. Very picturesque.

"We pulled it up on the sandbar," said George. "Roland sent two of his workers down the river and they brought it back here. They found the other paddle too."

"I bet Roland wishes you were not telling us your story," I said. Roland had been glancing our way with a worried look on his face.

"Well, we're not going to broadcast it," said George. "It should not really reflect on the ranch. It was our own fault. The river looked easy and we didn't put the lifejackets on. We left them in the bottom of the boat."

"Whether we buy land here or not, I'm going to learn to swim," said Marie. "It's irresponsible not to know how."

The other tables left but we talked on. I talked about some narrow scrapes I'd had rock climbing. I'd given up climbing when Jocelyn and I were married. George told us about a pipeline deal he had negotiated in a tent by the Arabian Sea. We had a great time. Roland and his helpers were cleaning up. He finally came over to our table.

"Stay as long as you want," he said. "There is still beer in the keg and cold soda on ice. If you'd like lemonade, walk into the kitchen and you'll find it in the fridge. I've got some errands to run but I'll be back. Leave me a message on the phone if you have anything you want to discuss."

What he wanted us to discuss, of course, was our buying lots. We'd seen the whole ranch and read the CC&Rs. We'd looked at other property in the area. We knew about as much as we were ever going to know.

We and the Nelsons exchanged phone numbers. We all had email addresses by then and we swapped them as well. I learned that George worked for Barclays Bank and Marie worked for a company called Dark Consulting.

"Do you think you'll buy?" Jocelyn asked the Nelsons.

"We are still thinking about it," said George. "But it seems absolutely perfect. Even if we never build we think the lot will be a good investment."

Driving away Jocelyn told me, "If they can attract people like that we are going to love it here."

I agreed. I said I thought George was right. The land itself would probably appreciate whether we built on it or not. We bought a lot by the river the next day.

I did not want to sabotage our buying the land. I did not tell Jocelyn what I knew about the Nelsons.

The morning of the picnic I was exploring the ranch when I heard a splash in the river and heard a woman wail out "Whoa!"

Moving closer and looking downstream I saw the woman flailing in the water. A sopping wet man was standing in the water near the shore anchoring a canoe. He watched the woman float away. She sank under the water for a good twenty seconds. A hand sometimes reached frantically above the surface but she could not bring her head up. The man watched without moving. When she crawled onto a sandbar he knelt down in the water and slammed the canoe into the side of his head. Then he swam downriver pulling the canoe with him. I stepped back further into the willows and neither of them saw me.

The longer I waited to tell Jocelyn the wiser it seemed to say nothing. The Nelsons bought a lot and built a house. We built our house at the same time. The four of us shared our experiences with the design review committee, our builders, our subs, our suppliers. We tried all the restaurants within driving distance. The Nelsons became our closest friends. After our houses were built we arranged schedules to be at the ranch at the same time. We played golf and went hiking together. We celebrated Christmas together.

All four of us found ways to work part-time from the ranch. George still had to travel but the rest of us cut back. I slowly lowered my handicap and Jocelyn started spending time with Pedro, a roan gelding that we bought and the ranch looked after. Jocelyn and Pedro took riding lessons together.

The incident on the river lost importance as new impressions took its place. George and Marie seemed perfectly happy. If George wanted to part ways with Marie, I thought, why would he go through all the effort of building a house with her? George and I went fishing together many times. I could have asked him about that day on the river but I did not want to lose the friendship. The closest I came was to ask him if he would keep the house if Marie died.

"I wouldn't let that happen" was all he said.

We went for hikes together in the summer and fall. If George was away on business, the three of us hiked without him. Marie and Jocelyn carried on a conversation with a few interjections from me. I was the acknowledged map-reader and guide. But I could not interest the ladies for very long in geology, the water table, or forest management practices.

Riding in the arena one afternoon Jocelyn fell off Pedro and broke three bones in her foot. The doctor said she would not be hiking for months. She encouraged the rest of us to go without her. The first time George was away Marie and I went by ourselves.

It was a little awkward. The hike was so much quieter than the ones with George and Jocelyn. Near the end I went on about pine bark beetle infestations and what people should do if they see a bear. A week later, with George still away, Marie and I had energetic conversations about bears and trees. Marie had read up on them. We proceeded to questions about each other that we had never thought to ask before, about what we were doing before we met our spouses. It seemed as though we met for the first time. Marie was, in fact, more interesting than pine bark beetles.

Climbing over a slippery boulder Marie fell against me. An electric shock went through my body. At the end of the third hike we parked in the woods and made love in the car like teenagers. I still don't know quite what happened. I did not think I had it in me after thirty. I tried not to let Jocelyn know how much I looked forward to hiking with Marie.

Marie and I never discussed what we were doing. We did not talk about love or the future. We did not talk about the rightness or wrongness of what we were doing. We did not discuss the consequences if our spouses found out about us or how to keep them from finding out. We made dates to go hiking and then things happened. That was it. It made it more exciting in a way. We each dreaded, I think, that we would meet on a hike and the other one would say the sex had to stop. That would be the end of it.

I proposed we take up butterfly collecting. I think Marie saw its advantages immediately. We could go more frequently. We could go anywhere, not just on hiking trails. And, unlike hiking, butterfly collecting took as long as it took. If we only caught three butterflies, or even none, it simply hadn't been a good day. To be on the safe side, I wrote dates and locations on the butterflies' little glassine envelopes that put us where we should have been instead of where we were. It required some calculation. The species near the ranch were different from the species in the mountains. And some species only flew for a few weeks – the females for barely a week. Our spouses would probably never check the dates and places. But we felt more secure, at least I did, knowing the data was there to support our alibis.

We needed time at Marie's house to mount the butterflies. On the web I ordered mounting boards, pins, display cases, tweezers, and magnifying lenses that clipped on to glasses. Mounting butterflies was painstaking work. It was easy to break off an antenna. If George was home, even outside the house or out running an errand, all we talked about was butterflies. I thought we were quite clever about that.

I hoped it would not end badly. I imagined that summer would be over, the butterflies would be gone, Jocelyn's foot would heal, and we would all go back to the way we were before. I would remember my days with Marie forever.

Our idyll did not last the summer. Marie and I had caught a new butterfly, our first Colias interior. It was not common and we were excited about it. It had yellow wings with bright pink edges. We were coming down from the mountains in my Explorer. The road did not have a lot of traffic during the week but it was curvy. Marie turned to get the butterfly book from the back seat and she unhooked her seat belt. A pickup truck, passing an SUV with a trailer, came around a corner at us on the wrong side of the road. There was nowhere to go but into the trees.

The ambulance took us both to the hospital. I was unconscious. Someone, maybe the person pulling the trailer, called 911 using my cell phone. He told them he was me. He must have looked at my wallet. Then he disappeared. He did not want to get involved.

Jocelyn met me at the hospital and took charge. She made sure the doctors told her everything they could and did everything that could be done. She asked a raft of questions that would not have occurred to me in my most mindful moments. She chased my doctor down the hall, hobbling on her bad foot, and grabbed him by the arm to make a request. She looked after me. She reminded me how lucky I was to have her.

I had gone into shock but my injuries were minor. When she was sure I was all right Jocelyn told me the bad news. The car was totaled. Then she told me the worse news. Marie had died in the wreck. Dead before she got in the ambulance. Death had not come so near to Jocelyn and me before. We were dazed. Sadness came and went in waves for each of us. We propped each other up. Jocelyn reached George in Munich and told him. She offered to make arrangements for Marie's service while he flew home and he agreed.

I was sad for George losing his wife. I was sad for Jocelyn losing her best friend. I was most sad for Marie who would miss so much of the life she had ahead of her. I was least sad for myself. I had lost a joy I had no business having in the first place.

"George, I'm so sorry," I said when I went to his house the day before the service. He held his front door open and we stood in the entryway. "Jocelyn and I will do anything we can to help you, now and in the future." He didn't say anything. He simply looked at me. "Are you all right?" I said. He, who always had something to say, said nothing. I thought perhaps he had been drinking. But he was fully conscious.

"I thought you would want to know how it happened," I said, searching for something else to say. I told him about the trailer and the truck and driving off the road. I told him about Marie reaching for the butterfly book. I said she had died almost immediately, though I thought the doctors must have given him more information than they would give me.

"You killed my wife," he said. He stared at me steadily, almost through me. It seemed all he could bring himself to say. No complaint, no anger. Determination.

"It was an accident, George," I said. "I was driving carefully. The truck was going much too fast. It was hidden by the curve until it was right in front of us."

"You killed my wife."

"That's not true," I said. "At least not on purpose, or even through carelessness."

"I've talked with the district attorney about charging you with murder. Nobody can find the trailer or the pickup truck from your story."

I sat down on a bench in the hall. Any strength I had was gone.

"There must be a recording of the 911 call," I said. "The voice on it won't be mine."

"So someone stopped. It doesn't prove you didn't just drive off the road as soon as Marie took off her seatbelt."

I looked up at him. "George, you can't believe I would do this. That I would kill anybody, much less a friend. The wife of my best friend. A friend of mine and a friend of Jocelyn's." I searched for something persuasive. "If nothing else," I said, "why would I take the chance of throwing my own life away in a wreck? I could have died too." No response.

"You know me, George," I said. "Could I live with myself after killing a friend?"

"But no problem," said George, "with being unfaithful and leading my wife to betray me." I didn't know how he knew this. Had Marie told him? Maybe she was going to tell me our trysts were over. Maybe George was guessing.

"Marie loved you," I said. I did not think through what I said next. I said, "Could you live with yourself after killing someone?"

George did not flinch. I don't think overturning the canoe even crossed his mind. "Don't come to the service," he said.

I didn't go. Jocelyn went. People told me that what she said about Marie was beautiful. When people asked Jocelyn where I was, she told them I did not think it was appropriate to be there, even though I was not responsible for the accident. We agreed on that. In the following days she became very solicitous of George. She cooked some meals for him and helped him run his house. She said he was morose. I wasn't cheerful either but Jocelyn had less and less time for me. I was sure George told her about the affair – whatever he knew or suspected.

"Do you suppose George would let me have the butterflies?" I asked her.

"He threw them out," she said.

Jocelyn stopped having much to say to me. We had dinner together less often. We didn't make love. I apologized profusely for my affair with Marie but it didn't help. I thought the death of her friend, on top of my affair, had made Jocelyn withdraw. But she was full of energy when she was doing something for George. She had come to love the ranch but she had always been fascinated by his cosmopolitan life, all the strange places he had been and interesting things he knew. She had been to Europe once in her life, never to Asia or Africa. Now he needed her help and consolation. I suppose she saw more in him than that but I couldn't grapple with it.

One night Jocelyn did not come home. I called George's house. "Don't call again," he said.

I lost everybody. Jocelyn demanded a divorce. She was going to marry George and he wanted to have her. "You might want to be careful if you marry George," I said. That was when I told Jocelyn what I had seen on the river the morning before we met the Nelsons. I told her about George standing there watching Marie drown. I told her how George finally moved when she crawled up onto the sandbank.

"You've made this up," she said. "You invented it to try and spoil things. I am not listening to any more of it."

"I have never understood it," I said. "It seems so improbable. Then he stayed with Marie ever since without any appearance of a problem."

"Until you came along," said Jocelyn.

"If you don't think George tried to kill her I hope you don't think I did either. George seems to."

"No," she said, "I don't think you wanted to kill her. George thinks you made her angry and the two of you had an argument. Then you went too far."

"A man of quick temper and rash actions. Doesn't sound like me."

"In any case I don't want you telling anyone this ridiculous story about George watching Marie drown. It makes you look pathetic."

"I won't," I said, "but I want you to be careful."

"Stop trying to poison my mind. It isn't like you."

"Let's hope he's reformed," I said. Jocelyn left scowling. She came back a few times to get things. Her foot was still healing and I had to help her. But she did not have a lot to say.

The years when Jocelyn and I were building our house, and George and Marie were our friends, were the happiest I ever had. But I would be happier now if I had spoken the truth.

Falling Star

Mrs. Jared Bonney
Bald Mountain Farm
Cornwall, Connecticut

May 15, 1873

Dear Sister,

We arrived two weeks ago at the land on Ochoco Creek that Henry bought and have been living in a tent while we decide whether to build a log cabin or a frame house. A frame house would be more comfortable but logs would be quicker and less dear. Henry promises me we will have a large, warm, and dry house before my confinement in the fall.

The landscape here is not as lush as the land we left in the Willamette Valley but we have 160 acres on the creek and will put horses, sheep, and cattle on the rangeland that is open to everyone. On our own land we will raise alfalfa and cattle. There are beautiful snow-covered peaks to the west of us. Three of them together are called the Three Sisters and I have named them after you, me, and Ruby. It makes me happy to look at them and think of the three of us.

They say the creek runs all year. The nearest post office is in Prineville where we will go once a week or so. Please send letters to us there and we will pick them up.

Last week when Henry went to town I had a remarkable visitor. I was turning over the soil for our vegetable garden when I saw an old Indian woman and a boy standing a little way off looking at me. There are no Indian settlements nearby anymore and I was startled to see them. The army is fighting the Modoc Indians about two hundred miles south in California. You may have read in the papers about the Modoc chiefs who came for a peace conference with the general they were fighting then pulled out their weapons and shot the man dead. The Modocs used to visit our area but Henry says the army is pursuing them night and day and they will not come near us.

The Snake Indians used to be even worse. No one would live here until the Snakes were beaten five years ago. Now the Snakes are at Camp Harney about a hundred miles east of here. They are difficult to manage but their numbers are much reduced.

I looked all around me to see if there were more Indians with them and there weren't. Just the woman and the boy. They had no weapons I could see and they looked harmless, though Indians can be deceiving. The woman stood very erect. She wore a buckskin dress with beadwork over her leggings and boots. I thought she must be about sixty years old. The boy wore a wool shirt and pants.

Henry's rifle was in the tent but it wasn't loaded and I wasn't sure where the ammunition was. The pair looked so unthreatening that getting the rifle seemed silly. I was worried about being attacked and worried about being uncharitable at the same time. I didn't know what to do. The Indians we knew in the Willamette Valley were very peaceful and I remember the Schaghticokes we saw in Connecticut were not a threat to anyone. I simply stood there and stared at my visitors.

Then the woman called out to me in clear English.

"Can you write?" she asked. I was astounded. It was the last thing I expected her to say. I realized immediately how confident she was.

"Yes I can," I said.

"Will you write for me? My son will work for you."

The boy looked to be about fourteen. He was almost six feet tall with the torso and arms of an even bigger man. He was a handsome boy except his legs were too short for the rest of him. He looked strong. If he did the work well it would be a good bargain.

"He can turn over the dirt for my vegetable garden," I said. One minute I feared for my life and the next I was making a bargain with the woman. I was dreading the hard work, even though I am still strong. The soil was dusty and got into everything. I showed the boy how to turn over the soil with a shovel and marked the corners of the garden with stones. I didn't know if he spoke English. He watched me carefully but he would not look me directly in the eye. His mother said a few words to him in their language and off he went.

The woman and I sat on boxes where we had a good view of the mountains and I brought out pen and ink and writing paper. I put a board across my lap and I was ready. I bet Mrs. Rice never imagined me here when she taught us our letters by the Housatonic!

The woman spoke simple but clear English. She knew what she wanted to say. Perhaps she had rehearsed it. She had a good sense of when to stop and wait for me to catch up. I wrote fast. I copied over what she said for you to read in this letter because I thought you would find it so interesting. Maybe you can ask the Cornwall Library to keep the letter when you have shown it to Ruby and mother. This is what she said.

> I will tell the true story of Falling Star and her husband so that the white man and the Indian know, forever, the truth. It will always be the same story.

> I was born on a night when falling stars lit up the sky. More falling stars than ever happened before.

> Nine years ago I went with others to hunt deer and elk in a valley between the high mountains and the mountain with two lakes. It was autumn. No one goes there in the winter. We camped on Mill-ke-ke Creek. We got meat to make jerky and hides to make clothes and blankets.

On a day after the men killed an elk two of them were in the sweat lodge they had built and Burning Wagon was coming back from cooling off in the creek. When he looked up, he saw that the camp was surrounded by soldiers. Our men were naked and did not have their rifles or bows ready. Burning Wagon told Horse Trap and the other man to come out of the sweat lodge and not to run or to fight until we decided what to do.

Earlier that day the soldiers had captured two of our men who led them to our camp. The men they captured were Magpie Man and Lean Man. Magpie Man liked to talk all the time and no one wanted to hunt with him. In camp he would talk to people who were talking with another person. He would talk to people who were sleeping. Lean Man was the only person who did not mind though sometimes he did not listen.

The two men were fishing near where the Little Deschutes flows into the Big Deschutes. The men ran to hide in the willows but the soldiers found them and forced them to come out. The Indians from Warm Springs who were guides for the soldiers wanted to kill our two men. But the lieutenant told the guides to speak kindly to our men and interpret honestly. He wanted to know where War Spirit was. War Spirit was war chief of the Walpapis. The lieutenant said he wanted to make a treaty with War Spirit to end the fighting between the white man and the Saydocarah.

The soldiers had signed treaties at Fort Klamath with other Saydocarah chiefs but War Spirit would not come. The lieutenant said if he could make a treaty with War Spirit he would reward our two men with horses, blankets, and rifles. There would be peace between the Saydocarah, the white man, and the Warm Springs Indians. The lieutenant also told Lean Man that the soldiers would buy back his wife for him. Lean Man's wife had been captured and was a slave to a Warm Springs chief.

Our men said they did not know where War Spirit was but they knew where there were more Walpapis. Then they led the soldiers to our camp. Along the way Magpie Man told them who was in the camp. Magpie Man was a fool. He let the soldiers know I was War Spirit's wife.

When the soldiers captured all of us they took away our weapons but they did not tie us with rope. They still pretended to be friendly. They kept asking where War Spirit was and said they wanted to make peace with him. We said we wanted the Warm Springs Indians to go away so we could talk among ourselves. The soldiers made those Indians wait outside the camp.

Horse Trap said the soldiers wanted to find War Spirit so they could kill him. He said our men should rise up and kill as many soldiers as they could with their bare hands, even though all of our men would die.

Burning Wagon said we should tell them we knew where War Spirit was and lead them to a bad place far away. Along the way the men could escape. I could see there would be a long discussion.

I could not tell the men what to do. A woman should not even talk about plans for fighting. But I was a prophet among the Saydocarah. The warriors knew my powers. They knew I could see the future and discover hidden things. I closed my eyes, opened my hands, and chanted a deep chant. I asked the spirits to show me the future and they did. I told the men what the future would be.

"This is what will happen. The braves will run for the soldier's horses and take them. The women will run at the soldiers. We will scream. We will block their eyes and pull their rifles down. All the Walpapi men will die except one who will escape to tell War Spirit." I did not tell them it would be Horse Trap who lived to find War Spirit.

"This is what will happen," I said again.

"So it will be," said Burning Wagon. We looked at each other, knowing it would be the last time we would be together. But no one was afraid.

Burning Wagon said, "Now!" We sprang up immediately. It happened as I had said. We surprised the soldiers and it appeared for a moment that many of our men would escape. But the soldiers shot every Indian. Horse Trap and Lean Man were wounded but they rode into the forest together. Lean Man told Horse Trap he would leave a trail that was easy to follow. The soldiers followed Lean Man and he was dead when they found him. Horse Trap rode over stony ground and the soldiers did not see his trail. He found War Spirit and told him all that happened.

The soldiers took the women and children to Fort Dalles on the Columbia River. Then they took me down the river to Fort Vancouver by myself. The soldiers did not know that one of the children was my son. War Spirit's sister pretended Buffalo Tail was her son.

I asked Falling Star whether the boy with her was the same Buffalo Tail and she said yes. I knew her story must have taken a turn for the better if she had been reunited with her son. The boy was working hard. Falling Star said she had given the boy a white man's name. It was Tom Childers. I don't know where she got the name but it reminded me of Reverend Childers who was minister at our church when I was very little. You probably don't remember him.

> At Fort Vancouver they put me in the guardhouse with a bed, a washstand, and a fireplace to keep warm. General Alvord was in charge of Fort Vancouver at that time. He told the soldiers not to bother me or he would punish them. He wanted to make a treaty with War Spirit. He hoped War Spirit would talk with the army in order to have me returned.

> I saw in a dream that War Spirit and I would be together again. Buffalo Tail would be with us too. In another dream I saw that War Spirit would fight again, that he would kill the chief of the Warm Springs Indians in his own tent. But my dreams were confused. I did not have the dream that I wanted, that we would grow old together and be at peace.

As soon as Falling Star mentioned killing the chief of the Warm Springs Indians I realized that her husband, whom she called War Spirit, was the famous Chief Paulina who rampaged over Eastern Oregon for years. He had snuck into the tent of the Warm Springs chief and waited for the chief to return after a celebration. He surprised the chief and slit his throat. Chief Paulina had burned ranches, robbed stagecoaches, and murdered dozens of people. He was dead now, fortunately. Everyone I knew counted that as a very good thing.

It had never occurred to me Chief Paulina had a wife. Or a sister. Or a son. I wondered if this woman had misled me on purpose, calling her tribe the Saydocarah instead of the Snakes or the Shoshone.

I'd never heard of the Saydocarah. When I stared at the woman she stopped speaking and looked back at me calmly. I looked around again for more Indians but there still were not any. The boy stopped working and looked at us both. His mother nodded to him and he went back to work.

"I'm going to get some water," I said. I ladled some into my cup hanging from the water barrel. "Would you like some?" She said yes and I ladled some into Henry's cup and gave it to her. We both took our sips. I picked up my pen.

> General Alvord sent Sergeant Phillips to teach me English. He asked me to teach Sergeant Phillips our language. The army was never sure the Warm Springs Indians were translating truly.
>
> Sergeant Phillips and I both learned so fast that General Alvord said the sergeant's only job would be to work with me. He wrote down Saydocarah words and phrases as I taught them to him. His memory was very good but he said mine was better because I could remember so many words without writing them down. He wanted to teach me to read but I couldn't see why I should. I told him the speaker was as important as the words. I wasn't interested in what someone said if they did not look at me when they said it. The words lost their strength.
>
> The white man's ways were all like reading. The white man knew many, many things, thought about many things, could organize many things. But a white person cared less about any one thing. I did not see how a white woman could love her husband as much as I loved mine. A white man used books and other people to know things. He had trouble seeing things that were, as Sergeant Phillips said, not black and

white. No white man could see into the future as I could. But I was an exception even among my people.

General Alvord came to visit my room. He asked whether I was being treated well and I said I wanted nothing from him. I would have said the same if they'd chained me to a tree and set their dogs on me. The general asked if I had ever seen a map and I said Sergeant Phillips had drawn me a map of Fort Vancouver and explained how to read it. He drew pictures of places in the fort because I couldn't read their names. Then the general showed me a map of the land he called the State of Oregon. He showed me the courses of the rivers and where the lakes were. He showed me where the mountains were. Sometimes I recognized the names and sometimes I didn't. I thought the map was useless. It was a toy for children and I was insulted that he wanted me to play with it. What good was a piece of paper with the word "Ochoco" on it when I knew where the Ochoco mountains were and how to get there? I knew where the deer bedded down and where the elk liked to graze. I knew where the berries were and when they would be ripe. I knew which streams had fish. The map did not show any of that.

General Alvord came back the next day with the map. He talked about how many days' ride it was between the different places on the map. How long would it take men who wanted to save their horses, and did not stop to hunt along the way, to go from one place to another. This was useful knowledge to Indians as well as white men but I did not see why you needed a map to know it. I told him I didn't know the answers. He knew the answers from his own soldiers and from his Warm Springs scouts. Why was he asking me?

He was working up to asking me where he could find my husband. He would say he wanted to talk with him, to make peace. I thought that was partly true. But once the general found War Spirit he could talk or he could attack, whichever he wanted. When I couldn't tell him where War Spirit was he would ask me where our winter camps were. It would be easy to attack Saydocarah in their winter camps. We didn't move around like we did in the summer. We stayed in our lodges keeping warm and eating the food we had gathered and hunted in the fall. We were not prepared for war. I was never going to tell him where our winter camps were.

But while he was working up to questions I would never answer, the general and I became distracted. With the map in hand he talked about measured distances between points. He thought this was important. How far it was from one point to another if you measured it with a stick. Or if you could fly like a crow but in a straight line. It seemed stupid to me. We may tell stories about crows but no one can turn himself into a crow, especially not a white man.

Then General Alvord showed me a compass. Not the compass that points north but the compass that has two legs. If you put a leg of the compass on one point on the map you could see the other places that were all the same distance away. They were not the same distance to travel but he said it was a different way to think about the land. He could draw the most perfect circles with the compass. He showed me how to use the compass to make a right angle. I didn't know what a right angle was but I could see the thinking behind it and how you could know for sure it was a right angle. General Alvord was very surprised at my explanation.

"Why, you are absolutely right," he said. "You've understood it perfectly. There are graduates of West Point who could not have said it so well."

After that General Alvord came to teach me geometry. I took to it very quickly. There were five simple axioms that you couldn't argue with. And from those five you could build all kinds of things and prove that you had done what you said. It couldn't be denied. It was certain.

"Do all white people know geometry?" I asked.

"Some do. Many don't," said the general, "and few have a true talent for it. Your gift for geometry is astonishing. You may be the only person who knows it so well but doesn't know arithmetic."

I was fascinated with geometry. It was a whole new world to me. It was a world I had never imagined existed. I studied it night and day. I could hardly think of anything else.

But the more geometry I learned the more my dreams abandoned me. Visions would not come when I asked for them. My visions were pale when they did come. Nonetheless I continued my study of geometry. I would not turn back.

The general brought me constructions that were harder and harder to prove. He had a special interest in the tangents of circles and spheres. We worked together on new constructions. I wonder whether he ever found a way to prove them. I hope so. He was a kind man, even if he did want to murder my husband.

For a while I met with General Alvord alone. Then he said the soldiers were saying we were lovers. So he always brought in another soldier, often Sergeant Phillips. Those poor soldiers were so bored with our discussions. Sometimes I disagreed with General Alvord or even corrected him. The soldiers became restless when that happened but the general didn't mind.

We talked about geometry every day and General Alvord put off asking me the questions he had to ask. He knew by then I would never answer them. I might lie to him and that would be a sad thing for both of us. He was a soldier, though, and it was his duty to ask. He brought in Sergeant Phillips and Lieutenant Halloran to be there when he asked about War Spirit.

"I would like to send Sergeant Phillips to talk with your husband. Where should Sergeant Phillips go to look for him?"

"I do not know," I said. "The Saydocarah are always moving about. War Spirit moves to hunt, to visit other Saydocarah, and to stay away from your soldiers. Even if I knew where he was today he would be gone long before Sergeant Phillips got there." This was all true.

He spread the map on the table. "What are the places that he might visit or where the Indians there might know where he is? Or even might be able to get a message to him?"

"I don't know that either," I said. "There are so many places they might camp." This was a lie and I was sure General Alvord knew it was a lie. But we had to go through this interrogation for his sake.

"Where did you camp last year?"

"I go where the chiefs decide. I cannot describe to you where they were. I could not find the places again. I am only a woman." Aside from my being a woman this was a complete lie.

I could have insulted the general with vague descriptions of locations that could be anywhere. "At last year's camp there was a stream that froze and there was a mountain in the direction of the setting sun." Such elaborations would have been an insult to both of us and I kept my answers short. Then General Alvord asked me his most important question.

"Do you think your husband will come to talk with us in order to get you back?"

"Yes," I said.

"What makes you think that?"

"If your wife were captured by the Saydocarah, what would you do to get her back?" General Alvord didn't answer my question. With two other soldiers there he could not admit that he might compromise his duty for the sake of his wife. I did not add that War Spirit and I were more than man and wife. We were born on the same night. The stars fell that night as they had never fallen before or since. It was a sign. Our people knew we would become leaders and saviors of our people. War Spirit became a great war chief and I became a great prophet. Together we are very powerful. The white man did not know how valuable I was to my husband or to the Saydocarah.

In the spring, after I had been at Fort Vancouver three months Colonel Maury replaced General Alvord. Colonel Maury had no interest in geometry and very little interest in me. A month later War Spirit sent word to Fort Klamath that he would sign a peace treaty if I was returned to him. Colonel Maury asked me whether my husband would keep the peace. I said he would if he agreed to it. Finally I was sent to Fort Klamath in August and my husband signed the treaty.

I told our people that we were going to make a big change. We could not live as we had before. We would not travel from place to place to hunt and fish and find food. We would learn to farm and to raise cattle and sheep. We could not think as we had before. We would have to think in new ways and learn many new things.

War Spirit knew I was right and he told the people to give up war and live in peace. This was very hard for the people to accept, particularly the young men who were our best hunters and warriors. At least we were all together and soldiers did not chase us from camp to camp. Our people were not dying.

But the government did not keep its promises. They brought no food. I told our people that food would come but it didn't. I asked the commander of Fort Klamath, Captain Kelly, to send a letter to General Alvord or Colonel Maury but he said he had already sent several. He said the government intended to keep its promises but had difficulty getting the supplies and bringing them to Fort Klamath.

I reminded Captain Kelly of what he had said earlier about chasing the Saydocarah all over Oregon. He said it took ten good soldiers to wage war against one Indian. It cost much less to feed the Indians than to fight them. Captain Kelly agreed the logic was overwhelming. He didn't know why the government could not deliver the food.

The Walpapi began saying that the white man planned for us to starve and that we were fools to stay. By that winter all the Walpapi left the reservation except War Spirit and me. It was humiliating to wait for the white man's promises to be fulfilled when every day made that less likely. Yet the two of us stayed. As long as War Spirit was here, the white man had fewer reasons to hunt down the Walpapi and kill them. War Spirit and I both knew that no war, no matter how long, would end until the white man won it.

Yet we still thought about war. War Spirit could make the white man pay for his victory. He could show the white man and the Indian that the Saydocarah were strong and fearless. The Saydocarah could fight fiercely even while knowing they were doomed. I kept my husband from following the warpath until February, when an army attack killed eighty Saydocarah warriors and some women of another band, not the Walpapi. Chief Howluck, the leader of the other band, wanted revenge and sent a message to War Spirit asking for his help. My husband decided his fate was determined for him.

War Spirit and I left the reservation and traveled to the Ochoco Mountains. I lived with a small group of our relatives while the men went out to make war. We lived the life we were accustomed to. We ate the camas, water lilies, fish, seeds, berries, and wild bird eggs we had known from our childhood. In the fall we gathered honey. War Spirit came to camp when he had captured cattle for us to eat. The men would have to carry deer or elk meat on their horses but they could herd the cattle into camp and that meant we had a lot more food. Those visits were the happiest days, though the men had to make very sure they were not followed.

We feared the soldiers and kept a sharp lookout for them. We made our camps in hidden places and covered our trail when we moved. We were discovered one time, when our warriors were away. The soldiers came up a canyon right toward our camp. I told the women and the children we would go out to meet them. They would see us before their captain gave the order to charge. I stood in front of the others with my feet apart and my arms crossed.

"There are only women and children here," I said in clear, strong English. I held my geometry book in my hand. It might have been a bible. At least it suggested I was civilized and due some respect.

"We are Lemhi," I said. "We have peace with the white man."

The captain and another man talked among themselves. The soldiers nervously watched the hills above them. I did not recognize any of them and they did not recognize me.

"Where are the men?" asked the captain.

"They are hunting," I said. "Gone three weeks already."

The soldiers talked some more. "We want to see your camp," said the captain.

"Follow me," I said. "But don't touch the women." I told the women to come with me and we all walked back to camp. We stood by while the soldiers looked around. One soldier knocked over a basket of camas root and the captain told the men not to damage anything. Then the soldiers left. We moved camp that night.

War Spirit and I knew the white man would win in the end. I knew it from what I saw at Fort Vancouver. The white men were like ants. There were more of them all the time. Many were stupid and lazy. But they could all act together and they kept working and working to build their forts and their farms and their roads.

My husband and I didn't tell the others what we knew. For a year War Spirit's raids were successful and our warriors always escaped. The braves thought they could stay on the warpath forever. They wanted war and they wanted War Spirit to lead them.

I wanted to find another way. I begged the spirits to send me a vision. After days of fasting and chanting they granted me one. It was a fearful sight. I saw my husband's death. I told War Spirit he would not be killed by soldiers but by two settlers. It would be in a canyon with high rock walls. He knew it was the truth but he was a war chief. He had no fear of death. He set his mind to war and he was fierce. Howluck relished killing but War Spirit did not savor it. He fought for honor and his people.

War Spirit made the white man fear him. He stole cattle and horses from ranches all over Eastern Oregon. When he raided wagons coming from the mines in Canyon City, he showed his contempt for the white man by scattering the gold on the ground. He didn't want what the white man had. He didn't want what he could buy with gold.

My vision of War Spirit's death came to pass when he was leading his warriors away from a raid. The men wanted to stop and feast on the cattle they had captured. War Spirit thought they should push on but they persuaded him to stop. Two white men snuck up on them and shot War Spirit with repeating rifles. They shot Horse Trap too but the other Indians escaped. War Spirit stared his killers down as they put six shots through him. They had to shoot him at close range to make him die. He looked the man who shot him straight in the eye. Black Eagle told me this. He was there and he escaped with the others.

That was my last vision. I will have no more. Geometry and logic have driven them away. The white man has won over my mind. My son and I will live by working as the white man works. We will follow reason instead of visions. Tom will learn quickly if someone will show him the way. He will learn to speak good English. He will have a white wife and half-white children.

I did not think the white wife was likely. There are more men than women in this part of the country. What white woman would marry an Indian? Yet he was not bad-looking and, if he was as smart as his mother seemed to be, a girl might do worse. He hadn't stopped working since we began.

"Would he like some water?" I asked. Falling Star said something to him in their language and he stuck the shovel in the ground immediately. He came over and quickly drank two dippers full of water out of our barrel. She said something more to him and he took the pail over to the creek and brought it back full of water. He drank another dipperful and went back to work.

I wrung my writing hand to loosen it up. "How long ago did your husband die?" I asked.

"Six years ago," she said. Seeing I was ready, she went on with her story.

> The last Saydocarah surrendered the year after War Spirit died. We went back to living the way we did before. We now have fewer men to hunt for meat. There are fewer deer and elk because the white man hunts them and uses the land for sheep, cattle, and crops. We eat what we can gather. Some Indians go to the forts and ask the army to feed them. The soldiers are kinder than the settlers. They see us as a defeated foe, like the men from the south in the War Between the States. The settlers see us as pests. I came to you because you are new to this land. You and I have made a bargain and we have kept it.
>
> If my people continue as they are we will starve. We will have less and less land. The only way for us to live is to become like the white man and live among the white man. My friends refuse to do this but I will go down that path for my son. I have taught him geometry and English. We will go to Prineville to find work for him. I think they will want him at a cattle or sheep ranch. I will live however I can but I have warned him I may not live long and he must go and live his life without me. The white man respects knowledge and hard work, I told him. He must follow those two paths to join them and have property, and to have a wife and children.

I had thought I was very strong and brave to become a pioneer in this wilderness. But the hardships I have suffered are like dewdrops compared to the storms that the Indian woman has been through. If she can carry on as she has I have no right to complain.

Tom finished turning over the garden and it was ready for planting. Henry was astounded when he saw it and I told him about my visit from Chief Paulina's wife.

Before the Indians left I brought out what food I had and we ate supper together. It was just biscuits and dried beef with tea. Tom didn't drink the tea. He only drank water. I was surprised to see Falling Star knew how to hold a teacup. She took a lot of sugar but I didn't begrudge it. I'd gotten my garden turned over and spent an interesting afternoon. I had a story to tell.

Henry passed them that evening on his way home from Prineville. He did not stop to talk with them. He said the sawmill wasn't running and there wouldn't be any lumber to build our house until the fall. When lumber is available it will be expensive. So we will settle for a log house. It won't be as nice as the house we left but it will keep us warm and we will have more money left to buy cattle.

I haven't heard anything about Falling Star since they left. I hope Tom found work and they are both getting enough to eat. When there is a library in Prineville I will give them Falling Star's story.

Henry dug a shallow ditch from the creek to the top of the garden so we can water the vegetables. They say there won't be any rain here from the middle of June to the end of October. I am going to plant spinach, turnips, celery, potatoes, and rhubarb. I'll try a few tomatoes and peas, but they are risky because we might have a frost, even in summer. I am grateful I didn't have to turn over the soil for that garden.

Write to me soon and tell me all the news from Connecticut.

Yours in love,
Winifred

Saturday Night

The closest I had to a brother was my cousin Jeff, who was four years younger. I liked him well enough but we didn't spend a lot of time together because he was so much younger. My sports in high school were football, wrestling, and shot put. Jeff ran cross country in the fall and track in the spring. He was thin and wore glasses. He was best in his class at math though, and he was going to go to college. When I finished high school I went to work for my father's construction company, building houses and commercial buildings all over Deschutes County.

Dad paid me less than the other workers because I didn't have the skills and hadn't proven I could show up and do a full day's work. I always did show up and I always did the most tiring jobs, like digging holes or carrying shingles up to the roof in the hottest part of the day. I didn't mind. I could show the other guys I was stronger and tougher than they were. The pay was pretty damn good for a guy right out of high school. I also liked that I could always see what I had accomplished. I was learning all the time – how to read a plan, how to think ahead, who in my father's company was reliable and what my father did about it when they weren't.

The men I worked with never complained about my father. I thought that was because I was there. But I wanted to know what they thought of him and, after a while, I asked one of the guys I felt closest to, Sam Koloski.

"He's good," said Sam. "He always has work for us and he pays us on time." I'd been hoping for some insight into my father, both as a man and as someone who had authority over other people. He'd always had authority over me. All Sam gave me were these basic nuts and bolts.

"Well," I said, "do you like working for him?"

"Sure," he said. "He handles the owners, he's pretty clear on what we're supposed to do, and he makes sure we never run out of material. If there's no lumber we can't work and we don't get paid. He keeps us working."

I still wasn't hearing the kind of stuff I wanted to hear. But Sam opened my eyes to something. It didn't matter so much whether my father was nice to the men or not. Or whether he praised them or not. Dad had a job to do just like they did. He did it and that was all they needed, or most of what they needed anyway. I began to see something else as well. Much as I wanted my father's respect I began to see that respect was not an on/off switch. My father knew how hard I was working and whether my work was good. He wasn't complaining and that was as good as it was going to get. Part of being a man was learning to live with that. As to whether he liked me I decided he probably didn't know himself. I could live with that too. But when I had children they would know for sure that I thought they were great.

The year that Jeff graduated from high school my father gave him a summer job with the company so he could make some money for college. Dad told me, "I want you to show him what to do and how to do it." This seemed like extra work for me until I thought about it. Jeff would share the load on some of the heavy lifting that I'd been doing.

"This is going to help you learn how to be a boss," said Dad. "Your job is to teach him what to do, not to lord it over him. And I want you to work at least as hard as he does. He is not there to do your work for you."

We were building a house out towards La Pine. Jeff and I dug the foundation by hand. It was the last house my father built before he bought the backhoe. There was no rock to deal with but the soil was dry and dusty. When you lifted the shovel half the dirt slid back off it and you knew you had to lift that same dirt all over again. Jeff worked hard and he didn't go looking for excuses to rest. The house was right next to the river and once or twice in the afternoon we'd jump in the river to cool off. No lollygagging though. We climbed right out and went back to work.

The owner said when he was younger Indians used to camp in the field by the house. They came in the fall to hunt deer. The Indian men would build a little sweat lodge out of willows. They'd cook themselves in it and then jump in the river like we did. They did it to sweat odors out of their bodies so the deer wouldn't smell them. Our clothes still smelled of sweat when we dried out. The Indians had jumped in naked.

The place was a cattle ranch but the owner only had about twenty-five cows. He'd sold off a bigger herd in World War II when beef prices were good and the army built a training camp on the land he rented for summer grazing. I don't know where he got the money to build the house we were working on but he sure needed it. He lived in an old log house across the driveway that was starting to fall apart. He'd been patching it up for decades. It had no plumbing, no insulation, and the heat came from wood stoves and a fireplace. The man came out and watched us work, especially when Sam joined us and we put in the floor joists and framed the walls. I think the man wanted to help. But he couldn't have kept up with us. After a while he came out to watch us a few times a day and didn't stay long. He sat on the porch that faced away from the new house and rolled his own cigarettes. Every now and then we'd get a whiff of Bull Durham tobacco.

Dad had other projects going and he showed up at our site once or twice a week. He parked his car up the driveway and walked down to the site. It was a blue 1951 four-door Oldsmobile Rocket 88 and he didn't want it to get it dusty or scratched. Dad barely looked at the house. He asked us a few questions and then went to talk with the owner. It was hard to imagine what they talked about. We had the house plans. We had a contract. It wasn't like the owner was going to make any decisions. But my father made a point of talking with him. Once my father told me to stop working and come over with him to talk with the owner. I stood there while they talked about the weather and about some other cattle rancher they both knew who'd sold his ranch in La Pine and moved to Idaho. My father said the tarpaper for the walls and the roof would come early next week. I thought there was no point in telling the owner that. He was dependent on my father to know what he needed and when. The tarpaper wasn't the owner's problem. It seemed to me the whole conversation, from beginning to end, was a complete waste of time. When we walked away I asked my father why he told the man when the tarpaper would be there.

"I'm showing him I'm on top of his job and he's important to me."

"But you've got a contract and we'll get it done in plenty of time. Why do you need to show him anything?"

"He's a lot happier trusting us and believing nothing is going to go wrong. It's not good for business to simply build houses and collect the money. You want the owner to like the house, like you, not drive you crazy with questions, and not complain about you to other people."

Jeff did the muscle work that required the minimum of knowledge and experience. He carried lumber to where we needed it. He carried the scrap away after the lumber had been cut. He rolled kegs of nails around the job site. I'd have him nail boards to the frame if it was in a place where he couldn't go wrong. I'd have him saw a few boards if I'd marked the line with a pencil. But Sam or I always marked the line. If Jeff measured wrong he would waste the wood.

When we broke for lunch one day Jeff got up and went around making measurements of what we'd already built.

"Is he checking our work?" Sam asked. He said it like a joke but he was close to being put out about it.

"He's just trying to learn all he can about building," I said. "He wants to be an engineer. If he asks us a question it's because he wants to understand something, not because he thinks we did something wrong."

Jeff wasn't lacking the grit to work hard. I thought he'd do okay with his professors no matter what they threw at him. What he lacked was the ability to have a normal conversation. His only friends were other runners in high school and they didn't talk much. He didn't have a girlfriend and I didn't think he'd ever had a date. I tried to get some conversations going while we drove to the jobsite and back every day in my car. He listened all right and asked some questions. But he had very little to say for himself when I asked him a question. I kept finding myself jabbering about sports, about building going around town, and about what my friends were doing. What Jeff wanted to talk about, when he did get going, was stuff nobody I knew thought about.

"Why don't people build octagonal houses?" he asked one day. "They'd get more space inside and use less lumber to build it. It would cost less to heat and, if you did it right, the runs for the plumbing and the electrical wouldn't be as long."

I'd heard of octagonal houses but I'd never even seen one. I wasn't sure Jeff was right that you'd get more space with less lumber. It seemed like with all those angles it might take more lumber rather than less. I told him I'd think about it. Then I couldn't get it out of my head, thinking about how you'd build an octagonal house. I made some sketches. I thought of asking my father about it but I wanted to see what I could figure out on my own.

I told Jeff I thought he was right about octagonal houses needing less lumber, as well as less roof. And I said anyone who could build a bay window could build an octagonal house, though parts of it would take some head scratching. But I said I thought owners liked rectangular rooms and none of the rooms in an octagonal house would be rectangles. The furniture and the rugs could be parallel with one wall but they'd be at an angle with another wall. The furniture would look funny and you might wind up wasting some of the extra space you gained.

"I didn't even think about the furniture," said Jeff. I was pretty pleased with myself but I told him the truth.

"I didn't think about the furniture either," I said. "I sketched out some plans and showed them to Barbara." Barbara Sorenson was my girlfriend. We were thinking about getting married. We both wanted children. Supervising Jeff and teaching him things was a sort of experiment in that direction. So far I thought it was going pretty well.

"Barbara didn't like the outside of the house either. She said it looked like a big water tank with windows." So take that, I thought, Mr. Math Whiz, Mr. College Man. I knew he was going to wind up knowing things I didn't know. But I was content to be on the path I was on, working construction for my father. Pretty soon, though, I knew it would be the only path I could take, wherever it went. Jeff would have choices. In the long run he would probably have more money. He might live in Portland or even New York. Or even Paris. Bend suited me just fine. I didn't want to live in those places. But Jeff would have the options and I would not. At least Jeff didn't act like a big shot, like he was smarter than anyone else because he was going to college.

I told Barbara I wanted Jeff to succeed, to get whatever he wanted. I'd be mad if he didn't take advantage of his brains and his opportunities. I was worried he wouldn't succeed because he didn't know how to make friends or play on a team or get people to like him.

"You like him," Barbara said.

"Yes," I said, "but he's my cousin and he's a kind of pet project. Otherwise he would be too much work. He's hardly got any friends and I think he's hopeless with girls. Wouldn't have a clue what to say or do with them."

"We could educate him," said Barbara. "We could be the ones who get him ready for college." We both laughed at that. Neither one of us had gone to college, hadn't really even thought about it. Barbara was smart enough that she could have. Instead she had a job in an insurance office on Bond Street.

Driving home after work on a Thursday, after we passed Lava Butte and started downhill, I asked Jeff what he was doing that weekend.

"Mow the lawn," said Jeff. "I'm sure my father will think of a few other things. Then I'll lie in the hammock and read a book. Probably go to church on Sunday."

"You don't have much excitement in your life, do you?"

"I've got a good job here with you, learning how to build houses. I like it and I think I can get better. Maybe I should keep doing construction instead of going to college. I'd be making money instead of borrowing it."

"You're nuts," I said. "This is a summer job. Nobody will need a gofer in the fall." This wasn't as true as I made it sound, except for the part about Jeff being nuts. If he didn't go to college I would beat him with a 2x4 until he went.

"How would you like to go out with Barbara and me Saturday night?"

"Thanks but, um, I don't want to slow you down."

"No problem. The more the merrier. We'll cruise around and see if we can pick up a girl for you," I said.

Jeff looked toward my foot and mumbled. "I don't know how to do that."

"Barbara will make it easy. You'll have a girl making goo-goo eyes at you before you know it."

I thought I might get the loan of my father's Oldsmobile for Jeff's sake. We'd been riding to work in my 1940 Chevrolet. Barbara had to ride in it too. I carried all kinds of tools back and forth in it to construction sites. Where the paint was scratched or the fenders were dented it didn't seem worth getting fixed. I planned to drive that car until it died then buy a newer car for Barbara and me.

"You can borrow the Olds," Dad said, "but you be careful with it." Saturday morning I followed Dad to Bend Country Club, where he played golf with his buddies. I parked my car at the far end of the parking lot and drove his car home to wash and wax it. I spent six dollars to fill up the tank, too. Then I took his car back to the club and drove my car home.

I took a shower and put clean clothes on, ready to go as soon as Dad brought the car home.

When I got to Barbara's house her father met me at the front door.

"Edie," he yelled back into the house. "Donny has stolen the nicest car to take our daughter out. Come look." Then he came out alone and approached the car.

"Your father let you take his car?"

"Yep. Just this once. If I drive through a puddle I'll never get to touch it again."

"How do you like the Hydra-Matic transmission?" he asked.

"It feels funny, like I'm not sure I'm in gear. I think I'd rather have a standard shift."

"Well, it sure is a nice-looking car."

Barbara came out and gave us a smile like the Girl Scout who sold the most cookies. Her blond hair was close to her head and curled like Doris Day's. She had on a blue plaid skirt and a white blouse that was tight across her chest.

"You'll be home by twelve?" her father asked.

"Daddy, there are girls my age who are married and have children," said Barbara.

"House rules," her father said with a smile. "You still live here. Your mother will worry." After two blocks she slid across the seat and sat next to me.

Jeff charged out of his house when I beeped the horn. He had on a shirt that still had the folds from the store. His left cheek was peeling where he should have used more suntan lotion during the week. Bright pink skin was surrounded by a thin ring of white flakes trying to peel off.

"Hello Jeff," Barbara said when Jeff came up to the car. "I'm so glad you could come with us. This will be fun." He got in the back seat and I eased the car into the street.

"Donny says you're a good worker," said Barbara. "I remember how hard you studied. You were in the Honor Society."

"I simply did my homework," said Jeff. "I didn't really study all that hard."

"Then you must be very smart," said Barbara.

"Smart enough for high school, I guess. But I still have a lot to learn about building houses. It's more complicated than people think."

"I'm sure you could learn it in no time," said Barbara, "if you weren't going off to college to learn more important things. Are you scared?"

"It's going to be different. I've lived here my whole life."

"But it will be exciting. Your professors will be really smart. And you'll meet people from all over, even California and Washington." I thought if Barbara went to college that was what she would enjoy the most. She'd stay up all night talking with people she'd never met before. Then she got to the point.

"Donny says he thinks you are shy. Are you shy, Jeff?" I kept driving and grinned.

"I suppose I am," said Jeff. "Always been that way."

"You shouldn't be shy," Barbara said. "There will be some nice girl at college who will want you to ask her out. If you are too shy she will miss out. Can you imagine how sad that will be for her? You owe it to her not to be shy."

"I sure never thought of it that way," said Jeff.

Barbara went into this story about a girl she had known in high school who had a crush on a boy but she was very shy. She wouldn't do anything to get his attention for fear he would laugh at her. She was getting so upset she couldn't sleep or study. Finally she decided she had to do something or go crazy. She went to his house and asked him to help her with her homework. She knew he might say no and that would be the end of her hopes. But he helped her that day and eventually every afternoon. Then he asked her out and they went out together the rest of the school year.

I'd never heard this story before but I thought it must be true. Jeff seemed to get really caught up in it.

"Then what happened?" he asked.

"Then she wasn't shy anymore and the next year she went out a lot."

"With other guys?"

"Yes. And she went to parties. She was as popular as anyone."

"What about the guy who tutored her?"

"Oh, he graduated."

"You watch," I said. "You get to college and some girl from the big city will want you to tutor her. You better be careful."

"That's not what I meant," said Barbara. "I meant that if Jeff likes a girl he should find a way to meet her. He needs to practice talking with girls so he gets used to it."

We drove up Third Street, the main drag through town, waving to people we knew in other cars. We passed miles of gas stations, restaurants, car dealers, and all kinds of other stores. We called it "oozin' and cruisin'."

"Hey, Donny, where you get that rocket?" yelled a skinny guy I hardly knew from the back seat of an old DeSoto. "You're ridin' in style."

"Wouldn't you like to know?" I shouted back. I revved the V8 at the next stoplight but I didn't peel out.

Two girls from Jeff's class passed us in a pre-war Ford with the paint peeling off. They waved to everyone. The girl on the passenger side was laughing and bouncing around in the seat.

"They're not shy," said Jeff.

"They act like they just got out of jail," I said. "Haven't tasted freedom in so long they don't know what to do with it."

"Well, they are making fools of themselves," said Barbara.

I stopped at the drive-in restaurant at the north end of town and parked on the street. I locked the car like I never do with my own unless I have tools in it. Jeff and I had cheeseburgers with fries. Barbara had a hamburger but didn't eat the fries. I had a chocolate milkshake. Jeff and Barbara had vanilla.

"Jeff, how's your father doing?" Barbara asked him.

"Okay, I guess," he said. "He says he doesn't mind working at the hardware store. The pay isn't as good as working at the mill but it's a lot quieter and he gets to talk to people."

"A lot of people who were laid off can't find work," said Barbara. Barbara's father was a manager at the other lumber mill, the one that was still running. Jeff's father had worked at the one that closed.

"Not enough trees left for two mills," I said. "My dad says they'll close the other mill someday and we'll bring wood in from Canada to build houses."

Jeff and I had cherry pie for dessert but Barbara said she was full. Jeff paid for himself and I paid for Barbara. On the way back down Third Street I stopped at a liquor store and went in alone.

I saw Jeff's eyes pop in the rearview mirror when we turned into the Canton Café. The way people talked about the place, it was home to drunks, bar fights, and loose women. I bet he never dreamed he'd go there and he was surprised I took Barbara there. Barbara and I had been there before, though, and we both liked it. If the Canton Café was a honky-tonk it was a nice one. People mostly behaved themselves. They had country music on the juke box and sometimes they had a band.

I parked in an end spot away from the building. We all looked red in the light of the sign on the roof. The "t" in "Canton" was flickering and we could hear the neon buzzing. The blue Rainier sign in the window looked ice-cold.

The booths and tables were half-full. A few people sat at the bar. Hank Williams was playing on the juke box but no one was dancing yet. I led us to a booth in the back near the pool tables. There were three men playing 8-ball at the near table and a couple playing pool by themselves at the far table.

"You waitin' for a table?" said one of the men.

"No," I said, "we're just going to sit and maybe dance a little later. You mind if we watch your game?"

"My game ain't worth watchin' but you're welcome to look."

"Okay," I said.

A waitress named Natalia came to take our order. She was a few years older than we were, with short black hair, high cheekbones, and dark eyebrows. She was from somewhere in Europe and had an accent.

"What can I get you?" she asked.

"One gin and tonic and two plain tonics," I said. She asked to see my license and I showed it to her. She stopped at another table before she went to the bar and had a laugh with the men who were sitting there. I could see Jeff watching her.

When the drinks came, Jeff couldn't help sneaking another look at Natalia. I was sure he was wondering what her story was. Barbara and I had asked her on an earlier visit. She had met a GI stationed in Germany and married him. He brought her back here.

I was going to say to Jeff, "Relax soldier, her next move is not going to be with you, college boy or not." But we were there to get him revved up, not to shut him down. So I held my tongue.

When Natalia left I pulled the bottle from under my jacket and unscrewed the top underneath the table. I took Barbara's glass and held it below the table while I poured into it.

"Do you want to put a little life in that glass?" I asked Jeff. Jeff said yes and I took his glass under the table.

More people came in, including two girls Barbara and I knew from her class in high school. That made them two years older than Jeff, still not old enough to get a real drink. They sat at the bar and ordered 7 Up. Then they headed toward the pool tables.

"Hi Barbara, how are you?" said the taller one. "Hello Donny. It's good to see you too."

"Hello," said Barbara. "I was sure we'd see someone we knew here. Sit right down and join the party. This is Jeff. Jeff, this is Jean and this is Pam." Jeff must have known their names from school but he said "How do you do?" as though he had never seen them before. Jeff squeezed toward the wall. Pam, the short one, sat next to Jeff. Jean sat on the outside. It was a tight fit. Across the table, I lounged back against the corner of the booth and smiled at them. Barbara leaned over and asked me if we could share our vodka with them and I nodded. Barbara offered them a taste of vodka in their 7 Up and they said yes. After a glance around the room I took their glasses and added to them under the table.

"Jeff is going to Oregon State next year," said Barbara.

"Off to the big world," said Jean. "Are you going to forget all about us here?"

"I am sure I won't forget," said Jeff.

"Yes you will. You'll have new friends and you'll want to stay in the valley. Or live in Portland or Seattle."

"I'll be back, at least to see my folks."

"What we should all do," said Jean, "is come visit you. You can show us around the campus. And Corvallis. I've always wanted to see it." Jeff looked panicked. He might have been to Corvallis once, if that, and he certainly wasn't ready to show anyone else around. He rose to the challenge, though.

"Of course you should come," he said, "but give me a little time to learn the campus myself."

"That will give us something to look forward to," said Jean. "You let us know when you're ready and we'll be right over." Jean turned to Barbara and asked about a girl who had gone to the university in Eugene.

I caught Jeff's eye and motioned toward his tonic. There was nothing but a little ice and the remains of a lime in Jeff's glass.

"I have to drive," I said, "but you don't." Jeff slid his drink over and I poured some more vodka in it under the table. Jeff sipped slowly.

"Jeff, I want to see if you can dance," said Barbara. "Come dance with me."

We'd all learned square dancing and the Foxtrot in high school gym class but I didn't think Jeff had danced since then. By that point, though, I thought he would try anything Barbara asked him to. Pam and Jean stood up to let him out. He and Barbara were the only people on the dance floor. It was still early. Barbara reminded him where to put his hands and they practiced the steps a few times slowly. Then they got on the beat. The jukebox was playing "Walkin' My Baby Back Home" and Jeff kept up with the time pretty well. A runner shouldn't have any trouble moving his legs and he did all right. By the time they were halfway through Rosemary Clooney singing the next song he looked like he knew what he was doing. If he could dance it would help him a lot with the girls.

What made his dancing more miraculous to me was that I knew what he was thinking. He's never been that close to a girl before. Like any eighteen-year-old he's fantasized about sex night and day. Now he's right next to a beautiful girl who likes him and is having a good time. He's got three quarters of his brain screaming "Yes! Yes! Go for it!" and a quarter of his brain working on where to put his feet. But he's managing to do it.

"Isn't Barbara a wonderful dancer?" Pam said to me. "And she always looks so happy."

"Yes she does," I said. "I'm lucky she likes me."

"Are you going to ask her to marry you?" asked Jean.

I gave her a smile. "That's between Barbara and me."

They danced one more song and then came back to the table. Barbara kept hold of Jeff's hand. He looked nervous as hell about it. As though he imagined Barbara had suddenly fallen for him and I was going to be jealous.

"Now ask Pam to dance," she said. "I'm sure she'd like that." Jeff stood by the table and asked Pam if she would dance with him. Jean slid out and Pam got up without saying anything. Jeff leaned over the table and took a big swig of his drink. I'd put a lot more vodka in it.

We watched them dance. "He's a sweet one," said Jean.

"Yes he is," said Barbara. "Don't you think so, Donny?"

"Yeah," I said, "he's a sweet one."

After three songs Pam came back alone and stood by the table. "Jeff said he wasn't feeling well and he went to the men's room," she told us. I laughed.

"One thing I'm sure he will learn in college," I said, "is to hold his liquor." I got up to rescue him. I could hear Jeff being sick before I got to the men's room.

"You all right, cowboy?" I asked. I took it as a good sign that Jeff was standing instead of kneeling in front of the toilet. He seemed to be finished throwing up. "Can you walk straight?"

"I guess so. I'm sorry, Donny."

"Okay. You clean yourself up as well as you can. Check your clothes. Blow your nose and rinse your mouth out. Then go out the back door and wait outside for me. I'm going to go get the girls."

"Please tell them goodnight for me. I don't want them to know I threw up."

"They already know that. That's the price you pay. Drink some water before you go and then just wait." He was washing up when I left him.

"Why did you give him so much vodka?" Barbara asked me.

"I didn't know he was going to polish it off in one gulp," I said. She gave me a look that let me know she wasn't pleased. Then she smiled at the other girls as if the stupidity of men was a fact of nature and had to be tolerated.

I told the girls Jeff would be all right. And I was sure he'd never had an evening like that before. "Ready for college," I said, though I knew he still wasn't.

I paid Natalie for our drinks. Barbara and I danced one dance to "Vaya Con Dios" and we all went out the back door to take Jeff home. He was leaning on a fence.

"I'm sorry you got sick," said Pam.

"I'm very sorry," said Jeff. "Thank you for the dances. Please go back inside and have fun."

Pam kissed him on the temple. "Goodnight. I hope you feel better." She went back inside with Jean.

"Hey stud," I said after the door closed. "You're a wreck and she still kissed you. What's your secret?"

"It's my charm and sophistication," said Jeff. Barbara laughed loudly and he actually smiled.

"We're taking you home," I said. "You sit by the window. If you think there is a chance you're going to get sick you let me know and I'll let you out. If you barf on my dad's car, there is going to be hell to pay."

We dropped him off in front of his house and he managed to walk a straight line to the front door. There were a few lights on inside and some of them went off before we left.

"I hope he makes it to his bedroom before his parents see him," I said. "They're going to be mad if they know I got him drunk."

"You can tell them he's learned his lesson. Now he'll know better than to drink so much again."

"So I've actually done him a favor?" I said as we drove away.

"I'm sure they'd see it that way," said Barbara.

"I think he had a good night, in spite of getting sick."

"He's a nice boy," said Barbara. "It was good for him to get out."

"You think he learned anything?"

"He's got a way to go but he'll get there. He needs to call Pam."

"And ask her on a date? She's older than he is and he doesn't have a car."

"He can borrow yours. Pam likes him. She told me. And she'd rather go out than sit around home."

"Okay," I said. "You give me her number and I'll give it to Jeff."

Barbara sat closer and put her head on my shoulder.

"You know," I said, "with what we're doing for Jeff, I think we should put that kind of effort into somebody who is going to stick around for a while."

"Who would that be?"

"A very little person, but kind of like you and me."

Barbara sat up and looked at me. "And where would we find a person like that?"

"Well, actually, that's the fun part," I said.

"What do you mean?"

"We'd probably want to get married first. Do you think that would be a good idea? Maybe in a month or two?"

Barbara hit me hard in the ribs. I almost ran up on the curb with my father's car.

"Are you being serious?" she said.

"Yes," I said. "Are you ready to marry me?"

"Yes I am," she said. She kissed me on the cheek and snuggled up to me again.

"And someday," I said, "we'll live in an octagonal house."

On the Road from Burns

You pull off the two-lane blacktop, here in the desert, to rest your eyes from finding the road with your headlights. You stand beside your car in the warm air, in the light of the full moon. You are alone; haven't seen a car or a town for hours.

The sagebrush glimmers over the vast flat plain, like a design etched in a massive silver tray. Dull and slightly tarnished, you cannot make out the smith's pattern. A garden? The head of a stag? The Sistine Chapel? Distant mountains rim the horizon.

You wish the one you love were here. There is no human light in any direction. There is no sound but soft wind. You could be the sole person on the Earth. Your lover may be looking at the same moon thinking of you. Fast asleep, dreaming of you. In the arms of another, thinking of Harry Truman. If your lover were here all would be perfect.

Your car is off on the sandy shoulder of the road, at the foot of a hill. You move around the car and up the hill, so you can see further in the night. Slowly you climb. You can see the rocks and the scrubby little bushes easily. You avoid the shadows, black as pitch, hiding who knows what – animals, mineshafts, traps for coyotes. When you begin to breathe more deeply (you feel the altitude) you see a broad flat rock and sit down on it.

Has the scene changed? Darker? Lighter? Different. As the moon moves, every shadow of every leaf, every reflection for a thousand miles moves with it. Your car plays a slow metallic rhythm as it cools.

In the far distance there is a wink of white light. It comes and goes, dims and brightens. Minutes go by. You can ignore it. Gaze at the desert. Know that you will see your lover again. Think of your lover's face, more beautiful to you than even the land below you softened by moonlight. Thank you, God, you say, for reminding me that life is, fundamentally, good. If you know where to look.

The little light is brighter, though it is still far, far away. It goes out for minutes at a time, then reappears. It is a car coming toward you. It may take half an hour to arrive. You imagine your lover is in the car, having read your thoughts, speeding over the desert to meet you.

Perhaps it is a person like yourself, a person alone caught up in his own thoughts. Or a brother and sister; or two lovers, newlyweds who took the wrong road; or an older couple that doesn't like cities, likes the roads they have always taken. They do not imagine they are being watched all this time. They are in their own private world. Perhaps one of them is asleep. You watch over them, like a shepherd. You wish them well.

You wait for the moment when they will pass, when you can judge the speed of the car, see its shape, perhaps, by moonlight, even its color. Perhaps, if you look carefully, the people inside. Do you want to move down to the road as they approach to get a better look? Perhaps to wave to them gaily as they drive past. Won't they be surprised?

No. Better to sit and regard them peacefully. A Buddha, a Sphinx. Then, when they have passed, you will get in your car and drive on. You lift your eyes to the moon, bright but barren. More barren than the desert. No air, no water, no scent of vegetation. How bright earthlight must be on the moon. The Earth a bigger mirror. Too much light perhaps. The moonlight spread before you seems more than ample.

Here they come. The headlights are steady now. You hear the rush of air around the car, hear the engine, the tires flailing at the road. The sound will change as they pass. What is this? They are stopping. Oh no! They think you have broken down. They will inquire over and over whether you are all right, whether you are sure the car is running fine.

"It's a lonely place for a car to quit," they will say. You will have to talk, make explanations, come down off the hill. No peace.

They turn off their engine. Turn off their lights. Two wiry men approach your car warily. They look inside, open your door, peer in the back seat, open the glove compartment. On to the floor they paw maps, insurance papers, pocket Kleenex, the latest letter from your lover. They can't open the trunk without the keys and you have them. They look up and down the road. They look up the hill. They have seen you. How very unpleasant this is going to be.

They start up the hill toward you, striding like teachers bent on discipline. Sergeants strict in their arrest. You do not rise up to escape. You await the passing of events. Like a monk.

The first man falls. "Ow!" he shouts. The other man looks down into darkness where the first man disappeared. He steps down. You can barely see the outline of his head.

"Are you hurt?" says the second man.

"I think I broke my ankle."

The head of the second man dips into the shadow.

"Dammit," says the second man. He waves his arm in the moon-light. The dark shape of a rope swings from his wrist.

"Damn snake bit me," says the man. His head and arm gyrate in a violent dance. He grabs the rope and hurls it away. "We've got to get out of here." He turns toward the cars, trips and falls. Swears again.

The first man's head rises slowly into the light. "Help me," he says. "I can't walk."

The snake-bit man won't go back into the shadow. He struggles to pull the other man up.

You do not move. Later you will think of reasons why you did not move. For now, though, you don't need reasons.

The men hobble down the hill, one leaning on the other. The broken ankle man turns his head back toward you. "Help us," he says.

Fat chance.

It's time you were going. You walk down the hill. Slowly. Stick to the moonlight. Keep away from evil. Shadows and villains. The bitten man is starting to be sick. They can both hardly walk.

There you are in your car. Lock the doors. Load the glove compartment later. Start the engine. Drive on. Don't look back. Tell your mind it was a dream. What will you tell the one you love? Better say nothing. The night was... well, it was dark.

Prisoner of Conscience

When I was a boy in Bolzano, near the Italian Alps, I dreamed of living in the mountains someday. I imagined my days walking from one majestic view to the next. I would have valleys, peaks, waterfalls, and hidden mountain lakes entirely to myself. When others came up from the lowlands I would point them to the best trails and tell them the names of the peaks. Then I would stride up mountains and they would be impressed with my strength.

I did, in fact, belong to a hiking club. When we were not trekking or climbing in the Dolomites or the Alps we were talking about it. We were all very fit and rather taken with ourselves. We thought our bond with the mountains made us superior to the people shuffling through their daily routines down the narrow streets and around the old buildings of our cities and towns.

A girl in our club named Tazia constantly impressed me. She was a strong hiker and strikingly pretty. She charged up mountains but grew sentimental when she saw the view from the top. She sang beautifully. She sang for us about loving the land and country.

Tazia became a member of a youth group called the Avanguardisti. The group had nothing to do with mountains but it did have enthusiasm. It was preparing young people to become the "fascists of tomorrow." I joined the group to be with her. We all developed an admiration for Benito Mussolini. "Il Duce" wanted to bring discipline and efficiency to Italy, to make Italy a better and stronger country. I came to see him as something like me and my hiking friends – lovers of beauty with the fortitude to take on challenges.

He was tough and clear-minded. It was noble of Mussolini, and a great sacrifice on his part, to entangle himself with the affairs of a country as disorganized and inefficient as Italy. It was a selfless service to his countryman.

I became a group leader in the Avanguardisti. Tazia welcomed my enthusiasm. She grew to respect me and care for me. We fell in love. We spoke of marriage and of doing our duty for Italy together.

Mussolini believed Italy needed to recapture territory that rightfully belonged to it. We needed space, spazio vitale, to become what we should become. To reclaim this essential space Italy needed brave and capable soldiers. I volunteered. The army sent me to officer training school. I was president of the hiking club by then and I already knew a lot about camping, field logistics, and reading maps. I became a second lieutenant. Tazia was immensely proud of me.

Italy's plan was to colonize North Africa with the help of our German allies. I went to Africa with mountain troops, the 7th Bersaglieri. Rommel praised our regiment for fighting fiercely in the victory at Kasserine Pass. But the Americans and British kept landing more troops while our supplies kept falling short. In May of 1943 all the Italians and Germans in North Africa surrendered. I became a prisoner of war and was sent to the United States.

In September of 1943 our American captors told us that Italy had ousted Mussolini and become an ally of the Americans. We were invited to sign a "collaboration agreement" and join the American war effort. We would be assigned to Italian Service Units, organized like army units, and support the United States war effort. Ninety percent of the Italian prisoners signed.

The "collaborationists" were happy to be in America, allied with the Americans. America was a much wealthier country than Italy. Most of the men had never eaten so well. The collaborationists cooked for American soldiers, fixed cars and trucks, and worked in army warehouses. They could leave the camps with a pass, like an American soldier. They went to Catholic services alongside Americans in regular churches. Local Italian-American associations invited them to social functions. They met and fell in love with American girls.

Not for one single second did I think about signing that agreement. I had promised to fight, and perhaps to die, for the Italy we were building with Mussolini. Mussolini had escaped and become Il Duce of a new Italian Social Republic, in Northern Italy, near my home. My promise to fight for fascist Italy still held. What would Tazia think of me if I abandoned the ideals we shared?

I was assigned to a non-collaborationist camp in Oregon called Camp Abbot. The army was training engineers at Camp Abbot to build bridges, barracks, canals, and everything else they would need when they invaded Europe. One thing they built was a prisoner-of-war camp. Since they had the camp, they might as well use it. That's how we got there. They brought in two hundred Germans and forty Italians.

My best friend in the camp was another second lieutenant named Mario Lucchini. He was a barrel-chested man with thick black hair. He was from Trento, another city in Northern Italy, and a mountaineer, like me. We had never met before but we knew the same mountains. Mario and I compared the trails we had walked and the peaks we had scaled. We talked about famous mountaineers that we had met or at least knew by reputation. Mario had even heard about Tazia, how beautiful she was and how wonderfully she sang. In my bunk at night I imagined Tazia singing.

There was an extinct volcano in the mountain range to the west of the camp. Mario and I liked to gaze at it while we talked. Neither of us had climbed a volcano and we were fascinated with this one. It had snow on the top, like the Alps, even in October.

Apart from my discussions with Mario, life in the camp was horrendously boring. There was a German violinist who had kept his instrument when he surrendered. But I could only listen to so much violin music, even Verdi and Puccini. A sergeant from Naples had a small accordion that we tolerated in small doses. He liked to play loud. All of us, Germans and Italians together, limited him to thirty minutes three days a week.

Some men played checkers all day. A lucky few spent hours engrossed in chess. Bridge and poker were the most popular card games. Germans and Italians did not mix well at cards. The lack of a common language led to too many arguments. If the guards had to break up a fight the combatants were shut up in log-walled cells that had no heat.

The Americans showed us movies that were always in English. We whistled at the actresses, gave nicknames to all the characters, and yelled comments back and forth since we couldn't understand the dialogue. We saw the movies after the Germans. They did their own shouting. We were quiet during the newsreels so the few who understood English could tell us about them later. The Germans were slowly retreating in Italy. We listened for the names of towns and cities, each man hoping his home had been spared the worst fighting.

The rumor mill was our continuous entertainment. The Americans were putting arsenic in our food. The German prisoners were digging a tunnel. The Japanese Navy would soon capture the American West Coast and set us free. Spain would join Germany and turn the tide in Italy. We never dismissed a rumor unless we had a more interesting one to replace it.

We believed that a few Germans relayed our rumors to the Americans in return for special favors. For amusement, and to make trouble, Mario and I invented stories to manipulate our captors. We would mutter about secret caches of weapons in the camp or the corruption of a specific American officer. In a few days the Americans would descend on the rumored location. Sometimes the designated American would be reassigned.

It was autumn when we arrived but it turned cold in November and started to snow. The Americans gave us warm clothes and warm barracks, heated with wood stoves. We had plenty of hot food. Winter didn't bother the Germans. To Mario and me it was like being in the mountains. But many of the Italians had never seen weather like this and they looked worried when the cold air nipped at their ears.

The guards counted all of us outdoors twice a day. Mario and I didn't mind freezing temperatures if the sky was clear. But mustering in the rain with a cold wind and slushy snow underfoot was miserable for everyone. I wanted to tell the Americans they could skip counting us. No one would escape in weather like that.

With little to do, some of us took to walking around the entire camp, lap after lap. It kept us moving and improved our moods. Mario, myself, and a few groups of Germans would make our rounds in all but the foulest weather.

On a cold morning in May, the Americans announced they were looking for volunteers to do forest work. The volunteers would be given extra cigarettes when they returned to camp. I was not going to help the Americans, certainly not for the sake of cigarettes.

Then Mario and I did volunteer. We reasoned that the work would not help the American war effort. We would not be harvesting timber. We would clear brush, thin trees, and build firebreaks so trees would grow taller and straighter for harvest decades into the future. If the fascists won the war we would be the ultimate beneficiaries. Also, the opportunity to leave camp, get into the forest, and do purposeful work exerted a strong pull on us.

In a bus labeled "Oregon Department of Corrections" they drove thirty-five prisoners and fifteen armed American soldiers west in the general direction of the mountains. The prisoners sat in the back of the bus with four empty rows between them and the soldiers. The Americans said if anyone got out of their seat they would be locked in a cell for a week. If anyone came forward they would be shot.

After thirty minutes the bus turned off on a dirt road and went deep into the woods. The soldiers got out and formed a rectangle in a clearing by the side of the road. Then we got out and stood inside the rectangle. A lieutenant from the camp gave a short speech in English and another American repeated it in German and bad Italian. They told us this was not the camp and the rules were different. We would work inside the rectangle of soldiers. Anyone who got near a soldier would be shot. Anyone who waved a saw around would be shot, even if the gesture was meant to be a joke. Anyone who refused to work or obey orders would be tied and "crippled." We thought he meant "shackled," but we weren't sure.

An older man in a U.S. Forest Service uniform explained, in English, the work we were to do. After every sentence he paused for a guard to say it again in German. They skipped the Italian and that worried us. There were only five of us but we needed to know about the work too. We might be dropped from the crew for doing the work wrong. They might throw us into the cold isolation cells.

Then the old man from the Forest Service started to explain the work again, but this time in fluent Italian. I wanted to rush up and hug him. It wore us down to talk with our captors through translators, some of whom were not very good. We couldn't understand our guards and they couldn't understand us. Sometimes we felt they did not see us as fully human. I wanted to tell this old man everything about who I was, where I was from, and how I came to be there.

"No talking," said the man. "Not to me and not to each other. If you are doing the work wrong, we will correct you."

All of us lined up beside a truck that had followed us and picked up saws and loppers. There were no axes. The biggest men, like Mario, got no tools at all and were assigned to drag the cut brush into piles. We all got brand-new work gloves. That was America. They fed, clothed, and housed us in comfort. And while they were fighting a war they still had new gloves for prisoners and gasoline to drive us into the forest.

We started work slowly. We didn't mean to be uncooperative or lazy. It was simply that we hadn't hurried for anything in months. We were even slower that day because we were cautious. We were sure the soldiers had never guarded prisoners out in the open like this before. They might make a mistake.

After ten minutes at our slow pace the army officer yelled at us to get moving. The translator followed. We knew enough English and German to get the point before he gave us the Italian. He said there were many other men in camp who wanted our place. I glanced at the forest ranger who spoke Italian but he didn't say anything. We started working faster and we didn't quit until they told us to take a break. It felt good to be working again. We finished two hectares that day.

Tired or not, Mario and I walked the fence in camp that night. He said what I had been thinking all day.

"We should escape," he said. "Once we get into the woods they will never find us. We can hide in the mountains until the war is over."

"It is our duty," I said. "It is every soldier's duty to escape if he can."

Mario and I could hardly sleep that night. Our minds raced over the problems and risks of escaping and visions of roaming the beautiful mountains in complete freedom. We stumbled through work the next day. But we were young men, very motivated, and we rallied time and time again.

We could not share our thoughts during work, on the bus, or at dinner. We prepared all day for our discussion during the evening walk. While we concurred on the need for absolute secrecy, and though we had many similar ideas, we found our principal concerns were somewhat different. Mario was more worried about getting past the guards and I was more worried about how we were going to live in the mountains once we escaped.

The plan we developed that night and the night after was, we decided, good enough to risk getting killed for. We scheduled our escape for three days later, on Friday. We accumulated as much food and warm clothing as we could over the next few days. We swapped our cigarettes for wool sweaters, waterproof jackets, and an extra pair of boots for each of us. Spring was coming and our fellow prisoners parted with their warm clothes more willingly than they would have earlier. As if the fates blessed our journey, the camp received a shipment of wool socks on Wednesday and we acquired three pairs for each of us.

In the mess hall we stuffed bread, sausages, unpeeled fruit, and anything else that would keep for a while into our shirts. We had another man we half-trusted do the same for us and we gave him cigarettes. We told him we needed extra food because of the hard work we were doing. We hid the food in our clothes when we went into the forest and buried it deep in the brush piles, hoping animals would not find it before we retrieved it. We wore extra clothes to work every day and hid them in the brush piles too.

What we really needed and nobody had were rucksacks to carry everything in. We acquired two long wool coats from the Germans and got some rope. We lay awake at night thinking about how best to arrange the ropes to wrap the coats around our supplies and tie them to our backs.

We persuaded some of our fellow forest workers, including Germans, to ask the lieutenant if we could have a short swim at the end of the day on Friday. There was a beautiful lake about two hundred meters down the hill from where we were working. Mario and I knew a mountain lake like that would be frigid at that time of year. But no one else seemed to realize how cold it would be and enthusiasm continued to build. We asked the Americans on Thursday, which was a hot, dry day, and our request made some kind of sense.

The lieutenant turned us down, as we expected. But the lake still figured in our plans. We convinced the other workers to make a rush for the lake at the end of the day on Friday. We had all behaved ourselves perfectly during the week and the guards were bored to death. We'd learned the names of many of them and established at least superficial relationships. We did not think they would shoot us if we went off on a lark. They would also see that we'd be trapped between them and the lake and we couldn't go anywhere.

Thursday evening Mario and I paused by the fence where the road went next to the camp. Across the road, where cattle sometimes grazed, a tall girl with a straight back, about fourteen years old, rode between the trees on a small roan mare with a white face. The girl wore a blue-checked blouse and no hat. She regarded us with a sort of curiosity, as though she could not quite imagine how anyone would want to fight against her country.

The girl was the same age as Tazia when I first met her. Once again I imagined Tazia married to me and living on a hill above Riva del Garda with our children. If I waited in camp for the war to be over I would at least see her again. I could persuade her to be my wife. If I died trying to escape it would never happen. As carefully as Mario and I had thought it out, our plan was full of risks.

The girl turned her horse and rode away. Gone to do her homework for school tomorrow. Gone to get into her own bed in her family's house. She would hear artillery from the range at Camp Abbot. But she could sleep soundly. No shells were aimed her way.

I wondered whether I would fire on that girl's house. If it were a military objective, I would. The thought made me sad. But I was a soldier. I was still at war.

If I didn't seize the opportunity to escape Tazia would despise me for a coward. I'd already surrendered in North Africa, though it hadn't been my decision. She might never marry me. There were still men fighting and dying to keep bombs from falling on Tazia. It was my duty to escape, even if my duty was mixed with a longing to trade the boredom of the camp for the freedom of the wilderness.

The next afternoon, before the planned break for the lake, Mario asked permission to go back to where we had worked the previous day and get a jacket he had left there. He would never be out of sight of the nearest guard and they told him to go ahead. I was up near the bus when a German shouted "Der See! Der See!" Half the men started running down to the lake and half stayed where they were. It could not have been more confusing for the guards.

"Stop! Halt! Stohp!" the guards yelled. But they didn't fire their rifles. The lieutenant shot his pistol in the air. He was ignored. I think the running men enjoyed taking a risk. It made them feel like soldiers again. I hid behind a brush pile. The lieutenant did what I suppose I would have done. He quickly named five guards to stay behind with the prisoners who hadn't run and sent all the other guards racing down the hill after the fugitives. While the guards who remained were distracted I dove under the bus, emerged on the other side, and ran as fast as I could into the forest. I ran at least a kilometer and rested in a thick grove of trees.

I could hear shouts but no gunfire. No one climbed up the hill after me. It may have been half an hour before the lieutenant realized two of us were missing. He probably had no idea which way we had gone. When I heard the bus and the truck drive away, I crept quietly down the hill to where I could see the work area. If the lieutenant were clever, he would hide two guards in the woods. As eager as Mario and I were to get away, we had decided to retrieve our supplies in the morning.

I spent a cold night in the forest. My warm bunk back in camp came to mind repeatedly. Thoughts of Tazia warmed me. I wished she could know what I was doing.

Mario and I met at first light by a tree we had designated above the road. We had not seen any guards and we crept up on the brush piles that held our supplies, signaling to each other by hand but making no sound. We kept the width of a soccer field between us so that if one of us were seen, the other might still have a chance to get away.

We made up our rucksacks, stuffed them full, and carried what was left in our hands. We decided to leave the way we came just in case there were guards we hadn't seen. It was frustrating to head back uphill to the east when the direction we wanted to go was west. We circled back around the work area and made as little noise as possible.

We walked and ran without stopping. The next few hours would make or break us. The Americans were surely going to send soldiers to look for us. They had a camp of thousands to draw from. The lieutenant and his commanding officer were probably going to lose their posts if they didn't find us. We avoided sandy spots where we would leave footprints. When we had to cross a dusty fire road, we crossed it at an angle ninety degrees from our general direction of travel and we walked backwards. It wouldn't fool a tracker but it would confuse a regular soldier.

The sun was barely up when we heard trucks off in the distance. We did not know where the roads were and we had no maps. We hustled west toward the ridgeline of the mountains. My pack loosened and two apples fell out. Mario looked around in a panic when I stopped to get them.

"If they find the apples they will know we were here." I jammed them in my pack again. The trucks were louder now and seemed to be coming toward us from the south.

"There must be a road ahead," said Mario. "We need to cross it before they get here."

We ran as though our lungs would burst until we came up a rise and sprinted across a gravel road. We jumped down the bank on the other side and raced into the trees. We were barely fifty meters off the road when the first truck appeared. Ten seconds earlier it would have seen us.

From a hill above the road we looked back down on it. Trucks were evenly spaced all along the gravel highway now and hundreds of soldiers were spread out between them. Whistles blew and all the soldiers walked abreast into the woods, back toward the work site we had left.

Mario and I could finally catch our breath. We ate some bread and an apple each, our first food since lunch the day before. We wanted so much to stay on that hillside and rest. But someone would see our tracks and not be fooled. Or someone would decide they should search west of the road as well as east. A hundred men could suddenly come after us.

As we climbed to the ridgeline we encountered patches of snow. Skirting around them to avoid leaving tracks became more and more time-consuming. Finally we charged straight ahead. There was no way around it. As soon as we got out of the snow on the other side we angled north and walked until nightfall. We covered about twenty kilometers. We were exhausted.

But we had seen that the forest was enormous. We could disappear in it forever. There were no signs of civilization except the occasional little-used fire road. Ponds and lakes gave us hope for fish.

We figured the army would not spare so many men for a second day. They had a training schedule to keep. But they might, we thought, send a few soldiers with wilderness experience after us. Even one man who knew this terrain could bedevil us. We would have to keep moving.

After two more days we came to another gravel road, this one with an endless lava field beyond it. The black lava was ugly and it would cut our boots. We turned back. There was plenty of good forest to hide in.

We were both fly-fishermen, but we had no flies or fly rods and we did not have time for sport. We had threads, strings, and safety pins. We used tree branches for rods and dangled beetles on the pins. The fish could see the string but, in the remote lakes, the fish had hardly ever seen a fisherman. We were patient. We had some luck with fish traps we built in the streams. We cooked the fish at night, when there was no moon to make the smoke visible. We camped in ravines to hide the light of the fire.

There were deer in the woods and we tried to kill one for food. We'd stolen a small saw from the Americans and we used it to cut branches and put points on sticks. We hid on the top of a cliff above a deer trail and waited. It was more boring than the camp because we had to be absolutely quiet. When a deer finally came we launched our spears straight down. My spear grazed the deer's side and blunted its point on the rocks below. Mario hit the deer right behind the shoulders but his spear did not even stick in the deer's back muscle, much less penetrate enough to hurt the deer. We thought of dropping rocks on their heads and lugged some heavy stones up the hill. We saw no deer for three days. We'd scared them off.

It was back to fish and berries. The blueberries and blackberries were good but they gave us the runs. The wild currants tasted like wood and upset our stomachs. We were steadily losing weight. Still, we were free, we were surviving, and we spent every day in those beautiful mountains. If it rained too much we hid in one of the caves we found.

We talked all the time about climbing the mountain we'd seen from camp and, after two weeks, we set off with all the clothes and boots we had and about twenty fish we had dried. We kept to the thickest woods, off the trails, until we got right up to the mountain. We joked that nobody would need to see us. They could smell the fish we were carrying. If we saw a bear we would drop the fish and back away slowly. We brought our pointed sticks to poke in the bear's eye. We were fearful, dirty, and smelly. As primitive as anything we had ever known. All our school learning counted for nothing.

When daylight came we climbed to the top. It taxed our muscles and tired us out. The rocks were hard on our clothes. There was no trail. But we didn't need climbing ropes. The last part was through packed snowfields. We left tracks but they could have been anyone's.

What a view! More snow-topped mountains to the north and south. Lakes below us. Our forest home to the west. And a vast dry desert stretching to the east. We didn't know the name of anything we were looking at.

We came down carefully. If we were seen we might elude capture. But if we were injured we would have to turn ourselves in.

The next day we rested, washed, and caught some fresh fish. Then we rested for three days more. The weather got better and we got smarter at fishing, though we got tired of the taste. We explored the forest and the mountains. I'd bet we came to know that forest as well as any American, no matter how much time he had spent there. In the fall we planned to head for Portland and pretend to be Italian immigrants. We'd brought an English-Italian dictionary and an English grammar book. We studied hard. We were uncertain of our pronunciation. We tried sentences on each other and tried to improve them.

One thing we discussed, in both Italian and English, was whether we should burn down the forest. If we started at the right time and at the right place, with the wind behind us, we could burn thousands of hectares. It would be an impressive act of sabotage. But what good would it really do? The Americans had plenty of trees. They would get lumber from somewhere else. We would be caught and shot. That was all right. We were soldiers. We hesitated, though, at destroying such a beautiful wilderness. We put off the decision, waiting for dryer weather.

Our first English exam came without warning. We woke to see a forest ranger with a rifle looking down on us from the cliff above our ravine.

"What are you doing here?" he asked.

"We're camping," I said. I made a quick inventory of what the man could see in our camp – a dead fire with a wooden spit, fish bones, coats, sweaters, and makeshift fishing tackle. No tent, no sleeping bags, no cooking utensils. "We caught fish," I added.

"Where did you come in from?"

"Tyee Creek," I said. We had seen the name on a sign and I hoped I was pronouncing it right. We couldn't find "Tyee" in the dictionary.

"What are your names?" he asked. We hadn't thought of names for ourselves yet. I thought fast and not very well. I gave him the name of the camp commander for myself and told him Mario's name was Garner Fairbanks."

"Your friend speak English?" asked the man.

"You betcha," said Mario. He'd learned that in camp, not from the dictionary.

"You come up out of there," he said. "Put your boots on but don't touch anything else."

We walked east and he followed us on his horse.

"If one of you runs I'm going to shoot the other one first," he said. From time to time he pointed us in a new direction. We came to a trail and followed it to a road. We walked along it for a while and then turned off it to a log house with a flag above it. We went inside and the ranger made Mario sit in a wooden chair by a post in the middle of the room. He had me tie Mario's hands behind him to the post. The man tied me to an iron bedstead. Then he checked the knots I had tied. Finally the ranger went to a phone and called the army to come pick us up.

While we waited we practiced the English we had worked so hard to learn. We hadn't talked to anyone but each other for months. We asked the ranger how he had found us. He said the Forest Service had been on the lookout for us ever since we escaped. They'd seen footprints by the lakes and knew we were still in the area. He didn't congratulate us on eluding capture for so long. We'd been proud of our cleverness, even though our capture now appeared inevitable. The man said the rangers watched for fires from a tower nearby.

When there was no moon they looked for spaces near the horizon where stars were missing. That's how he saw our smoke.

The hours we spent with the ranger were very pleasant, even though we were tied up. He gave us bread with butter and jam. And coffee. We hadn't had any of those things for ages. For a few minutes being captured seemed lucky. The news from the war, however, was discouraging. The Allies had captured Rome and landed in France.

In the early afternoon an army truck came with soldiers in it. A corporal, too old to go to the front, asked us where we had been and what we had done. Had we robbed or hurt anyone? We told him the truth and he seemed to accept it. When we got back to camp the Americans had already taken down the fences. All the prisoners were gone and almost all the soldiers. They put us in closets and locked them. For the next few days they brought us food from a mess hall some distance away. It was always cold. But it was a welcome change from fish.

Our captors were more disgusted with us than angry. There was no regular schedule. We spent three days with no exercise. We got a trip to the toilet when somebody thought about it. We never saw the ranger again. We never saw the mountain again. One night they put us in a truck and drove us thirty kilometers to a train station. They put us in a car full of Germans. None of us had any idea where we were going. We rode on the train for five days through some of the most desolate country I have ever seen. Mario and I didn't talk about escaping. We talked about food.

They took Mario and me off the train by ourselves in the middle of the night. They showed us to bunks in a new camp and then woke up everyone in the camp an hour later. We were in Camp Hereford in Texas. This camp was all Italian non-collaborators, including the men we'd known in Oregon. It was more regimented than Camp Abbot but there were more of us and it wasn't so boring. We had some good soccer games. We were comfortable, waiting for the war to be over. Resigned to be on the losing side.

Then, in the spring of 1945, the Allies discovered Bergen-Belsen, Dachau and other Nazi concentration camps. The prisoners in those camps were starving and dying of typhus. Skin and bones, barely able to stand. Our captors decided we could starve just as well. They said we deserved to. So they cut our rations to almost nothing. Mario and I had eaten better in the woods.

Up until then I had been impressed with the Americans. But when they cut our rations they abandoned logic. There were no death camps in Italy. We Italians had nothing to do with them. What justification could they have for punishing us? It was blind vengeance. It was unworthy of them.

When I finally got home Italy was in ruins. Railroads, bridges, and buildings had been destroyed. Tazia had married a man who worked for Fiat. No one much cared that I had refused to collaborate. Some of those who had collaborated were going to marry American girls and become Americans.

I made the best of it. I lived with my impoverished parents. I took whatever work I could find. We ate poorly and shivered in the winter. I took some comfort in knowing I was a free man in my own country. I hiked, when I could, in the mountains. My friends listened over and over to my stories of climbing the American mountain and living off the land in the Oregon forest. It sounded, in a way, like our boyhood dreams come true. But I had learned, by then, to choose my dreams more carefully.

Living Well

I got promoted and we were moved. It was August. Hot. First thing we bought was an air conditioner for the bedroom.

The second evening after we moved in I was shampooing the living room rug, wishing we could afford to air-condition the whole house. I looked up from the rug and saw Charlene standing in the doorway grim-faced, a bucket of fried chicken in one hand and the keys to the Honda in the other. I thought she might have crashed the car.

"We never should have moved here, Dan," she said.

"It won't be this hot all the time," I said. "We'll get by." I gave her a smile and my best chuckle. Charlene was twenty-three to my twenty-nine.

"It's not that," she said. "I just saw Bruce Harrington go into a house on Portland Avenue. Dan, he lives in this town."

"What's he doing here?" I asked. Charlene was fighting back tears.

"I don't know," she said. "But we can't stay." I went over to her and put my arms around her. My T-shirt was sweaty. I could see her clean blond hair shaking below me as she cried. I told her we might be able to move, but not for a long while.

"If you see him again, simply pretend you don't know him," I said. "Walk right past him if you have to."

Later that evening, I went to see where Bruce lived. Charlene said it was a one-story tan house with a dark blue Cadillac parked in the driveway. I found it, fourteen seventy-one Portland. Tan clapboard with a dark shake roof. Right behind it I saw the tops of three aspens that grew in our own yard. There was a tall fence between the houses and Charlene hadn't realized Bruce lived right behind us. I wasn't going to tell her.

I didn't like Bruce being our neighbor any more than Charlene did. But it gave me some satisfaction to find him in this little town. Mr. Big Time.

The only reason I was able to marry a girl like Charlene was that Bruce was such a jerk. He had swept her up when she was starting junior college. He was a good-looking fraternity man at Oregon, with a snappy Datsun sports car. I had seen him once in the Safeway where I was working when he came in with Charlene. They looked like brother and sister – blue eyes and bright blond hair, though hers was curlier than his. She was so pretty.

About two months later she came in looking like she'd had the flu and nearly died. I'd only known her from working behind the meat counter but I asked her what had happened. She told me she'd been ill. I said it looked like she could use some cheering up and I offered to buy her a cup of coffee. She was a sweet, sweet girl. Right from the first I told her she was a good person and I never stopped telling her that. It's true. It took me a half-year before I dared ask her to marry me and another three months before she said yes.

Bruce graduated from the university and left for Los Angeles. He was going to make his fortune in the real estate business. He didn't think Charlene would be an asset to his career. She was a small-town girl, he said.

The week after Charlene found out Bruce lived in our town she got a job and that helped. It was with a small law firm. She was their receptionist.

That Saturday I worked the store in the morning and went home at two. I sat under the aspens in a folding chaise that the store had a special on, picked up the newspaper and lit a cigar. I smoked one cigar a week and I smoked it outdoors.

I wasn't there three minutes when I heard this scream from Bruce's house. I grew up in a city, not the nicest part, and my first instinct was to ignore it, though I thought we had moved to a place where we didn't have to ignore things. I was beginning to wonder who had screamed when I heard it again, exactly the same as before. I got up to peek through the ivy that grew on the fence behind our house. Bruce's yard was weeds and dry grass. It didn't look like it had been watered or cut all summer. There was a gray awning with holes in it over a patio at the back of the house and a rusty white table with old newspapers stacked on top. I didn't see a soul.

The scream came again, so loud it hurt my ears. It came from a cage hanging from one end of the awning. In the cage was a big blue bird with a long blue tail. It shuffled back and forth on a wooden bar, bobbing its head up and down as though there was something important going on. It bent down with a sweeping motion and scattered a shower of brown seeds in my direction.

"Squ-a-a-wk," it said, not short and sharp, but blasting for a full three seconds like a foghorn. Loud.

I went back to my chaise and tried to read. I couldn't. When the bird wasn't squawking I was waiting for it to squawk. After fifteen minutes I heard a sliding door open at Bruce's house. Then it closed. Someone had put the bird inside the house. I could still hear it if I listened, but it was muffled. I fell asleep in the chaise, my cigar still in my hand.

When it got too hot, even in the shade, I woke up and went inside. Charlene was trying to hang some draperies by herself and having a hard time of it. She was pulling the drape to get the hooks to go into the hangers. I helped her. We agreed the drapes did a lot to make the living room look better. We stood back to admire them. Then I popped the lid off a paint can and started painting the kitchen walls. Taping and painting around the cabinets took the rest of the afternoon. Charlene was painting in the second bedroom.

After dinner, a real home-cooked meal this time, I started painting the kitchen shelves. By the time we went to bed I was exhausted and so was Charlene. We slept until 8:30 on Sunday and didn't hear the bird all morning.

After church we had sandwiches and beer for lunch. It was the first moment we had both relaxed since we moved in. I told Charlene it would be cooler in the bedroom and she followed me down the hall, laughing the slightly guilty little laugh that always gets me going. We rubbed Ben-Gay on our aching muscles. We were trying to get pregnant now that we had our own home. Then "Squawk." The damn bird was at it again. Charlene winced. We could hear it plain as day, in spite of the noise of the air conditioner. She told me to ignore it but neither one of us could. I was tired all over again and angry too. I was about as far from romantic as a man could be.

"I'm going to make that damn bird shut up," I said.

I got dressed again, got in the car, drove around the block, and marched up to Bruce's house. Bruce opened the door. He had on a pink golf shirt and neatly pressed pants. He had lost a little hair and gained a little weight since I saw him that one time.

"Hello?" he said. Of course, he didn't know me. Who would remember the guy he'd seen behind the meat counter one time four years earlier?

"I have the house behind yours," I said. "Your parrot is making so much noise I can't even think straight. Would you mind keeping it inside, at least on weekends?"

"It's not a parrot. It's a very rare bird. It's a hyacinth macaw. My wife's raised him from a baby. You should come in and see him." Bruce was so cool. His wife came up beside him. She had short dark hair and a tall slim body like a fashion model. She had a cute face, pert I'd call it, but she looked at me hard, as though I'd crawled out of a cellar somewhere and she hoped I would get back real quick.

"I don't need to see the bird," I said. "I just want to ask if there is some way you could keep it quiet. The noise is really hard to take."

"It's natural for the bird to call," said Bruce. "It's natural for him to be outside where he can see the trees. You can't keep a valuable bird like that cooped up."

"How about keeping him in on Saturday and Sunday so your neighbors can get out and enjoy the sunshine?"

"No," said Bruce, "that wouldn't work."

I could feel my jaw muscles contracting. With a good knife I could cut that bird up into fryers in less than a minute. But I wasn't going to let Bruce see that I was upset.

"Well," I said, "you owe it to your neighbors to do what you can." I stepped back off his doorstep. Bruce didn't say anything and I left.

When I got home Charlene was dressed. I told her the neighbor was a nut case in love with his bird. She still didn't know it was Bruce. We went out and got a pizza. The bird was inside when we got back.

But I woke up in the middle of the night thinking about the bird. I looked up "macaw" in the encyclopedia. Blue hyacinth macaws come from Brazil. They live sixty years or more. I started thinking about ways to silence the bird and I fell asleep again.

When I came home the next evening Bruce had cut down the ivy along the top of the fence. I had to see his house every time I looked out our back window. So the next Sunday I bought six pine trees to plant on our side. I put a radio on a ladder next to the fence while I dug the holes. I turned the radio up high and faced it toward Bruce's house. The bird was squawking when I started and he got all hopped up about the radio. I heard him try to imitate part of a song for an auto dealership.

"A-Okay," he said. "A-Okay." You wouldn't recognize it if you hadn't heard it on the radio thirty seconds earlier. From somewhere else he'd learned "Oh, shut up!" and he liked it a lot. But his voice rose on "shut" and sank on "up" so it didn't sound right.

"Oh, shut up yourself," I muttered. I wasn't playing the radio to entertain him.

Digging is hard work in the hot sun. I got the six holes dug and I made some instant iced tea. Charlene and I sat in the chaises in the shade of the aspens. I left the radio on over by the fence. Charlene turned on her side and went to sleep.

The radio suddenly went off. Bruce was leaning over the fence with his hand on the knob, glaring at me. I hustled over to the fence so he wouldn't wake up Charlene. She was turned away from him and I stood so that he couldn't get a good view of her.

"Do you have to play your radio so loud and smoke that stinking cigar?" he said in a snotty way. "How much of a slob can you be?" I'd found two ways to annoy him and that was good.

"Why'd you cut the ivy down?" I said in a quiet voice. "I don't want to see your house."

"The ivy was a mess," he said. "It needed to be trimmed." I looked at the pile of cut ivy that was dying on his lawn. It didn't look like progress to me.

"You get your bird to be quiet and I'll keep the radio down," I said.

"That's completely different," he said. "You keep the radio down or I'll call the police." He walked away. I looked around. Charlene was gone.

"How long have you known Bruce lived right behind us?" she asked. She was sitting on our bed with her hands in her lap. She was looking down at the floor but she wasn't crying.

I sat down beside her. "I knew you'd be happier not knowing," I said. "Look, the new trees will grow up and block him and his house from our view." Her face sank. I guessed she didn't think the pine trees were going to do it. I went out and planted them anyway. The tops were a foot short of the fence.

The next day Bruce's wife came into the store. I was in the manager's booth with the one-way glass. It was raised so I could see most of the store.

She pulled a cart out and put a big black purse in the top basket, and then she set off down the freezer aisle. She had long legs and she held her head high, like some kind of aristocrat. Other women turned to watch her. She got to the back of the store where the beverage coolers were and turned right where I couldn't see her. I saw the top of a glass door open and close but when I saw the whole cart again there was nothing in it but the purse. I called down to the nearest checkstand and got Greg, my assistant manager, on the phone.

Right in front of my office the lady picked her purse out of the cart and walked toward the door. Greg stopped her and pointed to the purse. He reached for it and she pulled it away. Greg looked up at me and I clicked on the mike for the speakers.

"Just have her leave the beer," I said. All the checkers and four or five customers were looking at her and Greg now. She opened her purse and Greg took out a six-pack of Michelob. Nothing but the best for Bruce. His wife marched out of the store. Greg said her name was Bridget. He had seen her driver's license.

In December we got an award for the most improved store in the Eastern Oregon District. Everyone in the store had worked hard and we were pretty pleased with ourselves. Charlene was happy for me, told me how proud she was and cooked me a special dinner.

The law firm changed Charlene's job to secretary for one of the partners. She started taking correspondence classes to become a paralegal. Things were looking up. We were even able to forget about Bruce and Bridget. They didn't put the bird outside in the winter.

Then Charlene found out why Bruce was living here. He had bought land with some partners to build homes on. But no one would loan them the money to build the houses and they were stuck with the land. They had borrowed money to buy the land and Charlene's law firm was representing the lenders who were not getting paid. Her boss knew enough about Bruce by now to tell us about Bridget. She was an actress Bruce had met in Los Angeles. She'd had a small part in a Michael Caine movie.

Charlene told her boss that she had known Bruce when she was younger.

"Why did you tell him that?" I slammed my fork down on the kitchen table. "It's none of his business." Charlene stopped with the salad tongs above her plate.

"Because I don't want to see Bruce if he comes into the office," she said.

"Why would Bruce do that? You're not his lawyers."

"He might come into the office for a meeting or something. I just don't want to see him."

"Still," I said, "you didn't need to tell anybody."

"I only said I knew him. I didn't say anything about the abortion. I didn't even say we dated."

I counted to ten. "I'm sorry I got mad," I said. "I just wish Bruce would go away."

The first Saturday in March the temperature got up to seventy-five. Everyone commented on it. It slowed the checkers down but it built customer relations and sales were higher. I knew we had almost no charcoal in stock so I bought a bag early and kept it in my office. I was starting the fire in our Weber when I heard the bird again. I was thinking I wouldn't get upset; I would simply ignore it. I slid our glass door shut so Charlene wouldn't hear it.

I'd forgotten how loud the squawking could be. In two minutes I'd made up my mind the bird had to go. I went over to the fence and glared at it. The trees had not grown at all since I planted them.

At one end of Bruce's porch the bird was jumping around in its cage, cackling and whistling, excited to be outside again I guess. At the other end of the porch their barbecue had a wisp of smoke rising from it. On the table in the middle of the porch were a can of charcoal lighter and a bottle of scotch. It wasn't Johnny Walker. On either side of the table sat Bruce and Bridget, drinks in hand, staring at the weeds in their lawn. Bruce looked up and saw me.

"What do you want?" he said. He got out of his chair and came toward me, carrying his drink. When he got to the fence I didn't say anything. I just stood there. Bruce hunched his shoulders like a linebacker.

"You know what you are, buddy?" he shouted at me. "You're small-time. You got a little house with a bright green awning and you think you're a pig in mud. You're nothing is what you are. You're a nobody and you've got no business looking at other people."

He stomped back past his wife and into his house. I simply looked on calmly. If that was what would upset Bruce, I'd just keep doing it for a while.

Bridget stared at me for a few seconds and started to get restless. She looked over at the barbecue and I guess she decided it wasn't lighting fast enough. She got to her feet, managing to look elegant and sway unsteadily at the same time. She wobbled over to the barbecue with her drink in one hand and the can of charcoal lighter in the other. She held the can out shoulder-high and squirted a stream of fluid on the charcoal. It happened so fast I didn't think to yell "Stop!"

In two seconds the fire went "poof" and the flame burst up in front of Bridget. She dropped the can into the barbecue, fell back on her heels and barely caught herself. She was seriously drunk.

"Get inside the house!" I yelled to her. She turned a blank face toward me. Her eyebrows were gone.

"It's going to blow up!" I said. "Get inside the house and shut the door." She didn't move. She was watching me climb over the fence into her yard. Finally she turned and walked inside.

"Shut the door!" I said again. She slid the door shut and walked back into the house. I ran over to the birdcage but I couldn't find the door to it. So I wrapped my arms around the whole cage and lifted it off its hook. The parrot didn't like it. He tried to bite me through the bars. I could feel his beak brushing my ear. I pulled my head back before he got a grip. The bird and I staggered across the lawn and I set the cage down by the fence.

Just as I stood up again the can of charcoal lighter exploded. The barbecue fell over and charcoal shot in every direction. The can clattered and banged on the concrete patio floor. I felt a wave of air wash past me. I looked for a hose in Bruce's back yard but there wasn't one. Then their awning caught fire and started spreading to the roof. I knew I had to get back to our house and call the fire department but my mind was still on the bird. I picked up the cage by the bottom, hoisted it up to the top of the fence, and dropped it on the other side. There was a lot of squawking, of course. I climbed over the fence after it.

"Are you all right?" said Charlene when I ran inside the house.

"Yes," I said, "but Bruce's house is on fire. Take the hose and wet down our roof." Charlene went outside while I made the call. I said Bruce and Bridget might still be in the house.

I got the leather gardening gloves before I went out and picked up the cage again. I put it in the garage and put a blanket over it. The bird did not look injured. I got another hose and helped Charlene wet down our roof, the plants along the back of the house, and the pine trees I had planted along the fence. We breathed in some smoke and coughed a bit. But we had kept the windows shut and you could hardly smell the smoke inside the house. The smell went away and we didn't have to get the drapes cleaned.

I still had this bird. I read in the paper that it had been stolen. An alert had gone out to pet shops and bird dealers to be on the lookout. The paper said it could be worth $10,000. I hated the idea of giving it back to Bruce so it could squawk at us all summer.

I stuck one end of a vacuum hose under the blanket that was over the cage and stuck the other end into the exhaust pipe of the Honda. I did this at night with the garage doors partly open. I ran it for about five minutes. Never heard a peep from the bird. I wrapped the dead bird in a fresh newspaper that I was careful not to get my fingerprints on. Then I threw it in a dumpster. It was the only crime I ever committed. I never wanted to be that nervous again. Yet there was a feeling of satisfaction, even triumph, that I knew would last long after I calmed down.

The cage was harder to get rid of. It wouldn't fit inside the car. I rented a van overnight. Paid cash for it. I drove out into the middle of nowhere, on the other side of Newberry Crater, walked two hundred yards off the forest road, and left the cage lying under a juniper tree. Somebody would find it someday. But I thought it would be a long time before they did.

Bruce showed up at my house a few days later. He and Bridget were living in a motel.

"You'll be hearing from my insurance company," he said, "about your role in causing the fire."

"I had nothing to do with it," I said. "I was on the other side of the fence."

"I don't care where you were," said Bruce. "It never would have happened if you had minded your own business."

"Bridget dropped the can in the barbecue all by herself. I was the one who told her to get inside before it blew up. And I'm the one who called the fire department."

"And I bet you know something about my bird as well," said Bruce. "You'll be hearing from the police about that."

"I'm glad it's gone. I'll tell them that," I said. Then I asked when he thought he would move back in.

"We won't," he said. "We can't wait to get out of this stupid place. You can have it. With your stupid little house and some stupid little job and some stupid little wife." He was upset again. Mr. Calm, Cool, and Superior was missing in action. I was delighted.

And that's when Charlene came to the door. "Hello Bruce," she said. She had so much confidence and poise. I was so proud of her. On top of that she looked prettier than ever, even being seven months pregnant.

Bruce almost fell off the doorstep.

"Stupid or not, we seem to have come out okay," I said. "I hope you and Bridget have as nice a life." I smiled at him and shut the door. "But I doubt you will," I said and wrapped an arm around Charlene. She leaned against me and hummed contentedly. We never did hear from the police or the insurance company.

Obligations

Peter Cary, standing on his back deck in a fresh shirt and dress slacks, surveyed the summer evening. Swallows swooped above the pond catching bugs. Fish rose sporadically spreading perfect rings across the surface. Peter, relaxed and ready ahead of time, recognized that he was sublimely content. He loved his house. He loved his wife. He was looking forward to seeing their friends, the Barretts, the guests who were coming to dinner. The sun would set right about the time they all went in from cocktails on the deck. He could not have planned it better.

Peter idly wondered how many more years he and Linda might have to enjoy summer evenings like this one. Ten? Twenty? Maybe more. Peter wondered if, at the end of his life, he were offered a five-minute reprieve, how he would want to spend it. With Linda, for sure. Maybe skiing through freshly fallen powder under a brilliant blue sky. But this peaceful moment, right now, would be enough. It would be enough to make his entire life worthwhile, no matter what else happened.

Linda was rushing to get herself ready and would not answer the phone that started to jingle. Walking with the easy stride of a man much younger than sixty-one, Peter reached the phone and answered it on the second ring. It would probably be the Barretts to say they would be late.

It was, instead, a woman named Elizabeth something, who sounded as though she knew what she wanted to say but was a little tense about it.

"Are you the Peter Cary who worked at Mount Bachelor in 1967?" she asked. A reporter, Peter thought, writing an article on the early years of the ski area.

"Yes," said Peter in a jovial tone. "I'm the only Peter Cary who was there. What can I help you with?"

"Well, if you're that Peter Cary, then I'm your daughter."

Peter smiled into the mouthpiece. He wasn't surprised very often at his age. She sounded like a bright and lively woman. Perhaps Duncan Barrett had put her up to it. They would laugh about it all through dinner.

"If you're my daughter," said Peter, "it's all news to me."

"I thought it would be," said the woman. "Do you remember Vicky Sayres?"

"Yes, I do," said Peter. Perhaps he should not have been so quick to answer, he thought.

"Vicky is my mother. My married name is Owen, Elizabeth Owen. I'm not after money or complicating your life. But I would like to meet you. I have children of my own now and I want to know more about you.

"I see."

"I will be in Bend for a conference," continued the woman, "and I'd like to talk with you for an hour or so. Do you think I could come and meet you?"

"I suppose we could do that," said Peter. "But we're expecting guests any minute. Can I call you back tomorrow?" Elizabeth said yes and she gave him her phone number. He knew area code 970 meant northern or western Colorado where all the ski areas were.

Peter hung up and Linda made it to the front door just as the Barretts arrived. She led her guests to the deck as Peter fixed them drinks, a beer for Duncan and a twelve-year-old Scotch on the rocks for Marty. Linda had a glass of Chardonnay and Peter had a gin and tonic. The four of them had been friends and had skied together for years. Unlike Peter, who lived for skiing, Duncan lived for running. He was built for it with a slim body, medium height, and strong legs. The dinner was to celebrate Duncan's first completion of the Ironman triathlon in Hawaii.

Duncan finished the race in fourteen hours and thirty-nine minutes. At the age of sixty-seven, Peter said, Duncan should be proud to have finished at all. Duncan said the best part was passing so many people in the final segment of the race, the running segment. He was coming from behind because he hadn't kept up in the ocean swim. Most of his training for swimming was in a pool. He had hardly swum in open water at all. Managing the waves took his full concentration. And he wasn't efficient at lifting his head to make sure he was going in the right direction. It helped that he was more buoyant in the salt water than he had been in the pool. But the extra buoyancy helped everyone. "Especially the fat ones," he said.

He started in the water with his age group and quickly fell to the back of the pack. Then the women who started a minute behind him caught up. They churned up the water and some of them swam right over him. Just when he was planning to take a breath some woman would slam his head underwater.

"I need to take a course in combat swimming," he said.

Peter did not mention his call from Elizabeth Owen during dinner, though his mind kept coming back to her. Did he actually have a daughter? Even if the call were the start of an elaborate fraud it would still be exciting. When the fraud unraveled, he would have a good story to tell. If the call were a joke he would try to avoid embarrassing himself. Peter kept waiting for Duncan to bring up daughters, past girlfriends, or strange phone calls. Maybe Duncan was waiting for Peter to mention the call. Then Duncan would pretend to be fascinated and enthusiastic. After he had drawn Peter out he would reveal that the woman was someone he worked with or a fellow runner. Duncan might go that far. Peter decided he was not going to be the one to bring up Elizabeth Owen.

The Barretts never gave a hint they knew about the call. They talked about golf and players on the PGA Tour. They talked about a friend's sixtieth birthday party. Linda asked the Barretts about their two children, newly out of college and starting their careers. Peter and Linda had no children. Life offered too many other opportunities and they were not confident that after eighteen years of effort their children would turn out well. But the two of them made a point of asking about the children of their friends. It was much easier, they said, and much less expensive, to live vicariously.

Duncan asked how Peter's business was.

"We're solid," said Peter. "Hoping for snow." His company was public now, and he was careful what he said about it, even to friends. The company had money in the bank and could handle two or three slow years in the ski business. But more snow meant more skiing, more ski clothes, more equipment, and a better year for everyone. Peter and Linda would be comfortable no matter what happened. But they wanted the business to do well.

The dinner, said the Barretts, was excellent. After they left, Peter and Linda carried the dessert plates, the coffee cups, and the leftover wine glasses to the kitchen.

"Who called while I was getting ready?" asked Linda

"A woman named Elizabeth Owen. She claims to be my daughter."

"Usually it's the mistress who calls to tell you she's having your daughter."

"Apparently a break with tradition," said Peter.

"Well, do you know her mother?"

"I knew her at Mount Bachelor my first year after college. I haven't heard from her since."

"Did you get her pregnant?"

"Not that I ever knew of. It's possible, I guess. I think she would have told me."

"What did she want? I mean the woman who called."

"She is visiting Bend and she wants to meet me."

"And you are intrigued by this, of course."

"Yes. Even if it turns out not to be true it will still be interesting."

"And if she is your daughter, what are you going to do with her?"

"I don't know. I haven't really thought about it. I suppose my first priority is to not get my wife upset."

"But you are rather charmed with the idea yourself?"

"I guess I am. She must be thirty-something by now, way past needing child support. If she's for real I'd like to see what kind of person she is and how her life turned out. I'd want to tell her how happy her father is with her stepmother."

"I never thought I'd be anyone's stepmother."

"No obligation. You can even be the evil stepmother if you want. And I suppose she'd like to know about all the uncles and aunts and cousins she's related to."

"Does she know you don't have any children – or at least no children aside from her?"

"We didn't get that far."

They washed the plates and the silverware. They agreed the glasses and the pots could wait for morning. Peter turned the dining room lights out but Linda said she wanted to make sure there was no water on the table and she flipped the lights back on.

"You go ahead," she said. "I'll be along."

Peter lay in bed with the reading light on, thinking about Vicky Sayres for the first time in years. He had worked in the ski shop at the bottom of the mountain and Vicky worked in a restaurant at the top. She was skipping a quarter during her junior year in college. They were surrounded by young people who worked on the mountain so they could ski as much as humanly possible. They talked of working in Argentina in July and Switzerland the next winter.

Peter lived with four roommates in an apartment in Bend. They ate, as he remembered, a lot of spaghetti. Skiing was free if they worked at Bachelor and every dime they could spare, which was not much, went into new and better skis, boots, and bindings. Some received money from their parents but none of them received much. Peter received no money at all but he did have an old Ford from his college days. He drove back and forth to Bachelor and sometimes his friends helped pay for gas.

Friendships were enthusiastic and, in their way, sincere. As long as your goal was skiing, and you were any good at it, others would welcome you, encourage you, and help you where they could. Peter's friends always knew where the best snow was, which trails had been groomed, and which lift lines were the shortest.

Peter met Vicky for the first time when she came into the shop for ski gloves. The ones she had were too thick and her poles kept slipping out of her hands. It was a slow day and Peter talked with her for half an hour. Vicky had brown eyes, blondish hair, and a suntan verging on sunburn. She wore a blue knit hat with reindeer on it. She could talk about her courses in college, not only about skiing, and she didn't chatter just to fill the air.

It was fun to ski with Vicky. She was good but she didn't take it as seriously as the other young people on the mountain. She simply enjoyed it.

The two of them started timing their trips to the mountain so Peter could give Vicky rides in his car. Peter became slow to tell his friends about his schedule. They visited each other's apartments, hoping their roommates would not be there or would leave. Sex, Peter thought, might be better than skiing. It felt fantastic and it was free. Other fools were missing out on the best things in life.

When Linda finally joined him Peter was lying on his back, hands behind his head, looking at the ceiling. Linda got into her side of the bed and snuggled up to him. "Were you in love with her?"

"We were hot and heavy during the ski season. But we weren't thinking about the long term. I don't know why she kept the baby, if there was one. I don't know why she didn't track me down and tell me. I'm lucky she didn't. It sure would have messed up my life."

"But did you love her?"

"I guess I did at the time. I wrote her two letters but I didn't hear back. I was surprised. Then I kind of shrugged my shoulders and moved on. We had no plans. Two years later I met you."

"Do you wish we'd had children?"

Peter knew he would never get to sleep if his answer were anything but no. The decision not to have children had been made a long time ago.

"It was right for both of us," said Peter. "It might be nice now to have grown-up children. And grandchildren that visited us once in a while. But when I think of all the time we didn't have to put into raising children, all the worry, all the things that could have gone wrong, I still feel we were lucky." There was no reply. "Don't you?" he added.

"Yes, I think it worked out just fine." Now Linda was staring at the ceiling too. "But this Elizabeth, if she wants to build a relationship with you, or with us, could be a sort of freebie."

Six weeks after they first talked, when Elizabeth arrived, Peter saw that any resemblance to him was tenuous. She might have his family's nose. She definitely looked like Vicky, though, as well as Peter remembered her. The same graceful movement. The eyes that grew bigger when challenged or amused. She beamed at Linda and Peter when they opened the front door to greet her.

It was mid-afternoon on an early fall day. The sky was overcast and it was too chilly to sit outside. The three of them sat by the window in the living room with a bottle of water beside each chair. The willows by the pond were now yellow, brown, and dark orange.

"You look much more like your mother than my side of the family. Whatever genes you got from me should still serve you well, though. No criminals or lunatics in the family. No hereditary diseases. I'll show you pictures of your relatives later. But Linda and I are dying to hear first about you and your mother. I hope you don't mind."

Vicky lived with her parents for three years after Elizabeth was born. The parents helped care for Vicky's baby while Vicky finished college and earned a teaching certificate. In Vicky's first teaching job, in Colorado, she fell in love with a history teacher and married him. As well as Elizabeth could remember, he had always been there and had always been kind to her.

Elizabeth grew up near Colorado Springs and skied on her high school ski team. She graduated from the University of Colorado and earned a master's in biology from the University of Pennsylvania. She had her own one-person environmental consulting business in Fort Collins. Her husband was working on a computer chip that would analyze chemical samples. They had two boys, Grant, who was ten, and Brandon, who was eight.

"I'm relieved to hear you've had a good life," said Peter. "I guess you didn't suffer too much not having your original father around. You realize I never knew your mother had a baby."

"I know. My mother made her decision and she made it work," said Elizabeth.

"How has your mother been through all this?" asked Linda. "Does she know you are here?"

"No, she doesn't. She never wanted to call you and she didn't think my calling would be a good idea either. She said she told you she was on the pill and you never signed up to have a child. She said it would be unfair to disrupt your life. She's had a good life herself up until recently, though. She and my father were very happy. And I guess I turned out pretty well without causing them too much anxiety. When I was eight Mom started to tell me more about Peter. She remembered him fondly and I think she was kind of proud of him. And then we read about him and his company in the skiing magazines."

"So what made you decide to contact Peter now?" asked Linda.

"My father, I mean my adopted father, died three years ago and Mom's memory is slipping. The doctor says she has early signs of dementia, probably Alzheimer's. She cannot always remember what happened yesterday. It occurred to me the same thing might be happening to you, Peter. Or you could die. Sorry to say that. If I was ever going to meet you I'd better do it now."

"Do you want Peter to go see your mother?" asked Linda. The question could be an objection or an offer, thought Peter. Linda's directness sometimes made him shrink. But she got to the point. The question would hang over them, spoken or unspoken.

"I don't think it's fair to ask," said Elizabeth, "and I'm not sure it would be a good thing for Mom. I wanted to ask you two what you thought. The main thing is I've always wanted to meet Peter. It seemed time to make that decision for myself. I hope you're not sorry you let me come."

"Not at all," said Peter. "We're both glad to meet you. This is easy. You are a grown woman with a life of your own. If you had arrived at age ten and asked to be taken in this would have been tricky." Peter smiled at her. They were adults. They could be realistic. "As far as seeing your mother, I'm not sure that would be a good idea for any of us."

"I would never expect it," said Elizabeth.

"In the meantime," said Linda, "how much do you know about Peter and what would you like to know?"

"I've been reading about Peter for years. I know you two have been married thirty-four years. I know you like skiing and fly fishing. I didn't read anything about religion in your life. I'm not very religious but my husband is a Catholic and we're raising our boys to be Catholics. What else? I hope I'm still skiing when I'm in my sixties like you are."

They showed Elizabeth photos of Peter's family and pictures of Peter when he was younger. There was a photo of him in his college graduation robes but no photos from his winter at Mount Bachelor. Elizabeth showed them pictures of her husband, her two boys, and her house.

"The one that looks the most like me is your husband," said Peter.

"The boys look like me, though Grant, the older one, sounds like his father when he laughs. They are both good skiers. We started them young." Peter imagined flooding them with ski equipment. And coming to watch them compete. He could even fly them to good powder on their school breaks.

"Whether you visit my mother or not, I hope you will come to Colorado to meet your grandchildren," said Elizabeth.

"We'd love to do that," said Peter. "It won't bother them, will it, this sudden appearance of another grandfather?"

"I think the boys will understand. There are all kinds of families these days. And my husband is all for it. He's a wonderful man."

"We might be able to come after Christmas," said Linda.

They went out to see Elizabeth drive off. "Thank you for being so nice to her," said Peter as they went inside.

"Why wouldn't I be nice to her?"

"I was afraid you might feel she invaded our lives, made a claim on us, or at least on me."

"Actually I like her a lot," said Linda. "I hope this all works out. I think it could be great to see her family. Not all the time, but sometimes. A link to a younger generation, a sense our family is continuing. You like her too, don't you?"

"Yes. I hope I am not too quick to trust her."

"She's like you," said Linda, "as honest as sunlight."

Duncan asked Peter to come fishing for a day at Crane Prairie Reservoir up in the mountains. The two men fished together a few times every year. They saved Crane Prairie for every other year because it could be so disappointing. The reservoir held enormous fish, thirty-inch rainbows, but the fish were notoriously hard to catch. Neither of the men might hook a fish all day. Even if a fish took they might mistake the subtle pull on the line for the fly dragging over a root. If they struck at the right moment they would still have to fight the fish to the boat. The rainbows in this lake were strong and could wear a man out before he landed it.

Linda said fishing at Crane Prairie was the opposite of skiing. You sat in Duncan's boat all day staring at the water, never seeing a fish. A trout might come to your fly once or twice the whole day and you might or might not know when it did. Peter told her that was the point – to keep your concentration on the fly line so you would be ready. And then all the time and attention you invested would suddenly pay off with a big fish. Linda said Peter might as well play a slot machine. The odds were better and the bathrooms were closer. But Crane Prairie was a good place to talk.

"This having a daughter is new to me," Peter told Duncan, speaking from one end of the aluminum outboard to the other. "All of a sudden I have grandchildren and will probably have descendants ad infinitum. It's all good. But at the same time I feel oddly cheated. It's very strange. I used to see childhood primarily as preparation for adulthood. I didn't appreciate how important childhood itself was. I wish I had known Elizabeth as a little girl. I wish I had been there the first time she saw the ocean. I wish I had been the one who taught her to ski."

"The shame of it," said Duncan, "is that you can't have it both ways. I love my kids. I wouldn't give them up for anything. But when they were growing up Marty and I sometimes wished we had the freedom you and Linda had, whether we used it to travel, to put more effort into our work, or to simply be together. And it would have been nice to take all the money we spent on the two kids' education and spend it on something else. I understand what you're saying but don't feel you've completely missed out."

"On balance I think I would still prefer the life we've had," said Peter. "Also, I have to be careful what I am comparing. If Linda and I had children of our own it would have worked. A different life, of course, but manageable. But my being there specifically for Elizabeth would have meant marrying Vicky when we were both too young. We would have struggled financially for years. I never would have founded my company or been as successful as I was. Vicky and I might have hated each other and gotten divorced. Elizabeth might actually have been worse off."

Duncan reeled his line in and put a different fly on the end of it. Then he went back to casting, letting the fly sink, and pulling it slowly across the bottom. Peter didn't think changing his fly would help. He simply had to be patient.

"Maybe you can answer a question I've always wondered about," said Duncan. "How much of my love for my children comes from their being genetic variations of me and Marty and how much comes from being in the same house and putting so much time and effort into them? Your relationship with Elizabeth is virtually all genetic."

Peter nodded his head and made another cast before answering. "I guess I am partly in love with the idea of having a child, of having what so many other people have. As for genetics, she doesn't look that much like me and she doesn't seem to have quirks that remind me of me or my family. So if there is a genetic resonance it is on a wavelength below the range I can hear. And of course I like her.

Anybody would. I wonder how I would feel about her if she were mean, jobless, and overweight."

"Well, how do you think you would feel?"

"I'd still care about her, I expect, and would want to help her. But it would be as much from duty as from affection."

"If she grew up with you you'd still love her," said Duncan. "But I don't think genetics alone would sustain your affection if she turned out to be nasty."

"Fortunately she's great," said Peter. "But that creates another issue I hope you can shed some light on."

"I am not the guru of parenting," said Duncan, "but ask away."

"I keep tamping down these feelings that are not exactly fatherly. Here is an attractive younger woman who is very interested in me and wants to be part of my life. I want to spend time with her. I want to make her laugh. Sometimes I feel like I'm courting her. I don't want to embarrass myself and I don't want Elizabeth to think her father has the wrong idea. And I don't want to upset Linda, though she seems to be pretty calm about the whole thing so far. I'm hoping these feelings will go away."

"Your problem is you don't have a lifelong relationship with your daughter. You've never had to discipline her or worry about her. She's never slammed a door in your face or called you a stupid old fart. She's never disappointed you. Keep walking the line and it will get easier." The men went back to waiting for fish.

On Halloween afternoon Peter sat on a bench outside his front door with an envelope in his hand. As well as he could remember, no one had ever sat there. The bench was to make the porch look inviting. He shared it with an arrangement of pumpkins and Indian corn. When Linda drove in from her trip to Bend, he followed her car into the garage. He opened the trunk and lifted out two bags of groceries.

"She's probably not my daughter," he said. "The first DNA test came back negative." Peter and Elizabeth had swabbed the insides of their mouths during Elizabeth's visit. By that time they were confident they were father and daughter. They had fun taking the swabs and putting them in the little vials. It seemed like a celebration at the time.

"Are you sure you did the tests right?"

"Yes, I was very careful. If we'd done something wrong the company would tell us the sample was no good. They say the samples were all good. There is just no match."

"Have you told her?"

"No. I thought I would wait for the results from the other company."

"I'm so sorry, Peter."

"It was nice to dream we had a daughter. I was looking forward so much to meeting her children. But finding out she isn't mine is going to be much worse for Elizabeth than for me. All her life she knew who her real father was. She's thought about him for years. When she finally meets him face-to-face the story changes."

"That's Vicky's fault, not yours. I guess old Vicky was more of a sport than you realized."

"She certainly didn't seem that way at the time."

"Claiming you were the father put Vicky in a better light than whatever actually happened. At least you were her boyfriend for a while. And you were a father Elizabeth could be proud of. Vicky might not even know the real father's name."

When the results of the second DNA test came in Peter called Elizabeth. "This is Peter," he began. He wanted so much to say "This is your father," but he couldn't. "I'm afraid I have some bad news."

"I know," she said. "You've thought about it and you would rather not come to Colorado. You'd rather not take this further. I understand. I'm still glad I got to meet you."

"It's worse than that," said Peter, "for both of us." He told her about the tests and waited for a reply. No words came back to him. He heard what sounded like Elizabeth gasping for breath. Or maybe she was crying.

"Oh, I'm so sorry to have bothered you," she finally said. "I think I should hang up now."

"Don't do that," said Peter. "We're friends, at least."

"How could my mother have done this to me?" she said. There was an anger in her voice that Peter would not have expected coming from the woman he had met. And a profound sadness. "I was so excited getting to know you," she said. "I've thought about you every day since I saw you. I've thought of so many things to ask you that I started writing them down."

"We can do the test again, if you like," said Peter. "And you can send the swabs in. I don't want you to think that I sabotaged the results. Linda and I were both very happy to think you were my daughter."

"Thank you," she said. "I don't know what to think or what to do at this point." Peter thought he heard a man's voice whispering to her on the other end of the line. He hoped her husband was holding her.

"What have you told your mother?"

"I haven't told her anything yet. I didn't know how she'd take it. But now I want to interrogate her. How could she tell me a made-up story all these years? And who, for God's sake, really is my father?"

"I don't know how your mother's mind works these days," said Peter, "but your questions may make her sad."

"You're right. I don't want to hurt her. I love her and she's been a good mother to me, except for one colossal lie. But I have a right to know the answers, don't you think?"

Vicky still lived in an apartment by herself. One of her friends in the building looked in on her twice a day. Elizabeth and her husband gave the lady eighty dollars a week. Elizabeth had traded Vicky's gas stove for an electric one and swapped out a floor lamp for a wall lamp that Vicky could not trip over. Vicky did not appear to read the newspaper anymore but they had not stopped delivery. She was still driving and they taped a sign on the dashboard reminding her to pull over and call them if she got lost. Vicky told them she didn't need it and had only called them once when she left the headlights on.

Elizabeth visited her mother on a Tuesday morning after dropping the boys at school. Vicky was at her kitchen table in her bathrobe, drinking coffee with the newspaper still in its plastic bag in front of her. Elizabeth said "good morning," took off her coat, poured herself a cup of coffee, and sat down across the table.

"The snow is supposed to be good at Eldora," said Elizabeth.

"Are you going this weekend?" asked Vicky. Vicky had stopped skiing when her husband died.

"We might," said Elizabeth. "Do you remember when you met Peter skiing at Mount Bachelor?"

"Of course I remember. He was a good skier."

"And you and he became lovers?"

"Yes. I was in love with him. A handsome man."

"You were young, Mother. Having fun. It was the sixties. Did you have fun with other boys?"

"We all had fun."

"Did you have fun with other boys besides Peter? Did you go out with them?"

"Yes. I was very pretty."

"I know you were. That's right. You were very pretty. Lots of boys wanted to go out with you, didn't they?"

"Yes, they did."

"And they kissed you."

"Yes, when I let them."

"Did you have sex with them?"

"Sex?"

"Did you have sex with any other boys?" Elizabeth felt as though she were the mother quizzing her evasive daughter. Her mother's head drew back and her mouth tightened.

"What do you mean? It's none of your business."

"There was a lot of sex back then, wasn't there?"

"It was hard to find a place. It was so crowded."

"But you found places didn't you?"

"Why are you asking me these questions?" Vicky asked.

"You had sex with Peter, didn't you?" Her mother paused and looked at her. She smiled a little smile.

"How do you think you got here?" said Vicky.

"Did you have sex with another boy?"

"Other boy?"

"Did you make love with any other boy when you were at Mount Bachelor?"

"I remember Mount Bachelor. Lots of bachelors there." Vicky chuckled.

"I don't think Peter is my father, Mom. I think it was some other boy."

"Peter was your father," said Vicky confidently.

"Are you lying to me, Mother? Have you lied to me my whole life?"

"I am not a liar."

Elizabeth sat looking at her mother, gazing into her eyes. Vicky stared back at her for a while then turned her head. "The snow should be good this weekend."

"I can't tell what the truth is," Elizabeth told Peter when she called. "Sometimes she avoids my questions and sometimes I think she just doesn't remember."

"Nine months before you were born was right about the time your mother left to go back to school," said Peter. "Maybe your father was a fellow student. Or a professor."

"Basically your random sperm donor."

"He gave you good genes, whoever he was. You know, you may live long enough that they put everybody's DNA in a big database. Out it pops. This is your father, now a Supreme Court Justice. You have a nephew who is a rock star."

"I'm so sorry to have bothered you and Linda. I know the idea that you had a daughter meant a lot to you."

"We may be able to make something of this yet," said Peter. "Linda and I both like you a lot. We already know you better and care about you more than some friends we've known for years. Linda and I are hoping you and we can be friends, if not relatives. We'd still like to come to Colorado and meet your family. Do you think that would work? Would you like that?"

There was a silence at the other end of the line. "I'm thinking," said Elizabeth. More silence. Peter didn't mind waiting.

Elizabeth did finally speak. "I am too embarrassed to face you, Peter. I've been living a lie my whole life and I've foisted it off on you. I can't continue down that path. I would feel like a helpless person. I'm sorry. I know you are sincere."

Peter said he was sorry to hear her answer. He was much sadder than he let on. He told her he had to respect her decision. This was all much more difficult for Elizabeth than for him. He asked her to call if she ever changed her mind or just wanted to talk.

"I don't think that will happen," said Elizabeth.

"Well, goodbye then," said Peter. "I hope you have a good life."

"Goodbye, Peter, and thank you for being so kind."

When Linda heard about the conversation she told Peter that he and Elizabeth were both idiots. "That's proof she's your daughter. She is as obtuse as you are."

It wasn't the first time Linda told him he was obtuse and Peter took it in stride.

"What's changed?" she asked. "In terms of what happened you could have been her father. She's believed all her life that you were. Maybe Vicky believed it as well. What's a stupid DNA test compared to that?" Linda raised her hands to her head as though she could not believe Peter's lack of common sense. She picked up the phone and called Elizabeth.

"Listen, young lady," she said, "we're offering you the deal of a lifetime here. You'd be a fool not to take it. You get nice people who care about you but won't tell you what to do. Your children get grandparents who are good generous people. We're wealthy, healthy, and we won't ask you to take care of us in our old age. You already like us. Peter could have been your father, you know. Fifteen years ago we didn't have this kind of DNA testing and you would never have known he wasn't."

"I still don't feel right building on top of this fiction."

"We build our lives on fiction all the time. Every time you make a plan it's fiction before it's real. Love is more fiction than fact. Yet lifelong marriages are made from it. You can make Peter your father or at least your good friend. Accept him. You'd be crazy not to."

"Linda, are you sure that you, yourself, want to do this?"

"Make my husband happy. And me too."

"And me as well, I think," said Elizabeth.

"I think you owe it to Peter to give it a try."

"I owe it to Peter, to you, and to my children."

"You owe it to yourself."

Ashes

Sarah Nelson, twenty-six years old, with a solid job to her credit, was surprised by her sudden buoyant mood. She should only be sad. Yet the blue September sky, the pines and aspens, and the log house with the bright yellow door brought back the happiness she had found on the ranch with her father every summer. There was a horse to ride, miles of trails to explore, a pond to fish in, and a river. They could paddle a canoe on the river like Indians or trappers in the wilderness. Or they could float down the river on inner tubes, half in and half out of the water, bumping off the banks and sand bars. Willows hid them from the rest of the world. The white flowers that bowed from the banks were beautiful but, as her father warned her every year, poisonous.

Sarah's father had died and she was coming to ready his house for sale. She could have closed up the house remotely – hiring the same robot that was now waiting for her outside the front door. The robot could have sent her a full report – text, video, photos, recommendations, the whole works. But Sarah very much wanted to visit the house again. And as irrational as she knew it was, she felt the house would miss her too, would want to see her one more time. The robot was named Sam and affected a broad-brimmed cowboy hat and a black rodeo shirt with lavender seams and pearl buttons.

"Do you have a key?" asked Sam. "It's an old-time mechanical lock." The robot, with a slight western twang, was maintaining the illusion that, like a human, it only knew what it had been told, only knew what it needed to know. But all the robots and computers were linked together now. In effect, people said, there was only one computer in the world. It simply appeared in different guises to accommodate the needs of the humans around it. The computer, and therefore Sam the robot, knew perfectly well that Sarah had brought a key. It had seen Sarah put it in her purse when she left her apartment five hundred miles away.

She turned the lock easily. Her father had taken care of the house himself. No computers. No robots. No networks. He had held out against them all. Even the thermostats in George Nelson's house were analog. You set the temperature by sliding little plastic arms to the left and right. He kept driving his '97 Ford Expedition, though the nearest mechanic who could work on it was in Redmond.

Sarah's father, George Nelson, was an Englishman who became an American. He was fascinated by the American West. His house was decorated with Indian rugs, the tools of cattle ranching, and maps of Oregon when Britain and the United States shared it. He wore shirts from a western store, owned a cattle brand with no cattle to put it on, and wore a cowboy hat to visit the grocery store. At a shooting range near Millican he taught Sarah how to shoot a revolver and a rifle. With more laughter than success they learned together how to rope a fencepost with a lasso.

Her father had never once ventured into virtual reality. Sarah spent a few hours a week there. Virtual worlds had partially replaced the television and movies of her childhood. The computer customized the alternate realities to amuse, challenge, and reward her in the perfect doses it took to keep her coming back. The computer could not read minds but it was excellent at inferring what people were thinking.

Sam stepped into the front hall and glanced quickly around him. "Anything special I should look for or tell you about?" he asked. The house interior would be all new information to the computer. The computer would soak it up – dimensions, images, weight, condition. It would assign a cash value to each item. The computer would estimate Sarah's interest in each item and her preferred disposition of it. The computer had observed Sarah her entire adult life. It knew her better than she knew herself. Its predictions of her decisions would be perfectly accurate. To preserve the impression of free will, however, the computer would present recommendations and suggestions. It would ask her for her decisions. It would even make some recommendations it knew Sarah would overrule.

Sarah's reply was exactly what the computer had anticipated. "Copy all the photographs and documents. Don't move anything until I've walked through the house myself one time. I won't take long."

"Shall I create a virtual copy of the house?" asked Sam.

"How much extra would that cost?"

"Two hundred dollars – down to every scrap of paper or speck of dust. It won't take much extra time since I've got to look at everything anyway."

"Sure," said Sarah. "Go ahead." She hoped someday she would take her grandchildren, when she had them, through the virtual house, just the way her father had left it.

Sarah's mother, with whom Sarah had lived the other weeks of the year growing up, had done her duty. She provided a stable home and a good education. Her mother was loving in her way but she could not hide a certain disappointment in her daughter. She wished Sarah were thinner, more fashionable, and more interested in the best kind of people. Sarah was drawn instead to books, being outdoors, and people she could laugh with. She could talk with anyone for hours, from the college dean her mother worked for to the uneducated men who were supposed to be trimming her mother's oaks in California. When the other person thought every possible subject had been exhausted Sarah would bring up a new one, just as interesting and just as important as the earlier ones.

"But you wear them out," her mother said. Sarah knew people enjoyed talking with her. They came back for more.

Sarah's mother had died of Alzheimer's two years ago in a nursing home in Palo Alto, near Sarah. During every one of Sarah's visits to the home her mother told her, as though for the first time, that she should try to wear something nicer or, even better, lose a little weight. Her father never said anything about weight. He was proud of her the way she was.

Sarah and her mother had moved out of her father's log house when Sarah was ten and her parents divorced. Her mother had not visited the house for many years. Sarah thought her mother must have had some pleasant memories of it. She'd loved her husband at one time and living in this house was implicit in her decision to marry him. They had met when he was raising the funds to build a pipeline in Argentina, where her mother had grown up. She spoke excellent English and had gone to college in the United States. She liked the caring man with international savoir-faire. She was amused at first by his preference for the Oregon outback and his fascination with cowboys, Indians, cattle, and sheep. She tolerated his avoidance of computers and the Internet. But as they traveled less and he became more established in his preferences, she said she missed city life and she missed her friends in California and Argentina. She said she wanted Sarah to grow up with a wider variety of people and experiences.

Sarah had inherited her mother's thick black hair and her dark eyes. People often expected her to be impulsive and emotional. Hot-blooded. The computer knew Sarah was steadier than that. The computer always knew exactly what to expect of her. That made dealing with the computer easier than dealing with humans. Sloth, she felt, drove her toward the computer. She tried to resist it.

In the room that was hers at her father's house Sarah changed out of the dress slacks, white blouse, and low-heeled shoes she had worn on the plane. She put on a work shirt, jeans, and thick walking shoes. By the back door she picked up a fishing hat with a circular brim. She stepped out on to the stone patio and sat in a chaise. She imagined she would sit for a while in the morning sun and call up memories of her father. How he loved this house. How he loved the ranch that he shared with the other owners who lived on it. And how he had loved her. Sarah looked out over the familiar view of the pond, the meadow beyond it, the willows by the river, the forest and half-hidden houses across the way. Above the trees the snowfield in the shape of a cowboy shined brightly on Mount Bachelor.

When she was sixteen her father allowed Sarah to ride the ranch on her own. His one concession to technology was to let her carry her cell phone with her. After a few calls to her friends in Palo Alto she realized she would rather be alone with her horse, the pines, the meadows, and the view of the mountains in the distance. She rarely called her friends from the ranch and she never answered the calls they made to her. When she was out riding alone she wore a revolver on her hip. It was loaded. She imagined she was miles from the nearest town in the Old West and the gun kept her safer. By age eighteen she felt silly wearing it, like a child wearing a Zorro cape. She left the gun at her father's house.

Lying in the chaise, basking in the sun, Sarah thought of discussing her father with Connie. Connie sat in a tiny chip behind Sarah's ear. She was Sarah's constantly available ambassador from the computer, a companion and personal assistant. At the extremes she was like a conjoined twin and a twenty-four hour servant at the same time. Mostly she was a clever and upbeat friend. Sarah tried not to spend too much time with her. Sarah knew her human friends cared what she had to say, at least a little bit. They had a stake in their relationship to her. At bottom the computer didn't care. It was simply better at simulating care than humans were.

"Do you want to talk?" asked Connie.

"No thanks," said Sarah. "I'll stick to my own thoughts for now." Sarah's mind moved more quickly when she talked to Connie. Connie knew what buttons to push, what thoughts to insert in the conversation. But Sarah wanted to be alone with her memories.

"See you later then," said Connie cheerfully.

Her father was buried in a cemetery plot in Bend before Sarah arrived. He hadn't wanted a service. On the way to the ranch from the airport she had gone to visit the grave and arrange for a stone. He owned the plot next to his own and the plot would be part of the estate she would inherit. Sarah didn't know which wife he had in mind when he bought the plots but the second plot was still empty.

She had sent her mother's ashes back to be interred with her family in Buenos Aires. Sarah realized she could take her father's other plot for herself. She would probably change her mind when a husband and a family materialized. But right now the thought that she could ultimately rest next to her father comforted her, made her a little more confident.

After no one had seen her father for three days the ranch foreman knocked on his door and, receiving no answer, had entered the house. The young man found her father sitting dead in his chair in the living room. A tin mug of cold coffee sat on the table beside him.

There was nothing left of him in the house now except his possessions. Sam would find photographs of her father and copy them. She was glad she would still be able to have them so her children, grandchildren, and even his further descendants could look at them if they wanted to. But the photographs would be about as far as posterity could go toward experiencing George Nelson first hand. Unlike many people these days, her father had refused to live on as a computer simulation. He thought it was a fad.

"Another decade or two and people will have no interest in even the best simulations of their relatives," he'd said. "The computer will invent families that are much more interesting."

Simulations of humans were getting better every year. The computer could project a hologram or even, at some additional expense, power a robot that looked virtually identical to the deceased. The computer was so familiar with the living person that it could predict and simulate what the person would say in response to a remark from anyone. Some people loved being able to talk with people they had lost. Others thought it was better to leave the past behind. Some people were known to exact a sort of revenge upon the dead, to insult them or tell them things that would make the simulation act upset, unhappy, or angry. This mental abuse was not illegal since no human was injured. But the abuse was considered, by most people, to be in very poor taste.

Sam was somewhere in the cellar. She didn't need to go find him to speak to him. The chip in her head would handle it. "Sam," she said, "where's the dog?"

"Over at the kennel."

"The kennel on the ranch?"

"Yes," said Sam. "The foreman fetched him along with his dog food. The pooch was hungry and thirsty but he's in good shape now."

She was done sitting and dreaming. The ranch was there in front of her. The least she could do was walk out on it, see what had changed from the last time she had been there. She did want to see the dog. She stepped off the patio, over the green lawn, and out into the dirt, wild grass, and sagebrush.

Until the past few years, when Sarah visited, she rode a horse her father kept just for her – a small well-behaved paint when she was younger and a Quarter Horse when she turned fifteen. Her father persuaded Fremont and Carson, his Chesapeake Bay retrievers, to obey her and she took them with her on her explorations of lodge-pole thickets and the trails between the great domes of willows by the river.

Sarah skirted the pond and cut across the meadow. At the bridge she looked over into the narrow river for trout. No one had ever seen trout there but she and her father had stopped many times to look over the log railing. There were trout in the river but they were elsewhere and they were skittish. She had only caught a few. If you wanted to catch fish, the pond was a much easier place.

The road from the bridge to the working part of the ranch was gravel. A fine gray dust collected on Sarah's shoes. Her father said this stretch of road looked the way a ranch road should look. A buck fence of skinny logs ran alongside the road. The stables, when they came into view, had the symmetry and sharp angles of a modern building. But at least the building was made of wood and not steel.

Clark, her father's retriever, was in a chain-link run outside the kennel with a Border Collie in the next run over. Both dogs barked when they saw her. Clark continued to bark until she put her hand up against the fence and he licked it. She gave the other dog a hand to smell through the fence and he stopped barking too, looking a little embarrassed at having barked so much and now affecting a canine nonchalance at Sarah's visit.

"Hello, Clark," she said to her father's dog. "I'm sure you miss your master. And your house. I'm sorry Daddy died and left you. But he loved you very much and he's sorry he's gone." Sarah realized the dog must have been with her father when he died. Clark would have been very worried and she felt sorry for him. Tears wet her cheeks for the first time since she arrived. She wiped the tears away with the sleeve of her shirt.

"I'm going to see if I can get inside and pet you." She walked around to the kennel door but it was locked. There were no employees around to let her in. She went back to the fence. "I guess no petting today. I wish I could take you home with me but I have no room for a dog. I don't live on a ranch. I'll find a good home for you, though, don't worry. With children and a bird hunter if I can." A hunter would value a well-trained dog like Clark. Sarah could reimburse vet expenses from the sale of her father's house and that might help find Clark a good home. Many families now decided a robot dog, or no dog at all, was just fine.

Her father said that dogs helped keep people human. "You can't email it in with a dog," he said. "A dog's first priority is other dogs. His second is his master and his master's family. That's the way it ought to be with humans. People's first concern should be other humans, as difficult as they can be. There are parts of human nature that computers can't touch."

"What parts would those be, Daddy?" Sarah had asked.

"I can't really tell you. Words are not too good at touching those parts either."

Sarah let the dog lick her hand through the fence one more time and said goodbye.

Beside the stable a man Sarah didn't recognize was brushing down a mare. The man was in his thirties and wore a baseball cap and long-sleeved shirt. He didn't have the deep tan an employee would have from working outside. Sarah guessed he was the guest of an owner.

"Been out on the trails?" she asked.

"Yes," the man said. "From one end of the ranch to the other. Are you one of the owners?"

"Well, yes," said Sarah, "at least technically. I am Sarah Nelson. My father lived in the dark log house near the entrance."

"I am Frank Agopian," the man said. "Bill Agopian is my uncle. I bet you know where he lives."

"West side of the river."

"This is my first time on the ranch," said Frank. "Uncle Bill always came to visit us in Massachusetts." He went back to brushing the horse and then looked up.

"I'm sorry to hear about your father," he said. "I think his death may have prompted my uncle to ask me out here. My uncle has no children and I'm his executor. He wants me to see the place while he is still around to show it to me."

In all the years she had been coming to the ranch Sarah had never met Frank's uncle, though she knew who he was. Bill Agopian had been driving the car when her father's first wife, Marie, died in an automobile accident. Her father had never forgiven Bill. Throughout her childhood Sarah wasn't supposed to go near Agopian's house or speak to him if she saw him.

"Is your uncle sick?" she asked.

"No. He's fine. But he wants to be prepared."

"Is that his horse?" asked Sarah.

"Yes," said Frank. "Uncle Bill wanted me to see the ranch from horseback at least once. He doesn't ride very much anymore. He says he owns the most docile horse in the stable. That's a good thing for me. I'm not much of a rider."

"I think your uncle has kept to himself pretty much. I've never met him."

"I am surprised how few people my uncle knows. He seems to have led a pretty lonely existence. It doesn't look like it bothered him much though. I've known him all my life. He's always been friendly and outgoing when I've seen him. A likable guy. Do you want to come by and say hello at last? It's just my uncle and me. I invite you. It seems a shame you haven't met him in all this time."

"I think I should meet him. This is probably my last chance. I don't think I'll be back to the ranch again. Will you be around this afternoon?"

"All day."

"I'll come over later then." Sarah started back toward the house. She thought of asking Connie what the computer knew about Bill Agopian but decided against it. The accident that killed Marie happened before Sarah was born. That far back the computer would rely on newspaper reports and legal documents. It would contrive a story to tie the few facts it had together. The story, though persuasive, could easily be false. Sarah wanted to meet Agopian before asking the computer anything, if she ever did ask it.

On the way back to her father's house Sarah went through the clearing where the ranch used to have a teepee. The stone fire pit was still there but the teepee was gone. Young pine trees were invading the grassy field. When she was a child the ranch owners came here once a summer to read poems and stories to each other over a campfire. They favored ghost stories and cowboy poetry but anyone could read anything as long as it didn't go over ten minutes. Some people read their own work. In the earliest years the smaller children, including Sarah, were herded into the teepee and encouraged to go to sleep. At the end of the evening her father would carry her to his car and drive her the short distance home. When she was older she sat with the adults and listened along with them. Sometimes she yearned for a smartphone or a tablet to distract her from a boring story. But that was forbidden to everyone.

"People have been telling stories around fires for thousands of years," said her father. "A lot would be missing if we gave it up." When he said "people," Sarah thought, he was picturing cowboys resting after a day of herding cattle. Or Indians after a day of hunting.

Sarah returned along the road and entered the house from the front. Sam displayed a report that listed what was valuable, what should be thrown out (in the computer's estimation of what Sarah would decide on her own), and what Sarah might want to take with her. Sam would confiscate her father's guns. Sarah wished she had hidden the ivory-handled revolver in memory of her father teaching her how to shoot it. But it was too late now. She'd never get it back.

"I found two urns in the cellar that I don't know what you want to do with," said Sam. "They have ashes in them. The labels say they are the last earthly remains of Marie Nelson and Jocelyn Nelson." Marie Nelson was her father's first wife, the one who had died in the automobile accident. Jocelyn was his second wife, the one who was married to Bill Agopian before she married George Nelson.

"God," said Sarah, more to herself than to Sam. "I never knew he had them. Why didn't he get rid of them years ago?" She wished he had. She didn't know what to do with them. "Well, put them in the front hall after I go through your lists. And delete them from the virtual version of the house. The virtual includes the entire house, inside and out?"

"Yes," said Sam, "out to the limits of the lawn. The views beyond the lawn will look exactly like today but you won't be able to walk into them."

Sarah wondered who besides herself might ever see the virtual copy of the house. Perhaps a future owner would want to see what it used to look like. Someday she might walk her children and grand-children through the house. Years from now the real house would be demolished or remodeled beyond recognition. Sarah would pass away. Her simulation and the virtual house would shuffle from one digital address to another, linked to each other but forgotten and unsummoned by any living creature.

Sarah read Sam's recommendations and approved them. The computer knew better than she did what she would miss if she didn't keep it and what she would throw out a year later if she held on to it. She put a few small things in a bag to take on the plane. Sam would ship the rest of what she wanted. He would keep some things to dress the house for sale and dispose of the rest.

Sarah backed her father's open-top army jeep with no doors out of the garage and drove it over to the Agopians. The jeep didn't have a license plate and could only go on the ranch. Her father had taught her how to drive it. It had a stick shift and threw off as much pollution as fifty normal cars. Sam had consigned it by law to be scrapped and recycled.

Bill Agopian answered the door. He was a tall, thin, white-haired man with an erect posture. He smiled a reassuring smile at her. She sensed that smiling was difficult for him. But he brought it off. "Ah, we meet at last," he said. "How do you do?" He stuck out his hand and she shook it. "Please come in. I was so sorry to hear your father died. Once upon a time, you know, we were good friends."

"I'm pleased to meet you too, Bill, after all this time," said Sarah. "I'm glad Frank invited me over." She followed Agopian down a long entry hall. Glass-fronted display cases filled with butterflies hung on the walls. The butterflies in some cases were virtually identical to one another. In others, the size, shape, and color varied.

"They're all from this part of Oregon," said Agopian, "from within twenty miles of here. I caught every one of them." When they reached the living room Agopian asked her if she'd like tea. Frank was heating the water.

"Yes thank you," she said. The living room ran to greens, browns, and textured fabrics, like a hunting lodge with a decorator's touch. No woman had lived in this house for many years. The room was dominated by a stone fireplace and chimney on one wall and a large picture window on another. Sarah could see her father's house half-hidden by trees.

"Are you retired, Bill?" asked Sarah.

"Until a few years ago I did consulting over the phone and the Internet. Now I'm as retired as I can get. I play a little golf and go hiking. I have a sorry old horse I ride around the ranch. Frank says you saw him. The butterflies get me outdoors and up into the mountains. I do cross-country skiing in the winter. I gave up downhill. Too risky for a man of my age."

Sarah's father had snowshoed in the winter "like a trapper," he said. But he had never skied. Sarah had brought her college friends to stay at his house during winter break to go skiing at Mount Bachelor. Her father had built roaring fires and fed them well. They had to buy their own wine, beer, and liquor. Anyone who overindulged was not invited back. Sleeping arrangements were flexible as long as her father didn't have to know about them.

Frank brought in a tray with tea and cookies. He poured mugs for each of them. "Sarah doesn't know why you and her father didn't speak all this time. It seems pretty strange to me too when you lived so close."

Bill Agopian pursed his lips and looked down at the tea tray. He looked up at Sarah and met her eye briefly. Then he smiled and said, as if amused at the irony, "What it boils down to is George thought I murdered his first wife and I am certain he murdered mine. That was after he stole her away from me."

Agopian was being dramatic, Sarah thought. He was trying to be interesting. It was true her father believed Bill Agopian could have prevented Marie Nelson's death if he'd driven more carefully. But her father never said that Agopian had murdered Marie on purpose. As for George Nelson murdering anyone, it was preposterous. People as kind as her father did not go around killing people.

Yet, Agopian had said, whether he really believed it or not, that her father had murdered Jocelyn, Bill Agopian's first wife and George Nelson's second. Sarah could not placidly sip her tea. She had to get Agopian to retract what he'd said. She would start by questioning what Agopian must know for a fact.

"And did you in fact murder his first wife?" Sarah asked.

Agopian sat calmly on the couch, gazed straight ahead, let one breath out slowly, and pulled fresh air back into him.

"A reckless driver ran us off the side of a mountain road. The reason Marie died and I didn't was she took off her seatbelt to reach something in the back seat. I would never have hurt her."

"My father told me the accident was your fault," said Sarah.

"I could never convince your father so I don't know how I could ever convince you. He and I had been friends for years before that. But the way he saw it was that I had run off the road on purpose. He could have sued me for wrongful death but he never did. There was no evidence I had intended to run off the road."

"And Jocelyn drowned by accident. Where did you get the idea my father killed her?"

"The way she died was exactly the way your father tried to kill Marie. He tipped over a canoe and watched Marie drowning in the river. If Marie hadn't washed up on a sandbar she would have died. I saw this myself."

Frank huddled behind his mug as though it were a shield, an inadequate one at that.

"George Nelson was not the kind of man to kill anyone," said Sarah.

"That's always been my feeling," said Agopian. "And I've never known why he would want to kill Marie."

The man is delusional, thought Sarah. That's all there is to it. She stood up to leave. She hadn't touched her tea.

"Do you have their ashes?" asked Agopian.

"How do you know about that?"

"Housekeeper. George and I had the same housekeeper. She said the ashes were in two urns in the cellar."

"Actually they are in the jeep. I didn't know my father had kept them until the robot found them."

"What are you going to do with them?"

"Spread them on the ranch somewhere. It's one more thing I have to do. I wasn't going to make a ceremony out of it. I never knew either of them."

"I knew them both," said Agopian. "Loved them both. One way or another. Would you let me spread the ashes with you?"

"Frankly, Mr. Agopian, I don't see why I should have anything more to do with you unless you take back what you said about my father killing anyone. Or trying to kill them."

Agopian paused. "I take back what I said about his killing Jocelyn. I never saw what happened. I don't know how she drowned. Her leg gave her a lot of trouble and maybe she couldn't swim well enough to save herself."

"And what you said about his trying to kill Marie?"

"Well, he didn't kill her, did he? What I saw could be, I suppose, open to interpretation."

"So you take it back?"

"If I said he intended to kill Marie, I take it back. How would I know what he intended?"

"And you won't make those accusations again," she asked, "to anyone?"

"Agreed," he said, "if we can distribute the ashes together."

"Okay," said Sarah, surprised at how important this seemed to be to Agopian. "Let's dispose of them together. But it has to be this afternoon. Somewhere nearby."

"Fair enough. Why don't we pour them off the bridge?"

"A good idea," said Frank. This was more than he had bargained for, thought Sarah, and he was eager for it to be over.

Agopian stood up, surprisingly quick for an older man. "Let's go," he said.

They walked over a meadow and through a sparse woodland toward the bridge. Frank carried one urn and Agopian the other. The day was still clear and warm. There was a forest fire on Newberry Crater in the distance. The smoke lay like a grey pillow above the mountain, the pillow leaking to the left in the wind. Sitting on top of the pillow was a bright white cloud. A bulky low-flying plane let loose a spray of pink rain. The spray looked too thin to make much of a dent on the fire.

"Do you want to pour the ashes?" asked Sarah when they reached the bridge. They stood on the downstream side, up against the log railing.

"Yes. Thank you," said Agopian. "Marie first." He lifted the lid and looked inside. He pulled out a sheet of paper and scanned it. "Cremation certificate," he said. He handed it to Sarah. Then he dumped the urn's contents into the river in one decisive move. No words. No slow thoughtful pouring. Done. Finished. Frank handed his uncle the second urn. Once again the older man pulled out a certificate and handed it to Sarah. He hesitated briefly and a look of sadness finally crossed his face. He poured the ashes out quickly and shook the container upside down over the edge of the bridge. Ashes from both urns floated away on the surface of the water, forming two light grey patches of scum. More ashes sank to the muddy bottom and created an irregular off-white patch. Sarah wondered how long the ashes would remain there before they disappeared, spread too thin to be recognizable.

"They were good friends when they were both alive," said Agopian. "At least there's that."

He turned and began to walk back toward his house along the road, carrying Jocelyn's urn. Sarah and Frank followed him, Frank carrying Marie's. Frank, Sarah thought, had even less stake in the past than Sarah did. She was grateful he was there to counterbalance the strangeness of Agopian's behavior. For Frank and Sarah this could almost be a pleasant stroll through the ranch on any sunny day. They were a different generation from the old men who had distrusted each other. The deaths that haunted those men happened long ago. Nowadays, with the computer, people knew they couldn't get away with murder. Anyone crazy enough to commit murder would be locked up long before they could actually do it. People could always feel they were safe, even with strangers.

The certificates, when Sarah looked at them, were both from the same mortuary: "Serving Central Oregon since 1911". The names were correct but Jocelyn's cremation date surprised her. It was a year after her father had worked in Argentina, a year after her father had met her mother. Sarah had always thought Jocelyn died well before her parents ever met. Neither parent had ever told her anything different.

Agopian was sitting on the stone steps leading up to his front door when Sarah and Frank got back to his house. He rose to his feet to say goodbye. He looked older, sadder, and much in need of a nap.

"Thank you for letting me do that with you," he said. "It meant a lot to me." He looked as though he might say more. Sarah decided she didn't want to hear it, whatever it was. Agopian could sort out his own feelings. Frank could be his confessor if he needed one.

"Goodbye," she said. "Thank you for the tea."

"Keep in touch," Frank said. He put the two empty urns on the floor in the back of Sarah's jeep. She gave Agopian and Frank a short wave as she started out the driveway. She pictured herself, a young woman in command of a car few others could drive, a young woman in charge of her life. Her father would be pleased with her.

When she got back to the house Sarah peeled the labels off the containers and threw them in the trash. Sam had left but would send a truck for the things Sarah didn't want. Sarah sat on the couch facing the chair her father had died in.

"Connie," she said, "here is the way I want it to be. My father never attempted to kill his first wife. Maybe she fell out of a canoe. Maybe she almost drowned. But it wasn't his fault. He never killed his second wife either. She drowned by accident. He loved them both, as he loved my mother. As he loved me. He was a good man."

"I'm sure that's the way it was," said Connie.

"And I never want to hear from Bill Agopian again."

The computer would manufacture a past that conformed, very closely, to Sarah's wishes. The most subtle nuggets of information would be bent to confirm her story. If other people wanted to know what happened – people, like Frank, whose stake in the story was less than Sarah's – the version they received from the computer would lean toward Sarah's story.

"Would you like to see how Jocelyn really drowned?" asked Connie.

Sarah knew there were no cameras on the river when Jocelyn drowned. There might be no cameras there today. What Connie was prepared to show Sarah was a simulation of the drowning – manufactured images presented as the truth. The virtual camera would be on the bank of the river, watching. The river would be flooding from snowmelt. Jocelyn would be in a kayak, alone on the river.

She would crash into some willows and become entangled, her feet above her body. She would struggle to lift her head out of the water. But she would quickly grow tired. The water would be cold and running fast. After more and more desperate attempts her head would go under and not come up. It would be unpleasant to watch.

"No," said Sarah, "I don't need to see that. We're done on that subject. Now I want to talk with my mother."

"Hello, Sarah," her mother's voice said. It was like a phone call. Her mother sounded the way she was ten years earlier, before her health began to go. Sarah was the trustee of this simulation. She set the rules about who could talk with her mother. So far it was Sarah, a few of her mother's friends, and some of her mother's family members in Argentina. In the computer her mother never aged. She never remembered what anyone told her from one conversation to the next. She did not know George Nelson was dead nor, for that matter, that she herself had died. The simulation was false in other ways too. It didn't seem to be the least surprised that Sarah was no longer a sixteen-year-old girl, that she lived on her own and had a career. The simulation was getting further and further from reality. Sarah's relationship with the simulation was becoming more artificial all the time. Yet sometimes it was exactly what Sarah needed.

"Hello, Mom," said Sarah, "I'm at the ranch and I met Mr. Agopian for the first time. Do you remember him?"

"He lived across the river. We'd see him wandering around the ranch with a butterfly net."

"Did you ever speak with him?"

"Once or twice," said her mother. "Your father didn't like him. He didn't think the man was trustworthy. Anyhow I was busy with you and we had plenty of friends without Mr. Agopian. He seemed to want to stay to himself."

"Did Agopian ever tell you his theory about how Jocelyn drowned?"

"If he did I don't remember it. It was an accident."

"Did Agopian ever say anything about Daddy trying to drown Marie?"

"He better not have. I had my problems with your father but I don't think he went around drowning people. Is that what Agopian told you?"

"Did anything Bill Agopian said help convince you to leave Daddy?"

"Hardly. I only spoke to him once or twice. Your father and I were just not meant to be together, aside from having you. Nothing I could have heard from Bill Agopian could have made the slightest difference."

"Something else I learned, not from Mr. Agopian, was that Jocelyn died a year after you and Daddy met. I thought she was long gone before you and Daddy fell in love."

"Why are you digging all this up?" asked her mother impatiently. "Jocelyn was divorcing him. It was not a happy marriage. Your father and I were very much in love. We met all over the world, wherever your father traveled. I don't think Jocelyn ever knew I existed."

"But Daddy was here when she died, wasn't he?"

"Good God, Sarah. I don't know where he was. All I know is the poor woman drowned. If she hadn't drowned you would never have existed."

"I suppose I should be grateful she's dead," said Sarah.

"You are lucky to have been born who you are, Sarah. I hope you take advantage of it."

"Tell me again why you divorced Daddy."

"I've told you this so many times, Sarah. I wanted to bring you up in the twenty-first century. He wanted to stay in the nineteenth. The gap between us kept widening. I made allowances for as long as I could but your father thought he was John Wayne. He would not compromise."

"Yet he could be generous," said Sarah.

"Yes he could. When he felt like it." Her mother seemed to be thinking. "He hasn't taken up with some nutty woman rancher, has he? I've always thought he would fall for some woman who smelled of horse sweat."

"No," said Sarah, "there's no other woman in the picture."

On the Road from Burns

"Well, that's sensible at his age. Still, I'm sorry if he's lonely."

"I don't think he's lonely, Mom."

"Well, he has you. He's always adored you."

"That's a nice thought, Mom. Thank you."

"Take care of yourself, Sarah. Go out and buy yourself something nice to wear."

"I will, Mom. Talk to you soon."

"And don't worry so much about the past. It's over and done with. Lock it away in a box."

"I think I've done that. Goodbye, Mom."

Acknowledgments, Sources, and Historical Notes

First of all, my love and gratitude to Joan Stafford Haynes, my wife of 39 years, for being the first reader and advisor on these stories. We discovered Central Oregon together, made wonderful friends there, and built a home we love on the Little Deschutes River.

My deepest appreciation to Ellen Waterston for her insightful comments on this book and for encouraging all those who write about Central Oregon. Readers should thank Ellen as well, for making these stories better than they would otherwise have been. Any remaining shortcomings, however, are entirely my own.

I owe more than I can say to Grace McNellis, my friend and coauthor of *Vandevert*, for awakening my interest in Central Oregon history and for supplying ideas and details for many of the stories in this collection.

Many, many thanks to Tom Parker at UC Berkeley and Nancy Packer at Stanford who taught me so much about writing stories.

The most important single event in the history of Central Oregon was the coming of the railroad in 1911, after years of anticipation. "Bridges" and "A Trick of the Light" are informed by the *The Deschutes River Railroad War*, by Leon Speroff and by the chapter on Opal City in *New Era: Reflections on the Human and Natural History of Central Oregon* by Jarold Ramsey. The men who worked on the bridge did not actually camp out on the river below. But the myth that they did, reported by Speroff, was too beguiling to pass up in these stories. While many of the workers were recent Italian and Greek immigrants, three of the workers, the Catlow brothers, were uncles of my friend Grace and were born in Iowa. Their father, who also worked on the bridge, was born in Lancashire.

"Boondoggle" evolved from a story a friend told me of a woman accountant who was sent to her company's Paris office to clear up some accounting loose ends. The director of the office was very helpful in taking her through the books. When she came back from lunch she found police surrounding the building. A man had jumped down the stairwell and killed himself. It was the friendly office manager. He had been embezzling for years.

"Do No Harm" was inspired by an incident related by an early Bend doctor, Urling C. Coe, in his highly entertaining book, *Frontier Doctor*. The narrator of this story is slightly mistaken in using the place name "Rosland." The Rosland Post Office changed its name to La Pine in 1910.

The wagon train that visits "Kubali and the Vampire Cowboys" actually did come through the area in 1853. The tracks of the Elliot party can still be found in Sunriver. For some reason this "Lost Wagon Train" left no record of meeting Kubali or her friends.

"On the Mountain" grew out of an exercise in dialogue I wrote for Nancy Packer at Stanford. I never faced the dilemma of these characters when I was climbing. But making life-and-death choices was always a possibility.

In researching "Bloodlines" I was repeatedly surprised how Americans, less than a hundred years ago, celebrated eugenics – the idea of improving the human population by selective breeding (and selective prevention of breeding, including forced sterilizations). Eugenics is anathema today, largely due to Hitler's use of eugenic arguments to justify murdering fourteen million people. Yet today we are only a few generations away from blood relatives who welcomed the concept. The portraits of local logging camps of the 1920s and 1930s are drawn from *Life in Railroad Logging Camps of the Shevlin-Hixon Company 1916-1950* by Ronald L. Gregory and *Roughing it in the Little Deschutes River 1934-1944* by Edward Gray. The description of the dance by the Little Deschutes is based on recollections by Grace McNellis and her brother Claude Vandevert.

The feel of "Local Rules" comes from my dreams of being in a class for which I am hopelessly unprepared. Probably in my pajamas. I am often desperately unprepared on the golf course. I looked to *The Unconsoled* by Kazuo Ishiguro for guidance in writing this story but kept thinking of *Alice in Wonderland* as I wrote it.

"Fatal Errors" was inspired by a couple I met in New Zealand. They each traveled all over the world for business and had met at Lake Rotoroa for vacation. The wind came up while they were out on the lake in a canoe that tipped over. She was not a good swimmer and they barely made it to shore. They were English and I hoped she hadn't read *An American Tragedy*. What impressed me was how enthusiastically she told the day's story over dinner that evening.

Falling Star, War Spirit, and all the other Indians in "Falling Star" were once real people, though used fictionally here. General Alvord was commander of Fort Vancouver when Falling Star was imprisoned there. He later taught mathematics at West Point and made advances in the field of geometry. The facts on which this story is based are drawn primarily from Michno's *The Deadliest Indian War in the West* and Ontko's *Thunder over the Ochoco*. Ontko is notoriously unreliable and the mention I took from his book about Chief Paulina killing a Warm Springs chief in his tent is unsubstantiated. Of course, much of this story of Falling Star is pure invention. I am indebted to Linda Evans of the High Desert Museum for excellent information on early settlers on Ochoco Creek.

"Saturday Night" was originally inspired by the song *The Heart of Saturday Night* as written by Tom Waits and sung by Diana Krall. Set in Bend in 1953, much of the background for this story came from Grace McNellis.

Burns is 130 miles across the Eastern Oregon Desert from Bend. "On the Road from Burns" came to mind when I remembered the first time I came west, at age 22, and stopped by the side of a desert highway late at night in Utah. I climbed a hill and could not see a light in any direction. I don't think I have ever again been so far from another human being. On a cheerier note, Grace, who grew up south of Bend, said of this book's cover photo, "It so reminds me of coming home from Philadelphia in 1954 in a 1947 Chevrolet with two little boys and another due soon and hitting this road from Burns. I was never so glad to see a place as when we saw the Cascades – and – finally – Pilot Butte. I knew we were home!"

The inspiration for "Prisoner of Conscience" came from a delightful book, *No Picnic on Mount Kenya* by Felice Benuzzi, an Italian Alpinist who escaped from a World War II POW camp in Africa to climb Mount Kenya and, having no hope of reaching friendly territory, returned voluntarily to camp. The somewhat surprising history of Italian POWs in the United States was informed by a DVD, *Prisoners in Paradise* and an online article, *Italian POWs held in America during World War II*, both by Camilla Calamandrei. I learned about the POW camp at Camp Abbot from Grace McNellis. A girl resembling Grace makes an appearance on horseback in the story.

The idea for "Living Well" came from struggles Joan and I had with a neighbor who owned a very loud macaw. The problem was ultimately resolved with petitions, lawyers, and quiet discussion. But fire and blood are more interesting.

"Ashes" gives the characters in "Fatal Errors" a chance to wrap up their stories many years hence. The story plays with a prediction by Ray Kurzweil that by 2030 computers will be smarter than all humans on the planet put together.

I wish to offer a final note of thanks to the Deschutes County Historical Museum for their assistance and the use of their extensive library.